PART I

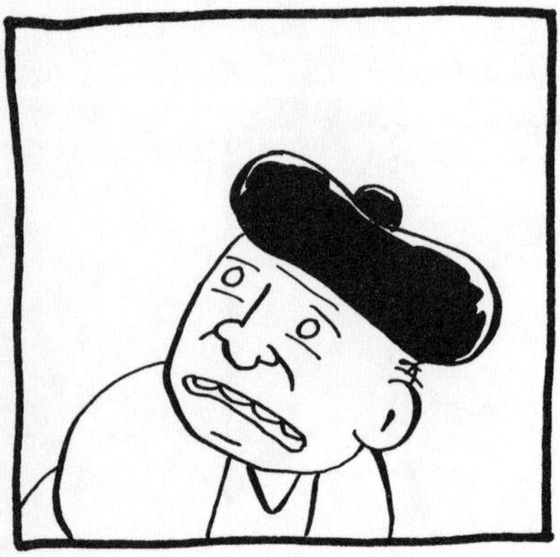

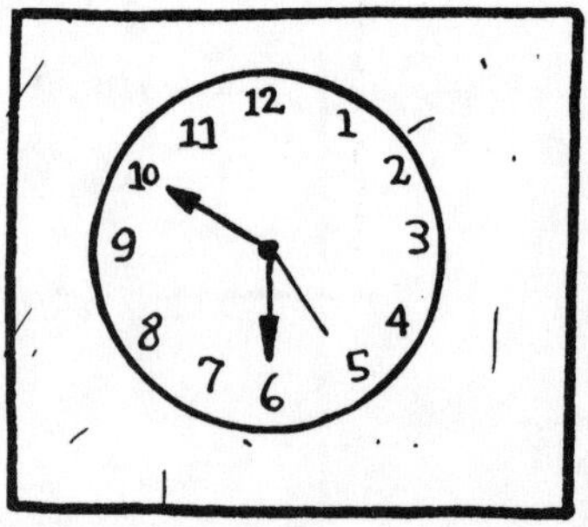

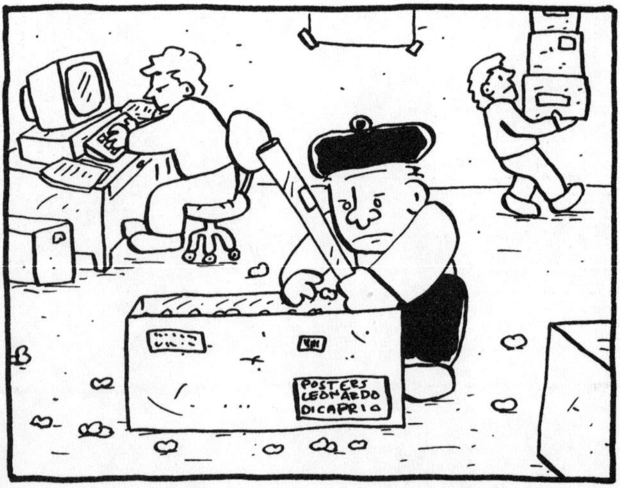
POSTERS LEONARDO DICAPRIO

ZZZZTTTTT

DIATTAVIO POSTERS
WHOLESALE · RETAIL
ART · NATURE · CELEBRITY

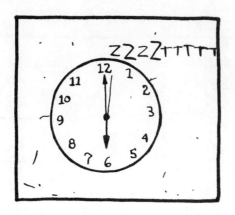

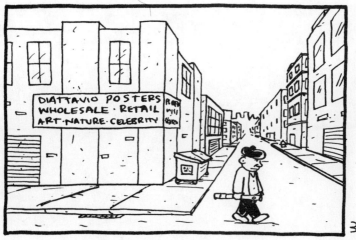

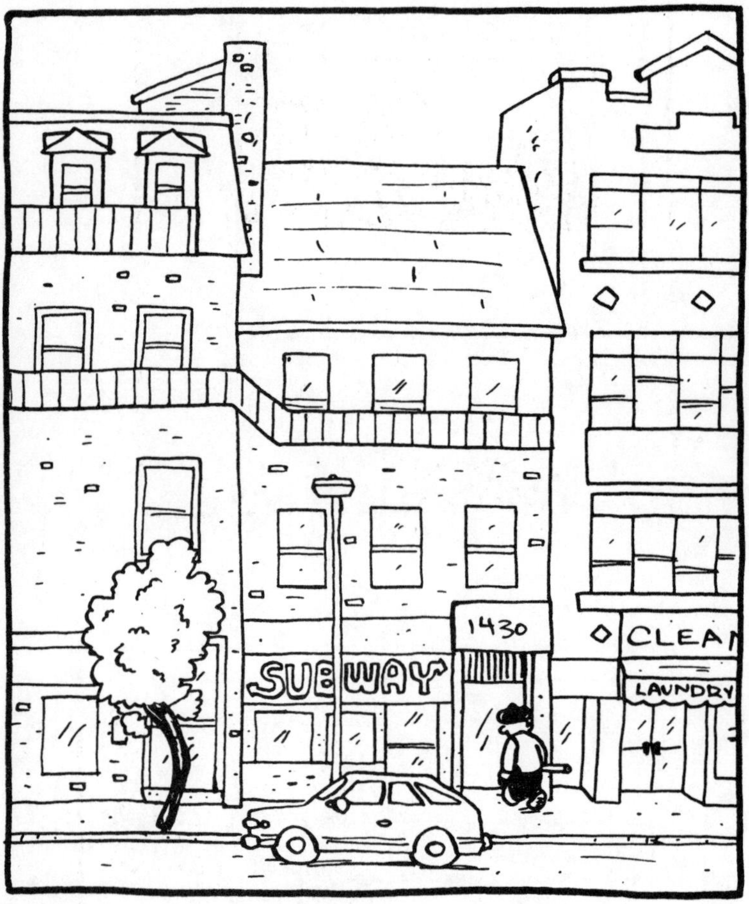

1430
SUBWAY
CLEA
LAUNDRY

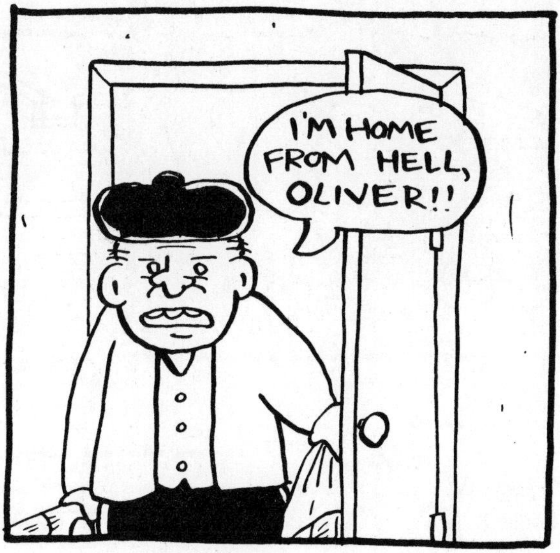
I'M HOME FROM HELL, OLIVER!!

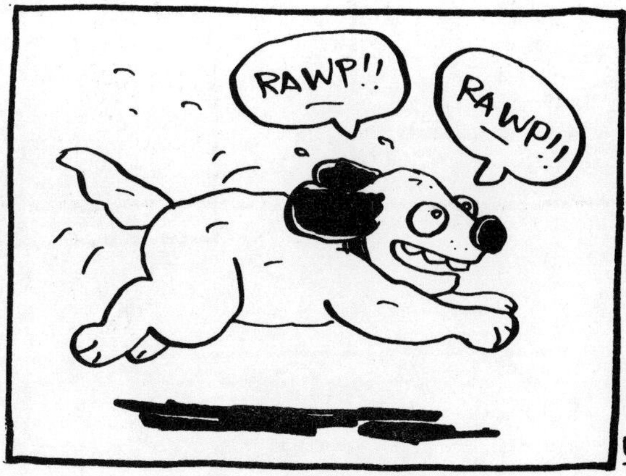
RAWP!!
RAWP!!

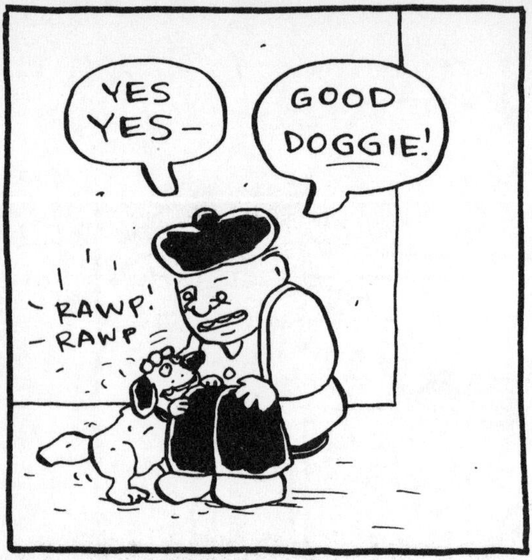
YES YES-
GOOD DOGGIE!
RAWP!
RAWP

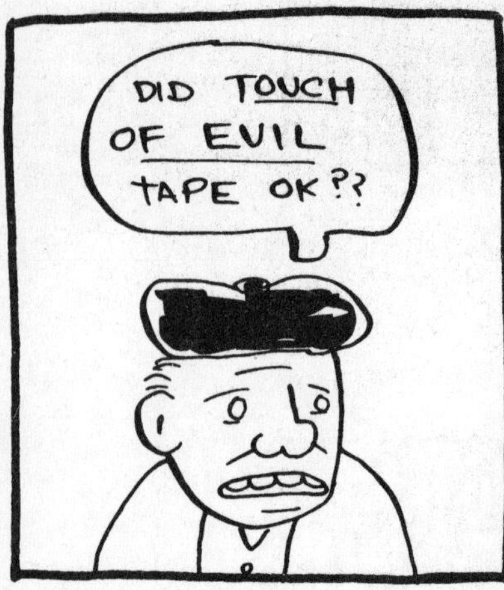
DID TOUCH OF EVIL TAPE OK??

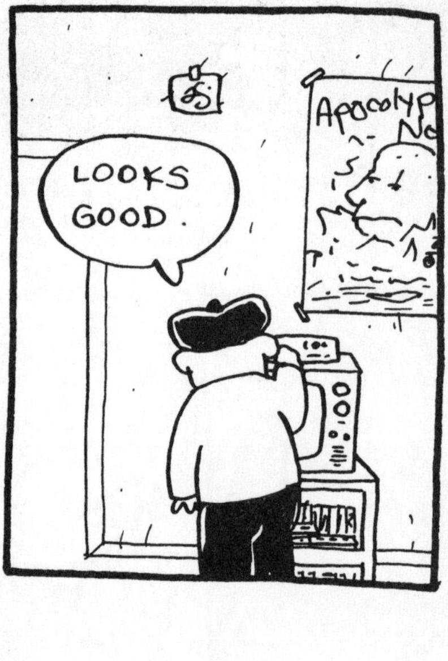
LOOKS GOOD.

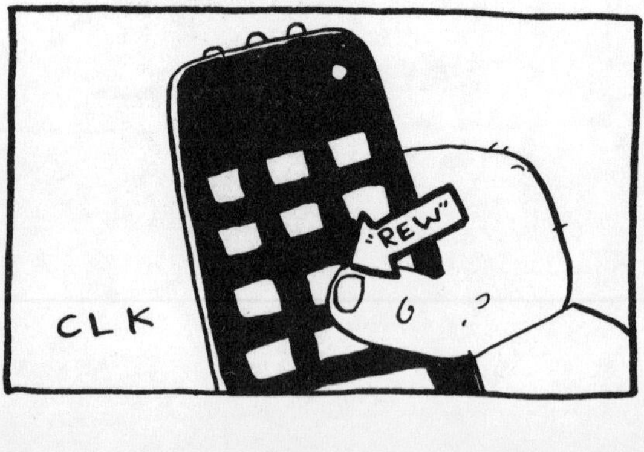
"REW"
CLK

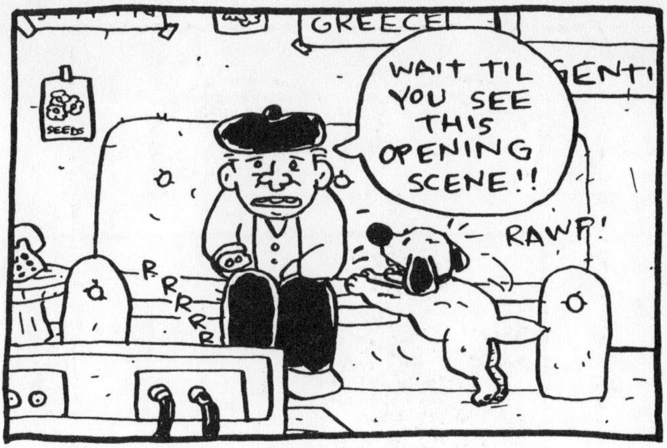
GREECE
SEEDS
GENTI
WAIT TIL YOU SEE THIS OPENING SCENE!!
RRRRRR
RAWP!

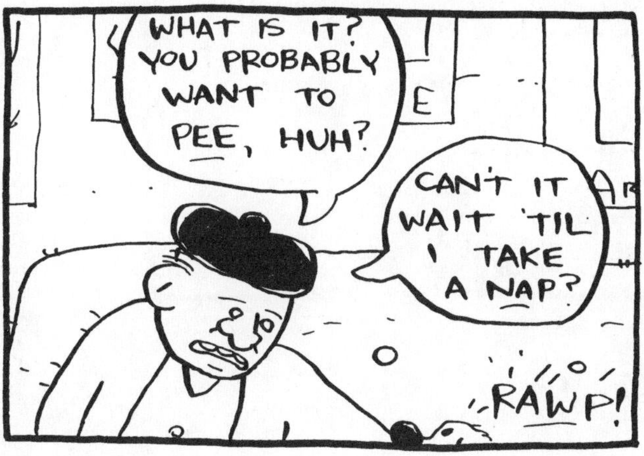
WHAT IS IT? YOU PROBABLY WANT TO PEE, HUH?
CAN'T IT WAIT 'TIL I TAKE A NAP?
RAWP!

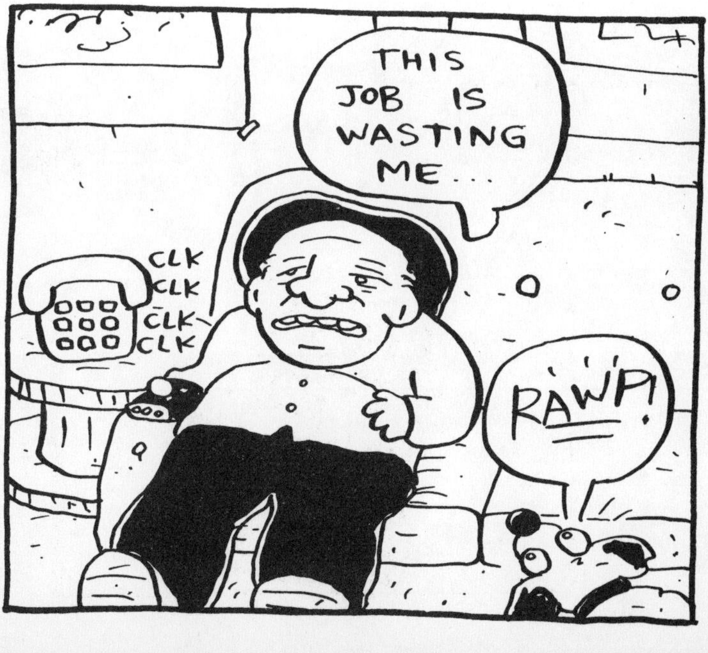
THIS JOB IS WASTING ME...
CLK CLK CLK CLK
RAWP!

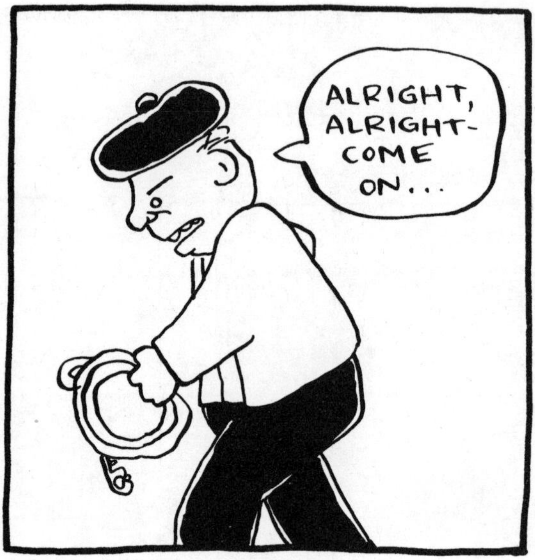
ALRIGHT, ALRIGHT- COME ON...

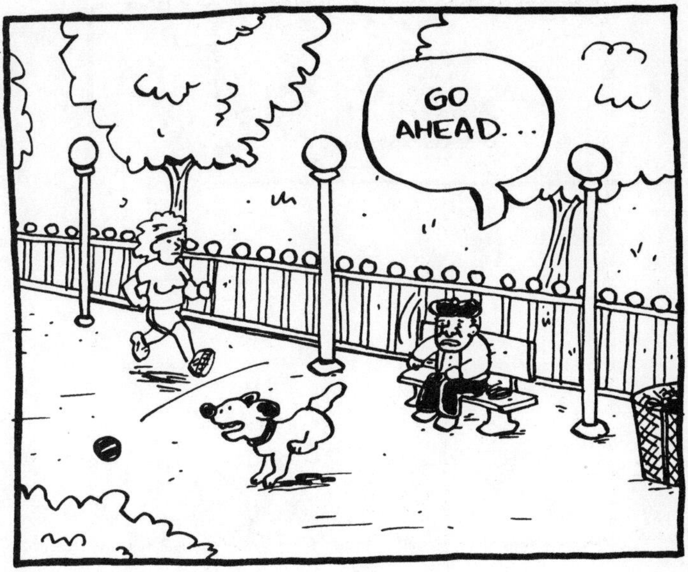
GO AHEAD...

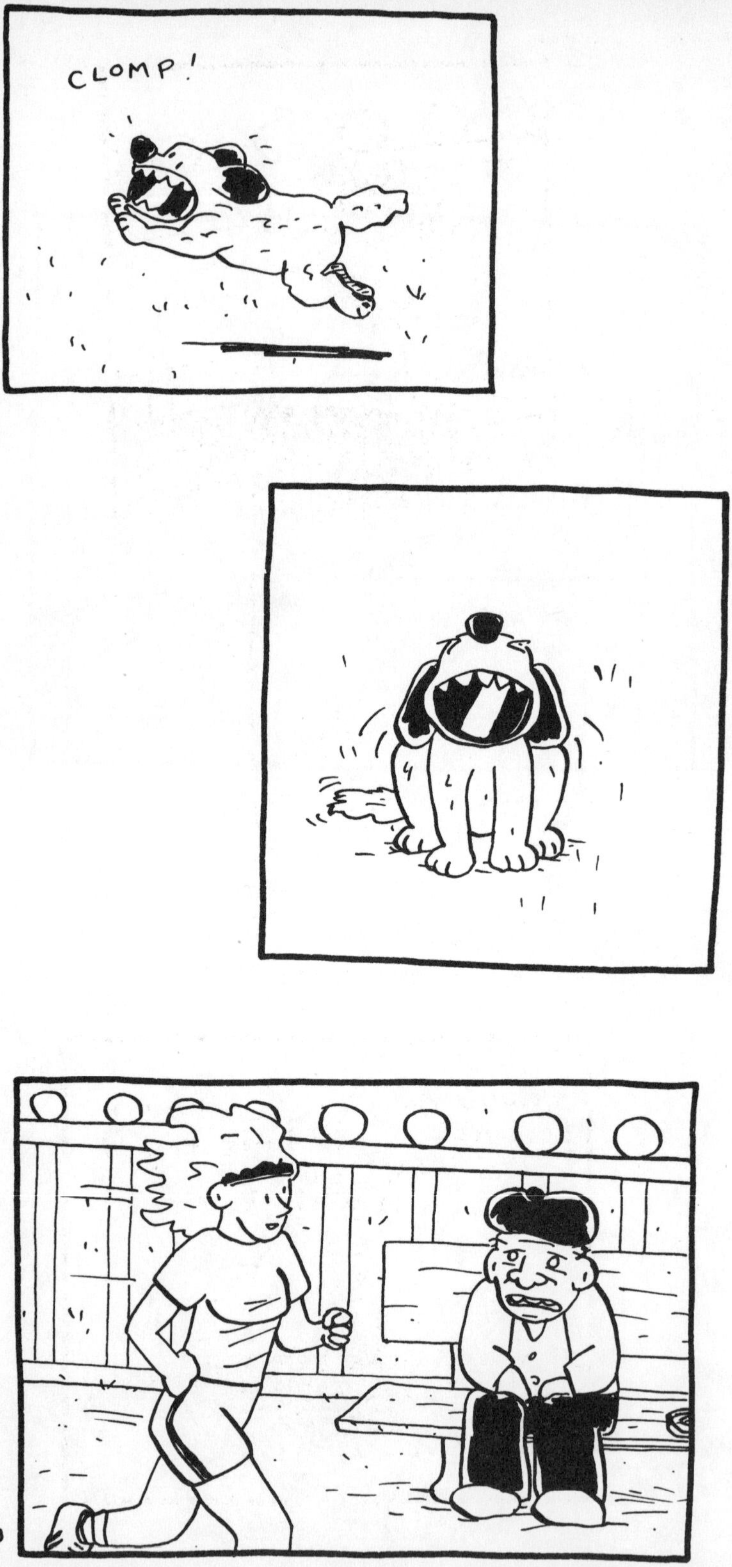
CLOMP!

GOOD BOY! ALL FINISHED?
GIVE ME THE BALL!

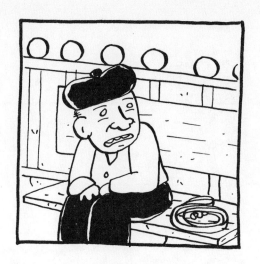

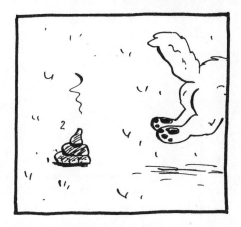

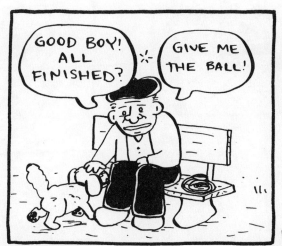

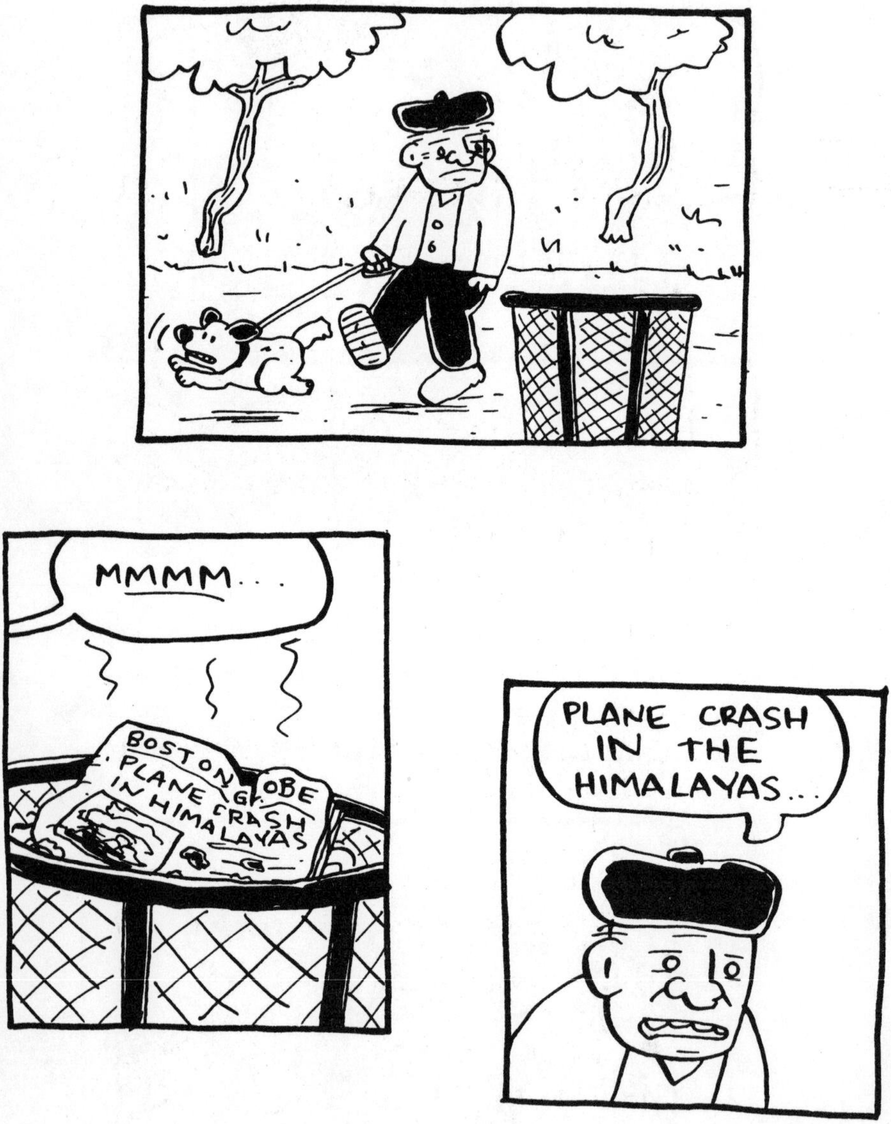
MMMM...
BOSTON
PLANE CRASH
IN HIMALAYAS
PLANE CRASH IN THE HIMALAYAS...

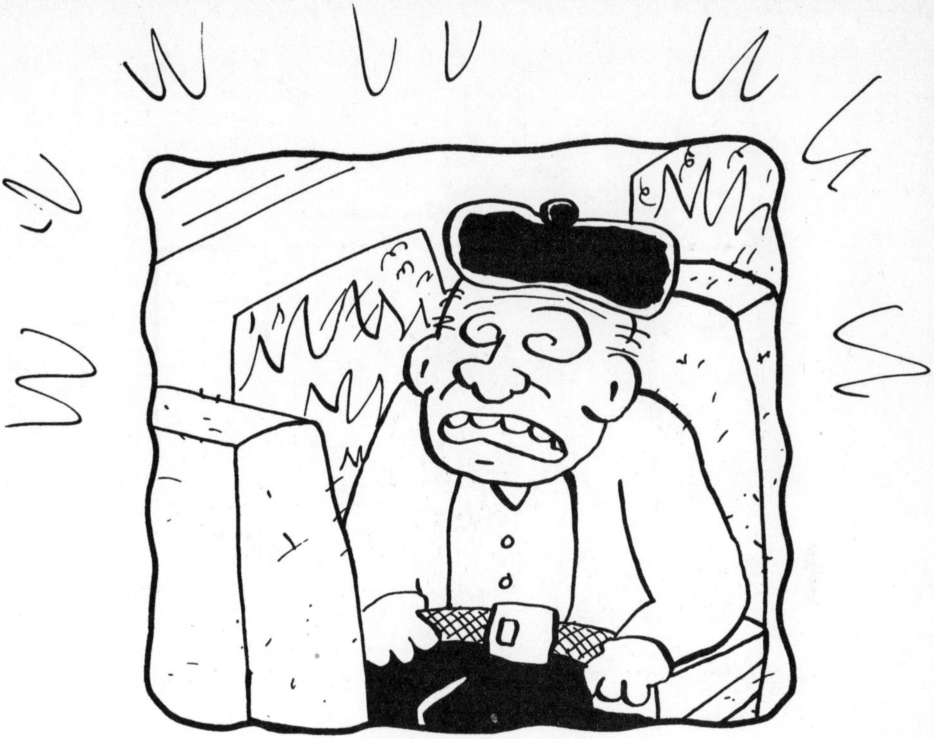

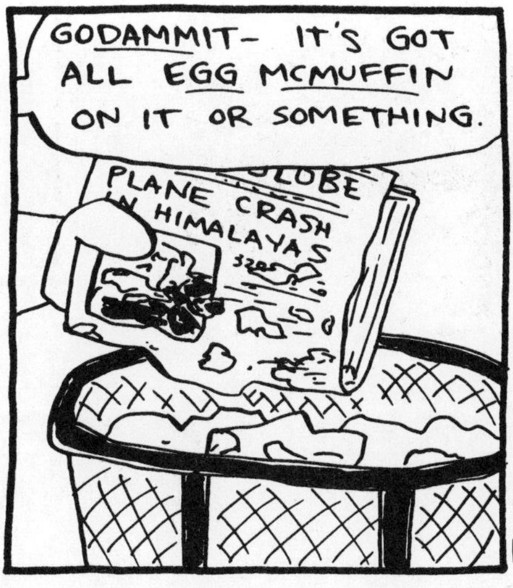
GODAMMIT- IT'S GOT ALL EGG MCMUFFIN ON IT OR SOMETHING.
PLANE CRASH
HIMALAYAS

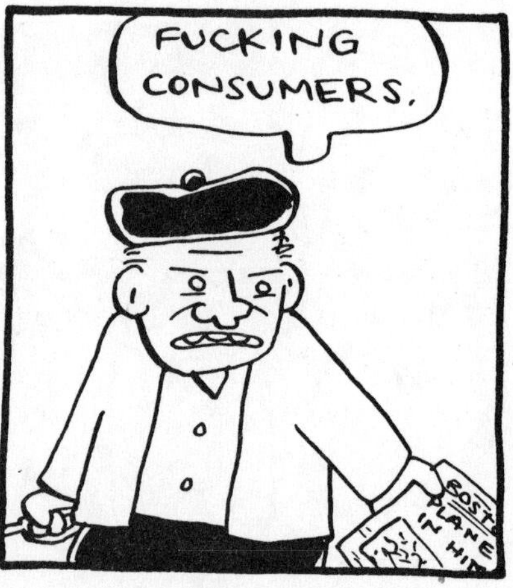
FUCKING CONSUMERS.

15

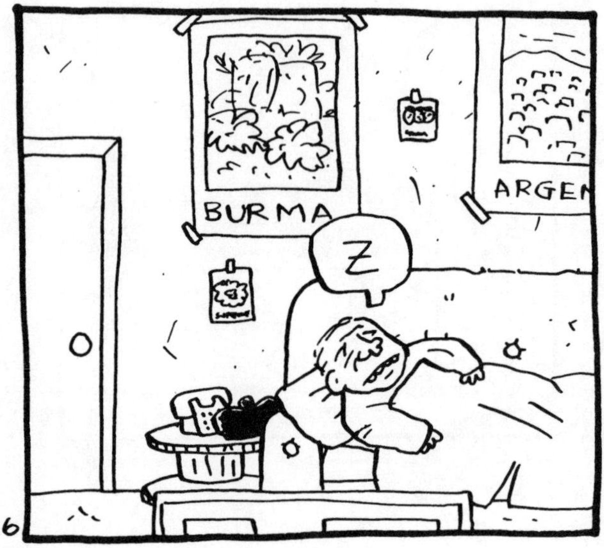
BURMA
ARGEN
Z

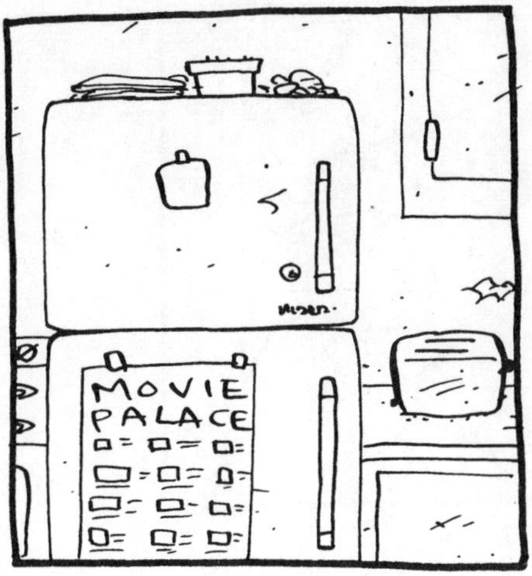
MOVIE
PALACE

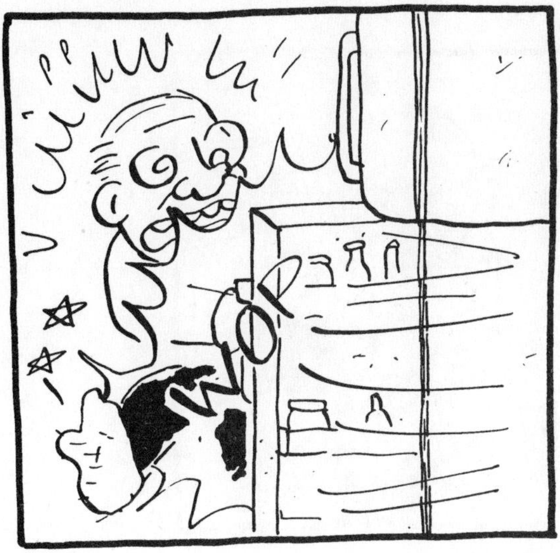
WOP

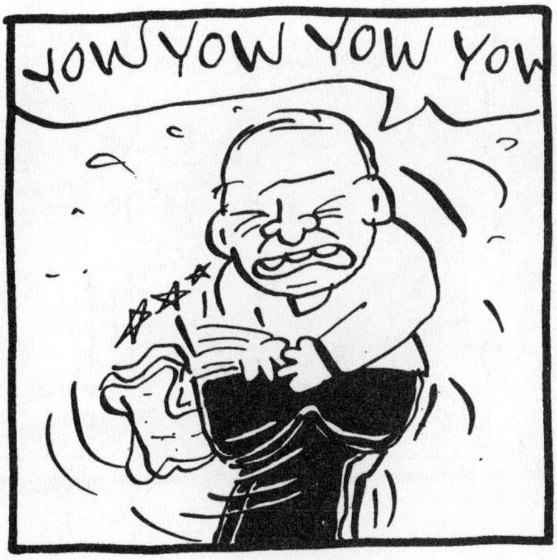
YOW YOW YOW YOW

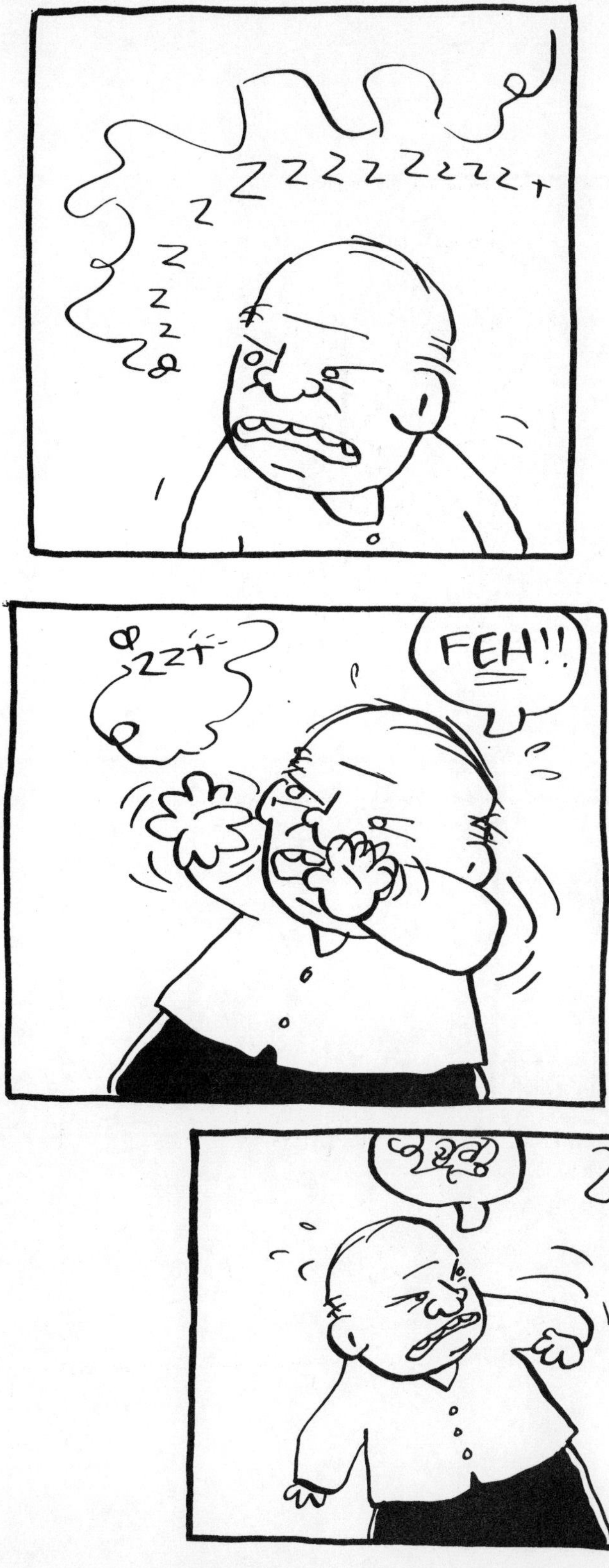
FEH!!

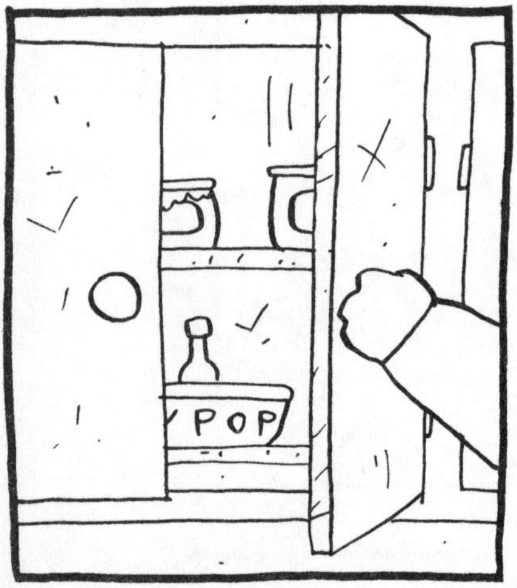
YPOP

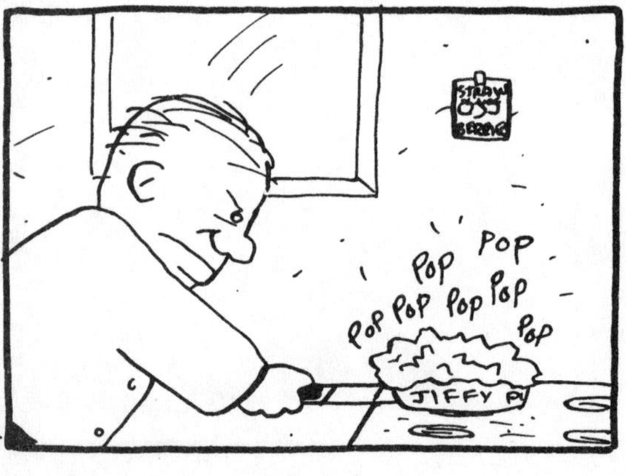
Pop POP
Pop Pop Pop Pop
Pop
JIFFY P

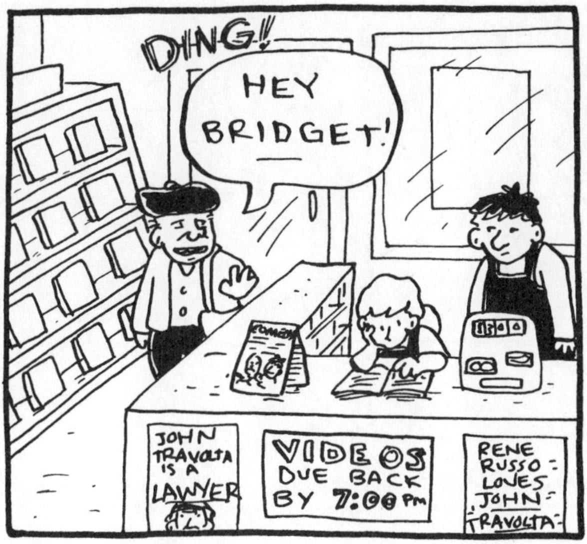
DING!
HEY BRIDGET!
JOHN TRAVOLTA IS A LAWYER
VIDEOS DUE BACK BY 7:00 PM
RENE RUSSO LOVES JOHN TRAVOLTA

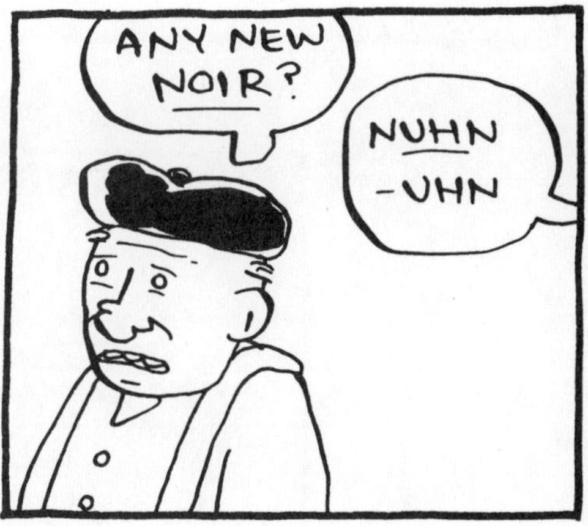
ANY NEW NOIR?
NUHN -UHN

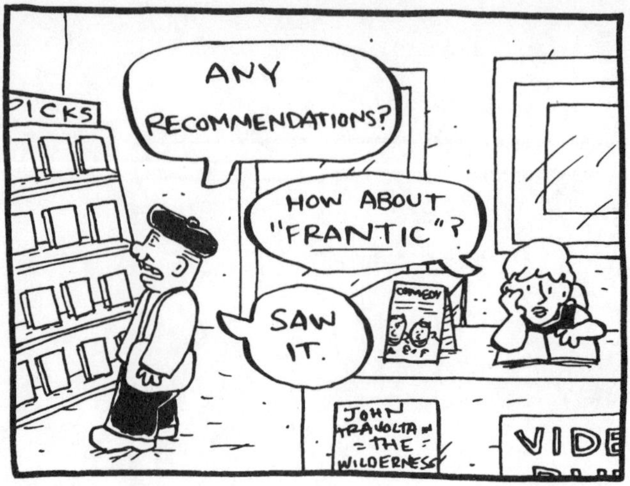
ANY RECOMMENDATIONS?
HOW ABOUT "FRANTIC"?
SAW IT.
JOHN TRAVOLTA IN THE WILDERNESS

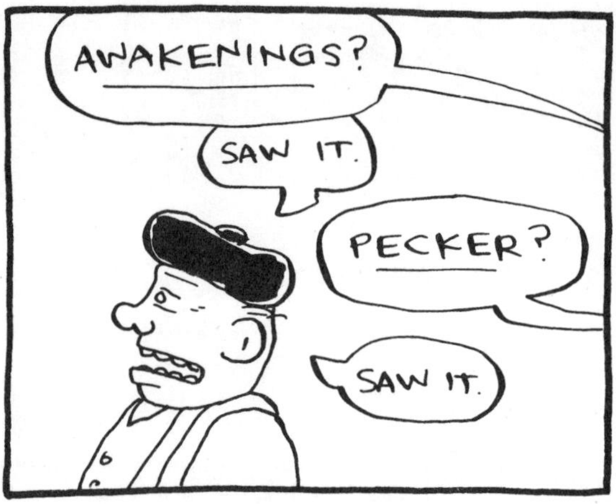
AWAKENINGS?
SAW IT.
PECKER?
SAW IT.

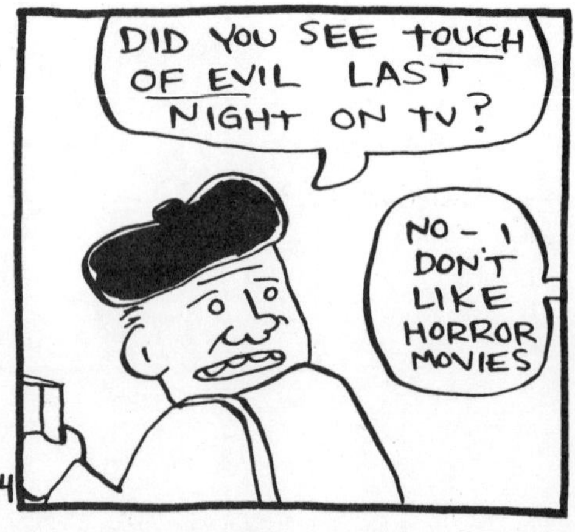
DID YOU SEE TOUCH OF EVIL LAST NIGHT ON TV?
NO - I DON'T LIKE HORROR MOVIES

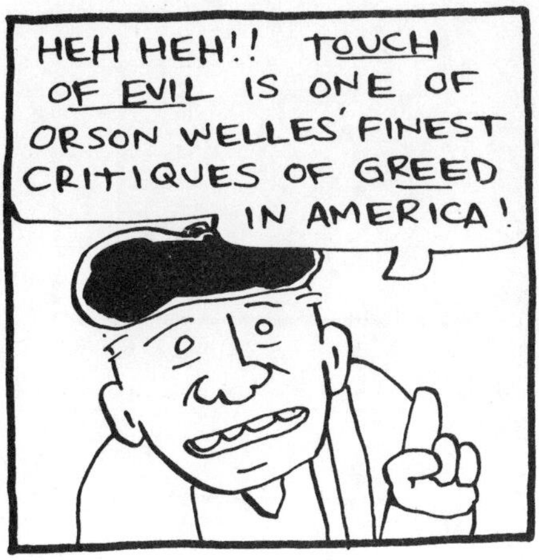
HEH HEH!! TOUCH OF EVIL IS ONE OF ORSON WELLES' FINEST CRITIQUES OF GREED IN AMERICA!

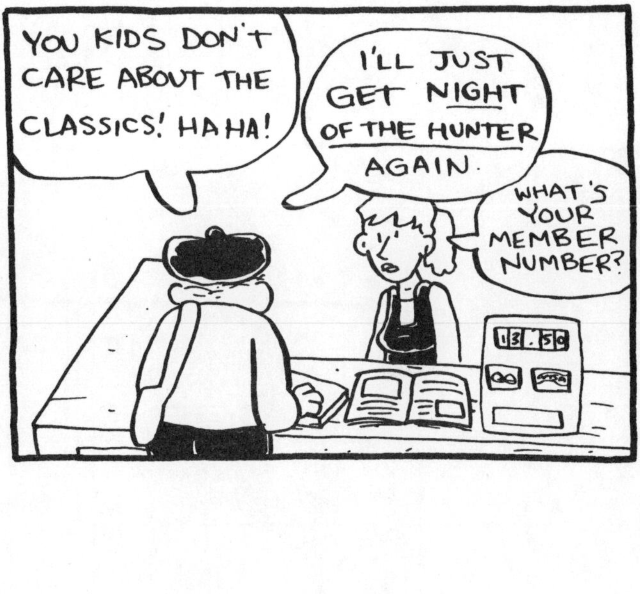
YOU KIDS DON'T CARE ABOUT THE CLASSICS! HAHA!
I'LL JUST GET NIGHT OF THE HUNTER AGAIN.
WHAT'S YOUR MEMBER NUMBER?
13.50

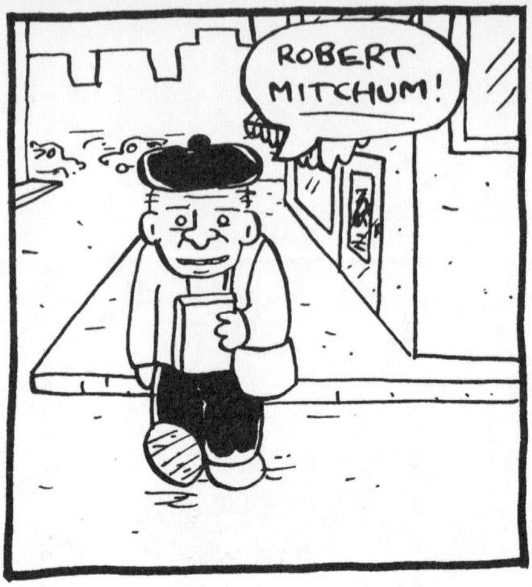
ROBERT MITCHUM!

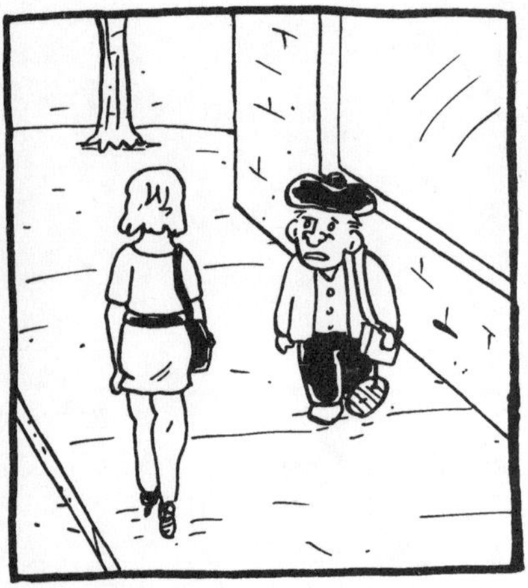

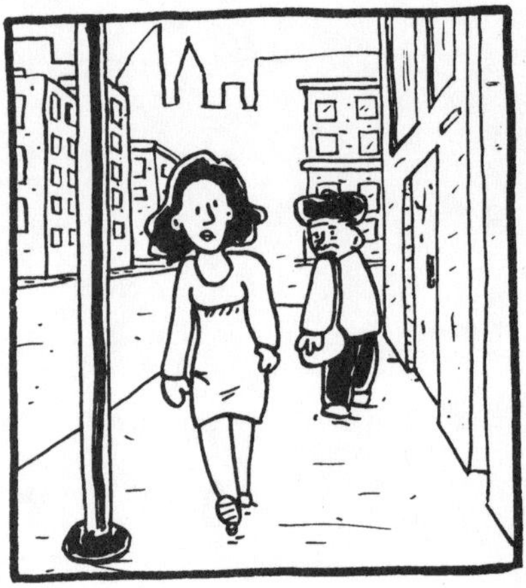

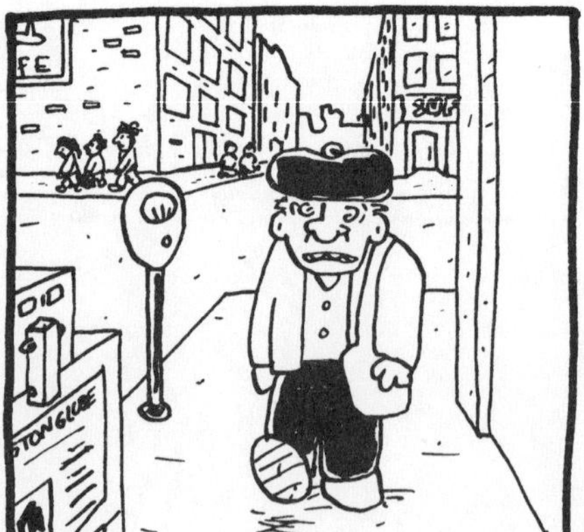

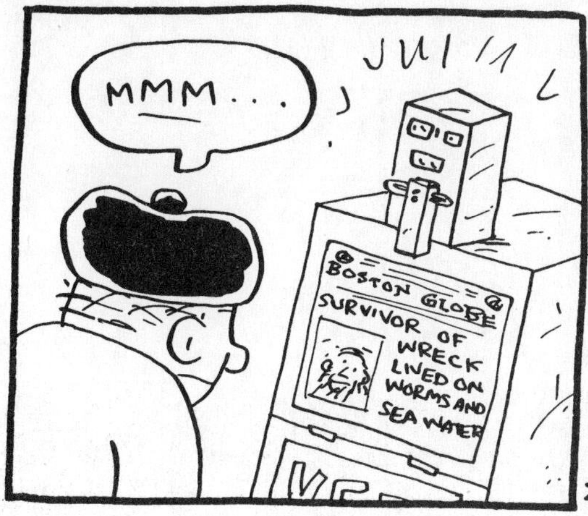
MMM...
BOSTON GLOBE
SURVIVOR OF WRECK LIVED ON WORMS AND SEA WATER

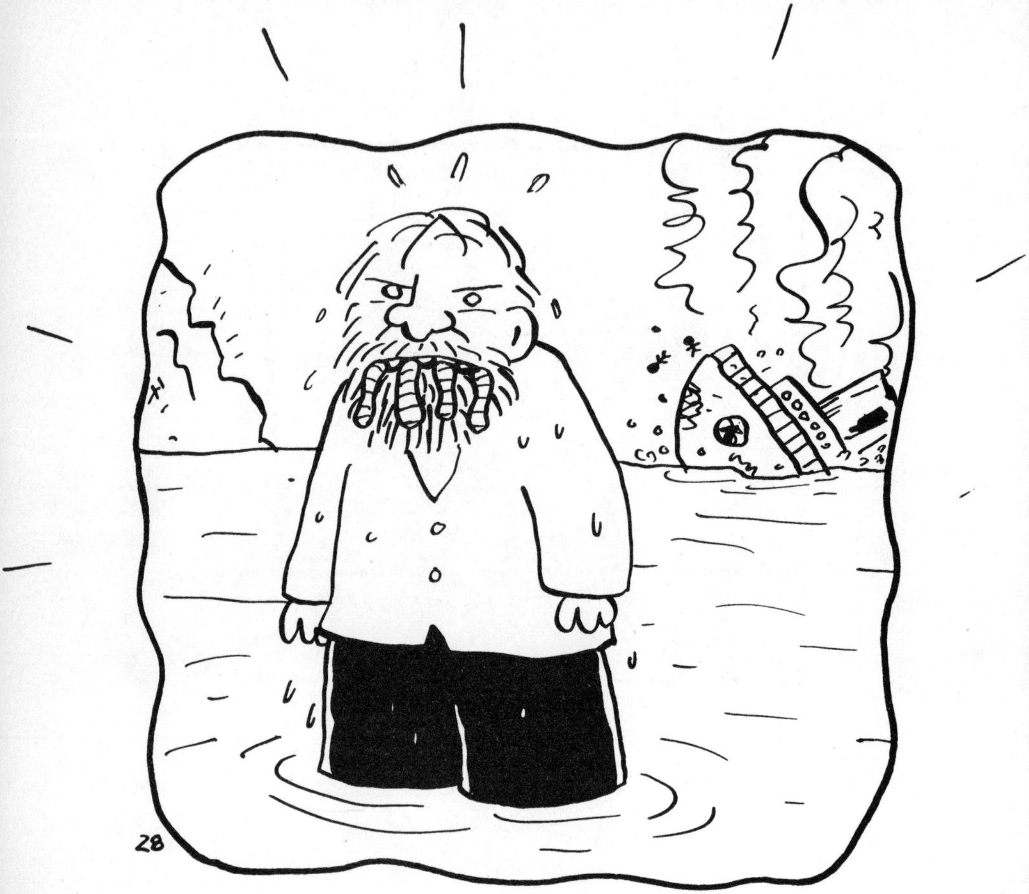

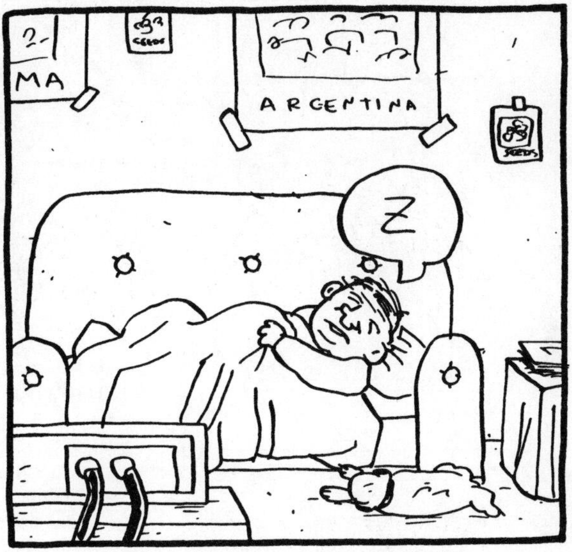
MA
ARGENTINA
Z

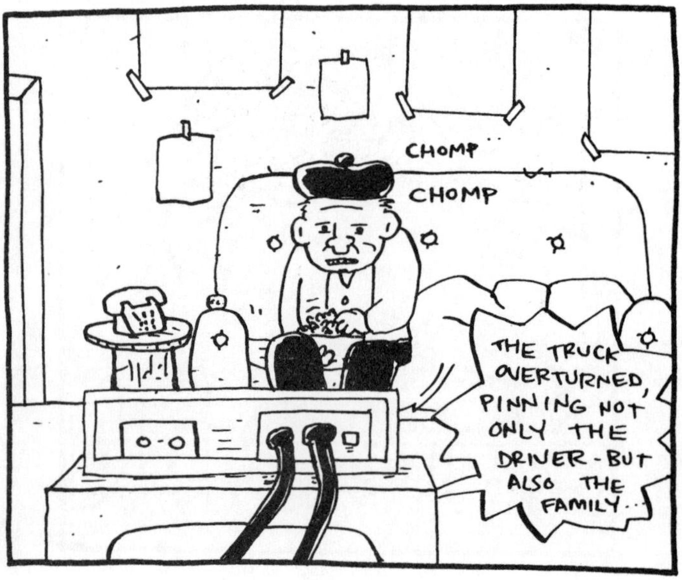
CHOMP
CHOMP
THE TRUCK OVERTURNED, PINNING NOT ONLY THE DRIVER - BUT ALSO THE FAMILY...

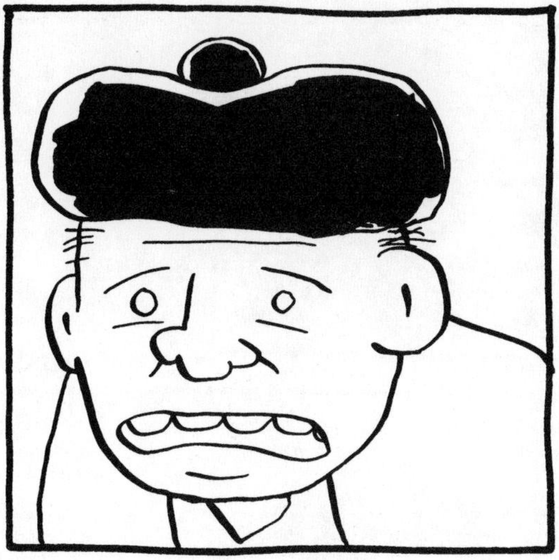

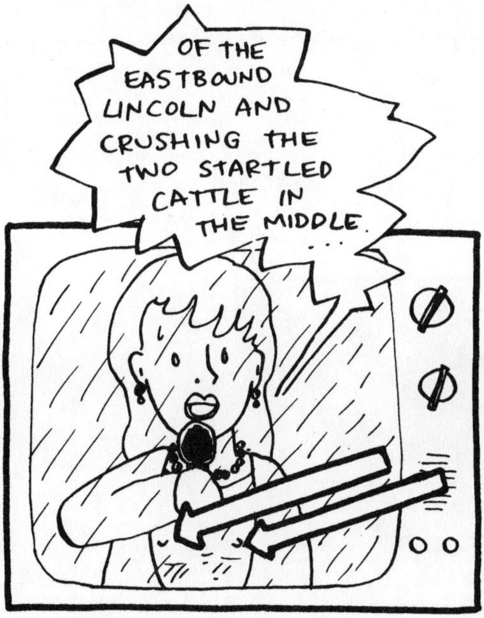
OF THE EASTBOUND LINCOLN AND CRUSHING THE TWO STARTLED CATTLE IN THE MIDDLE. . . .

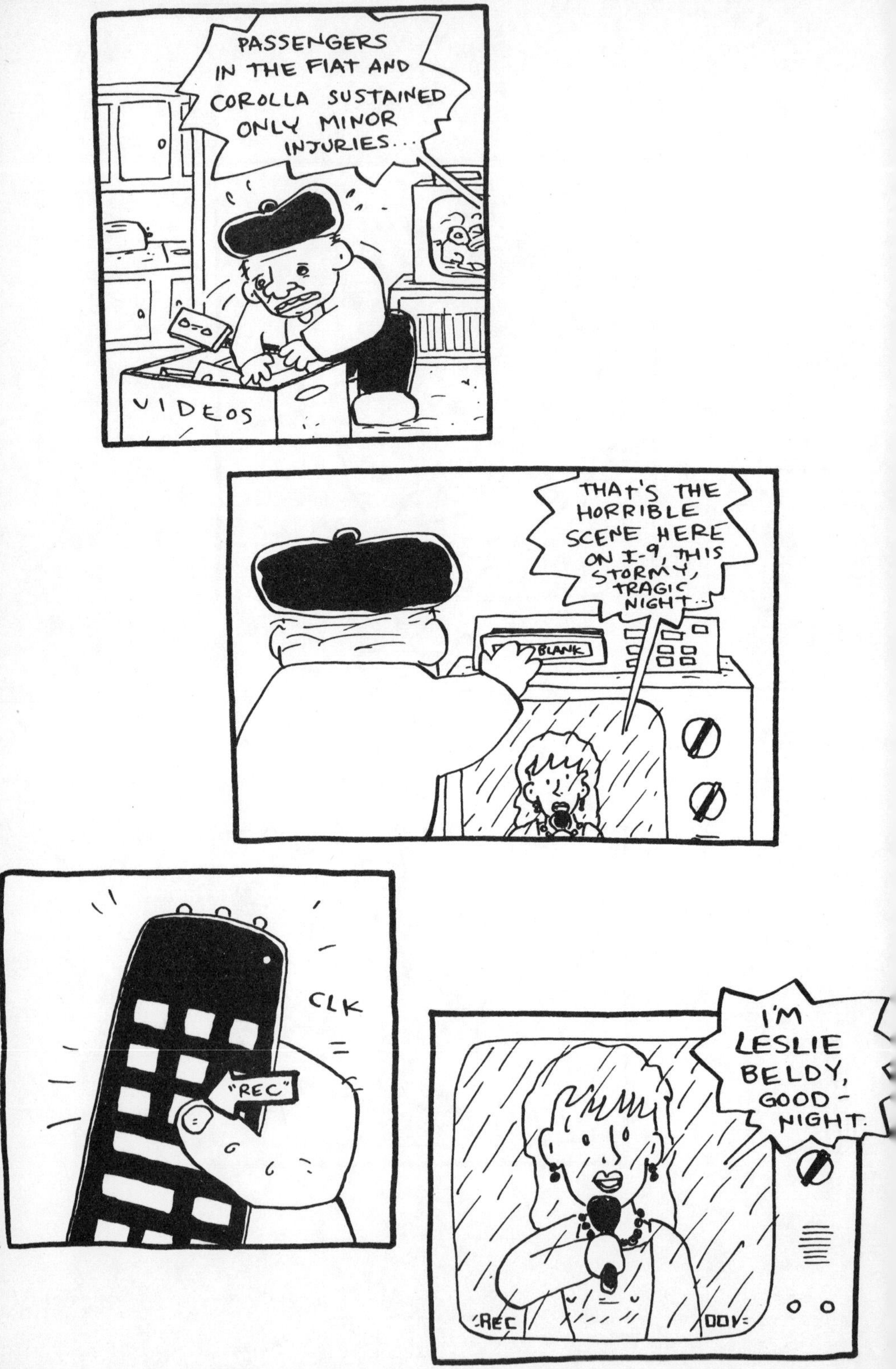
PASSENGERS IN THE FIAT AND COROLLA SUSTAINED ONLY MINOR INJURIES...
VIDEOS
THAT'S THE HORRIBLE SCENE HERE ON I-9, THIS STORMY, TRAGIC NIGHT...
BLANK
CLK
"REC"
I'M LESLIE BELDY, GOOD-NIGHT.
REC

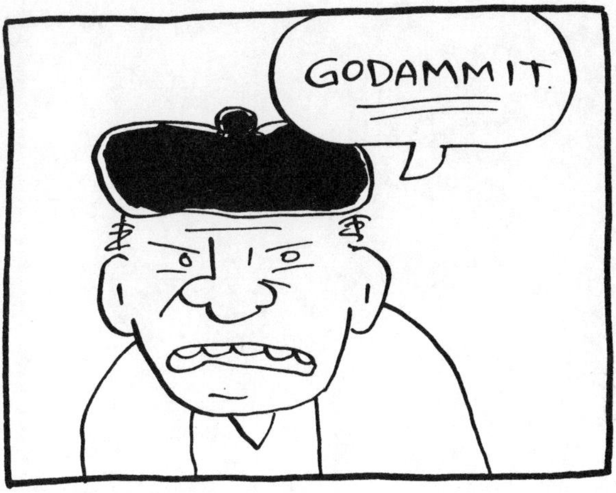
GODAMMIT.

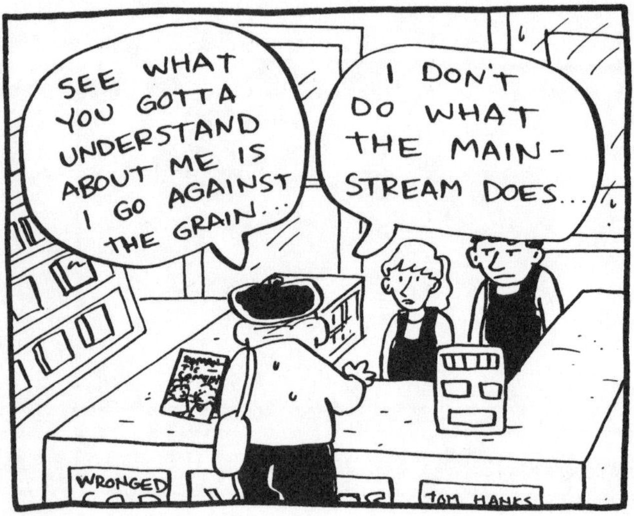
SEE WHAT YOU GOTTA UNDERSTAND ABOUT ME IS I GO AGAINST THE GRAIN...
I DON'T DO WHAT THE MAIN-STREAM DOES...
WRONGED
TOM HANKS

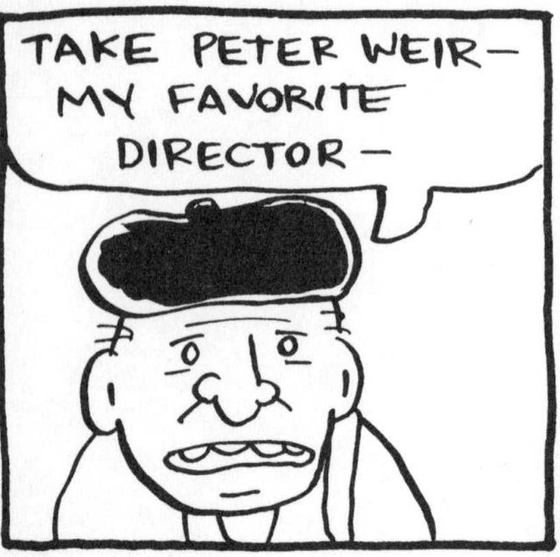
TAKE PETER WEIR– MY FAVORITE DIRECTOR–

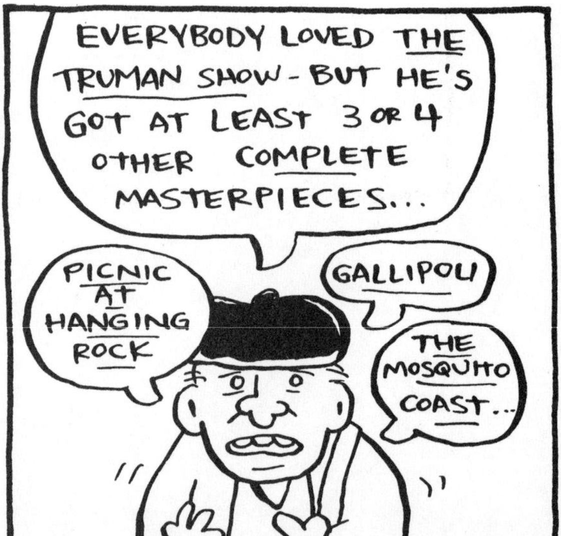
EVERYBODY LOVED THE TRUMAN SHOW - BUT HE'S GOT AT LEAST 3 OR 4 OTHER COMPLETE MASTERPIECES...
PICNIC AT HANGING ROCK
GALLIPOLI
THE MOSQUITO COAST...

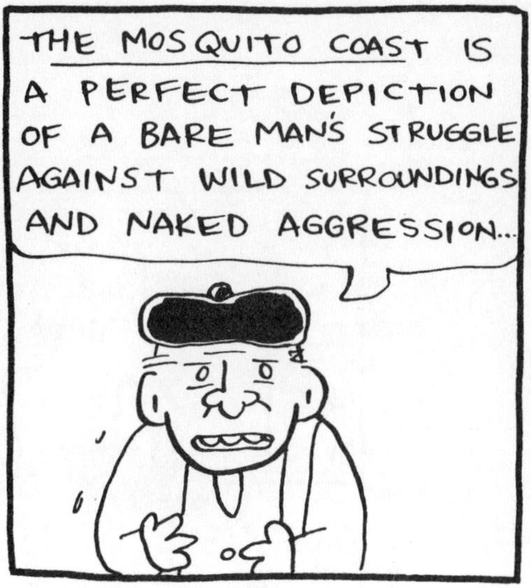
THE MOSQUITO COAST IS A PERFECT DEPICTION OF A BARE MAN'S STRUGGLE AGAINST WILD SURROUNDINGS AND NAKED AGGRESSION...

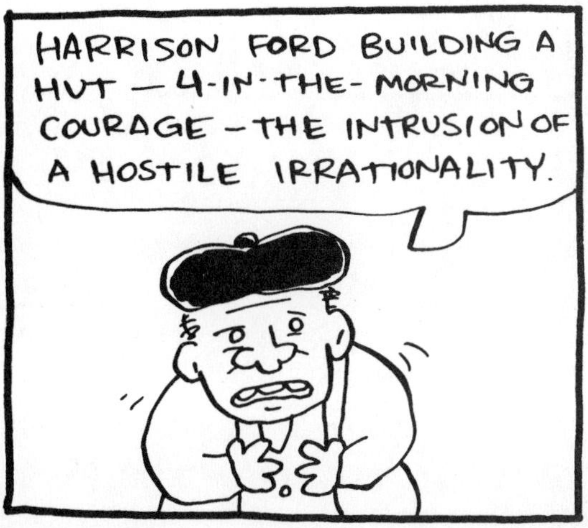
HARRISON FORD BUILDING A HUT — 4-IN-THE-MORNING COURAGE — THE INTRUSION OF A HOSTILE IRRATIONALITY.

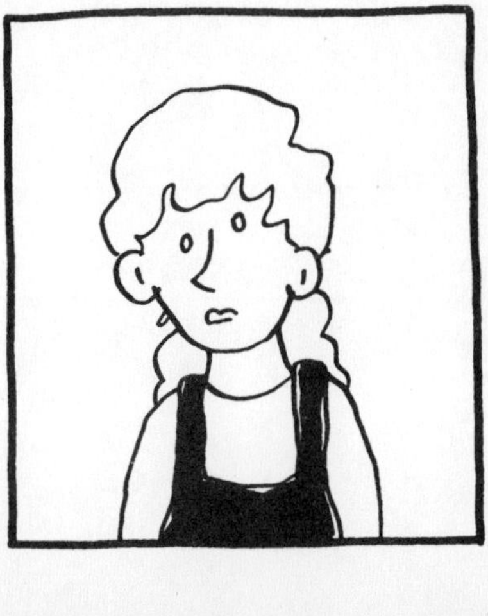

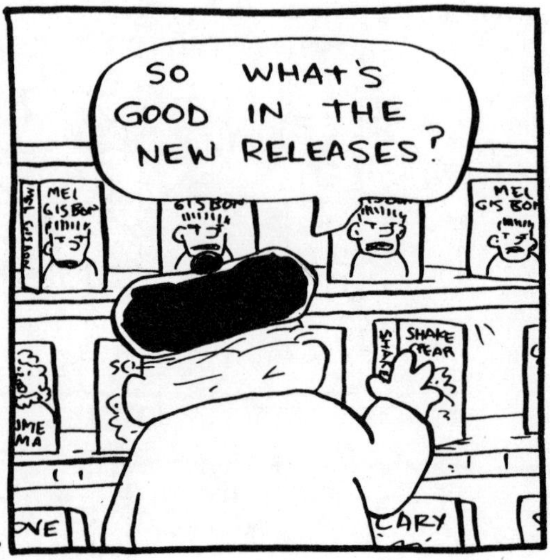
SO WHAT'S GOOD IN THE NEW RELEASES?

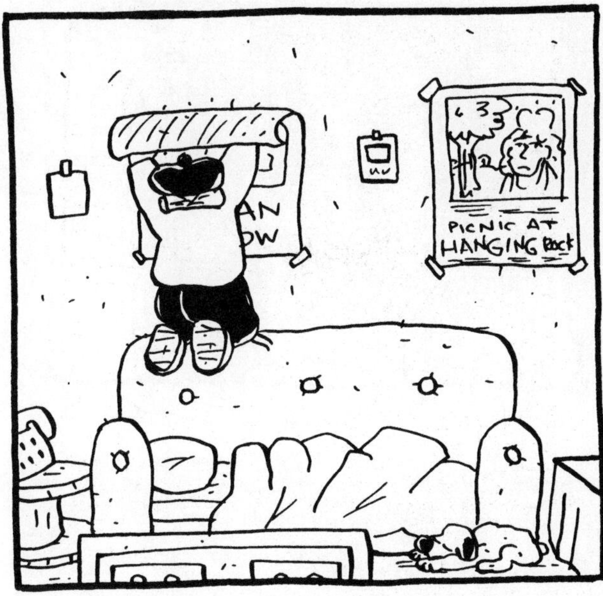
PICNIC AT
HANGING Rock

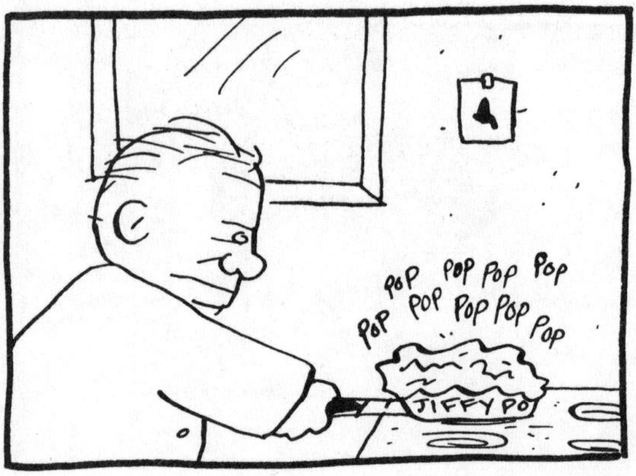
POP POP POP POP POP
POP POP POP POP POP
JIFFY PO

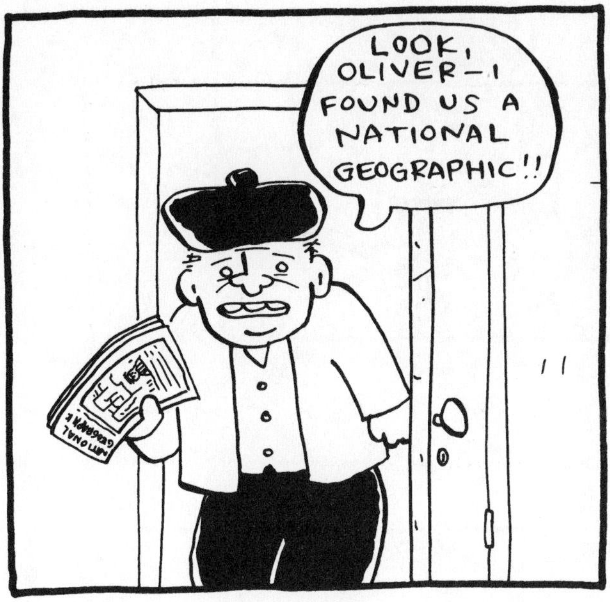
LOOK, OLIVER—I FOUND US A NATIONAL GEOGRAPHIC!!

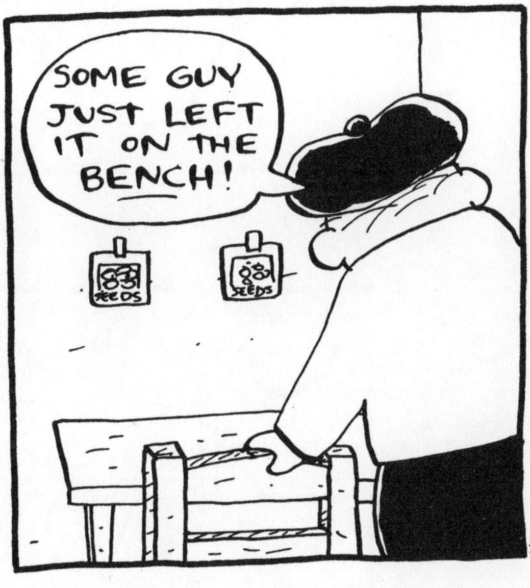
SOME GUY JUST LEFT IT ON THE BENCH!
SEEDS
SEEDS

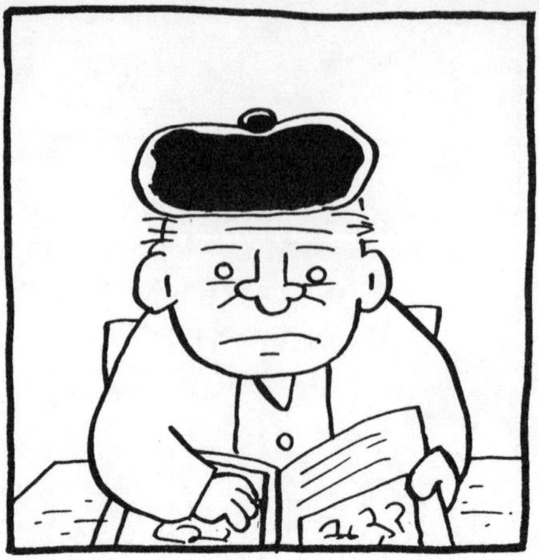

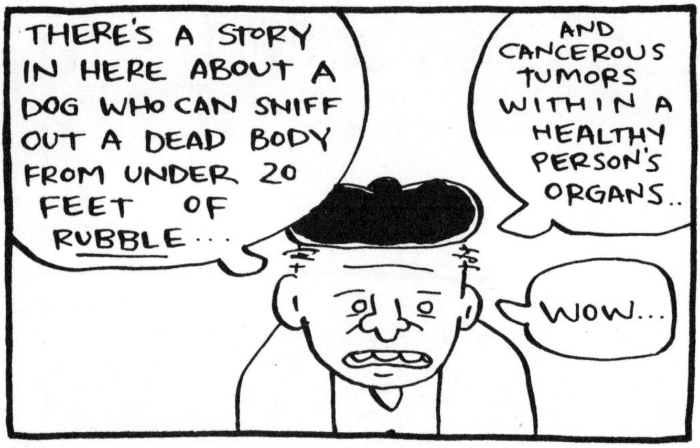
THERE'S A STORY IN HERE ABOUT A DOG WHO CAN SNIFF OUT A DEAD BODY FROM UNDER 20 FEET OF RUBBLE...
AND CANCEROUS TUMORS WITHIN A HEALTHY PERSON'S ORGANS..
WOW...

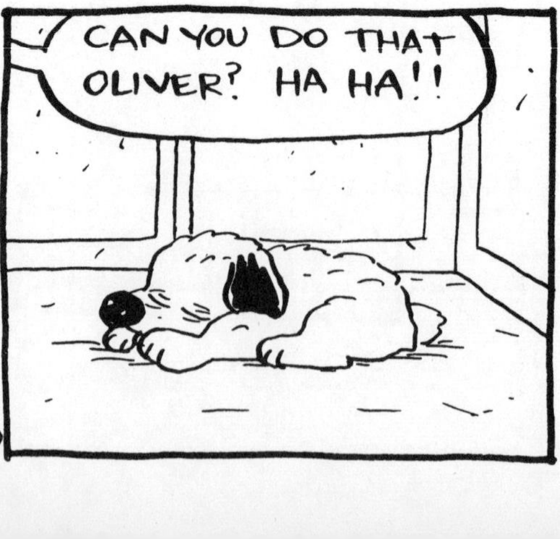
CAN YOU DO THAT OLIVER? HA HA!!

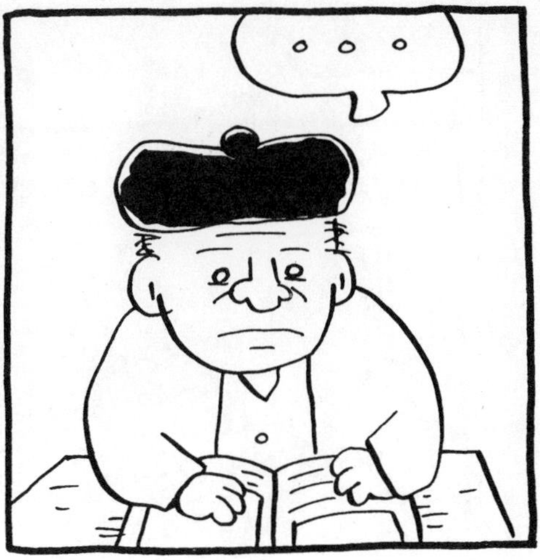

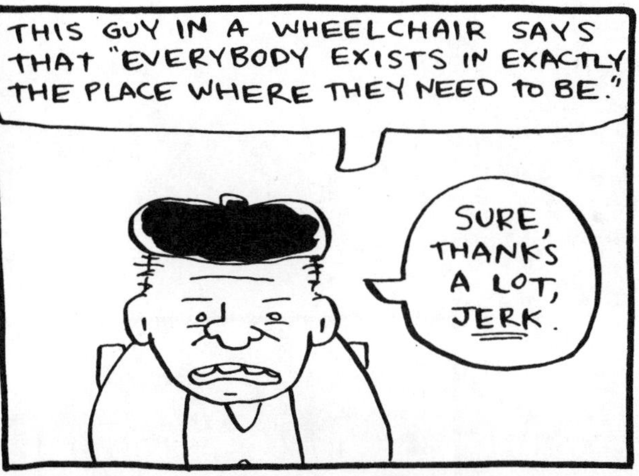
THIS GUY IN A WHEELCHAIR SAYS THAT "EVERYBODY EXISTS IN EXACTLY THE PLACE WHERE THEY NEED TO BE."
SURE, THANKS A LOT, JERK.

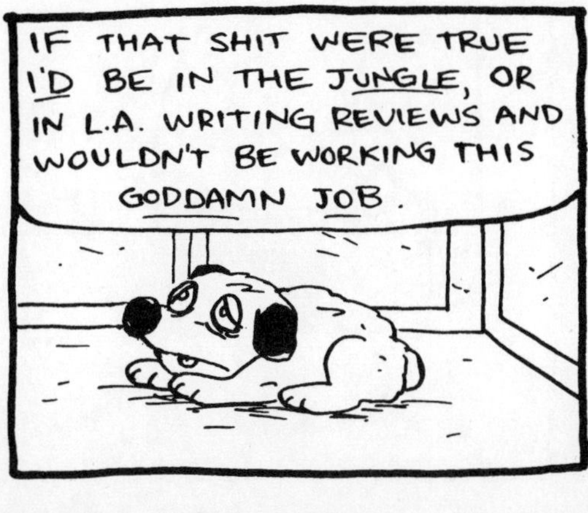
IF THAT SHIT WERE TRUE I'D BE IN THE JUNGLE, OR IN L.A. WRITING REVIEWS AND WOULDN'T BE WORKING THIS GODDAMN JOB.

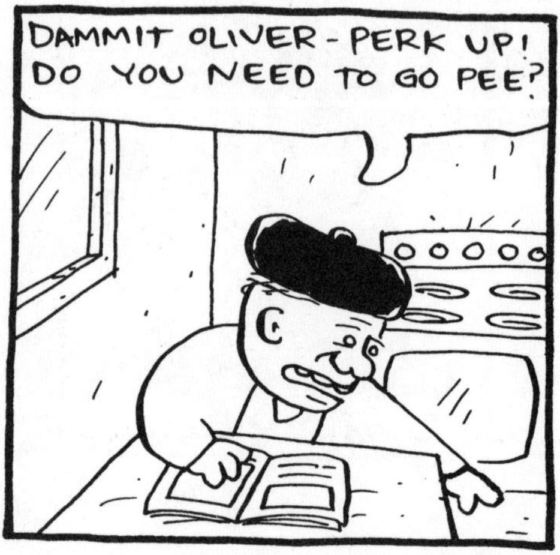
DAMMIT OLIVER - PERK UP!
DO YOU NEED TO GO PEE?

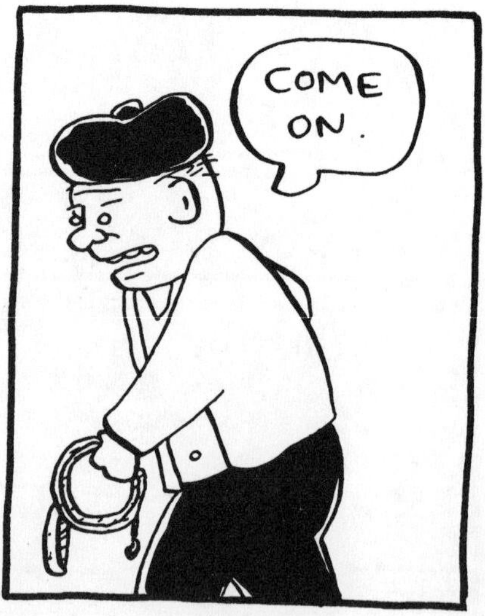
COME ON.

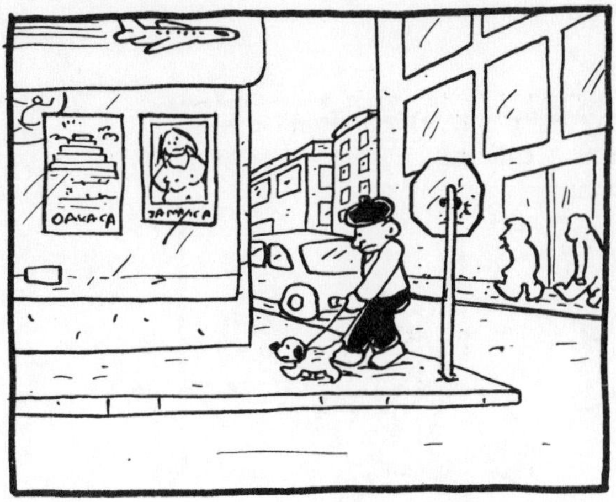
OAXACA
JAMAICA

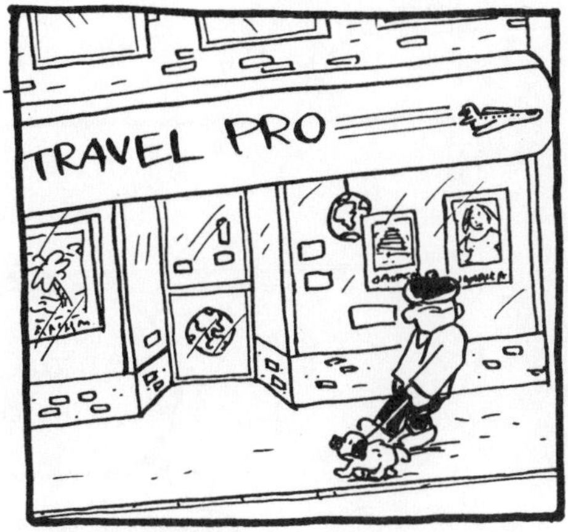
TRAVEL PRO

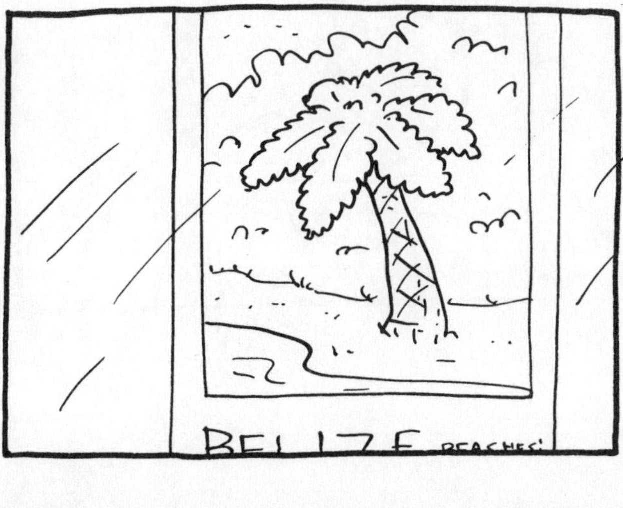
BELIZE BEACHES!

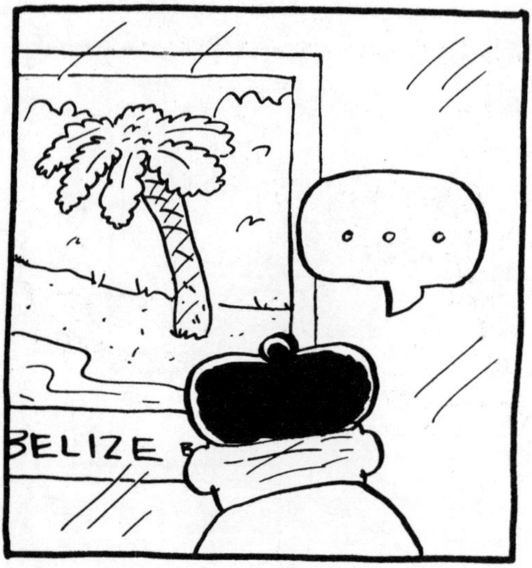
BELIZE
...

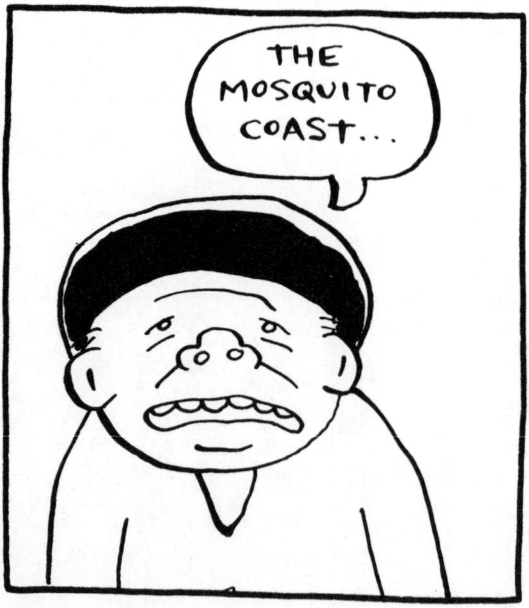
THE MOSQUITO COAST...

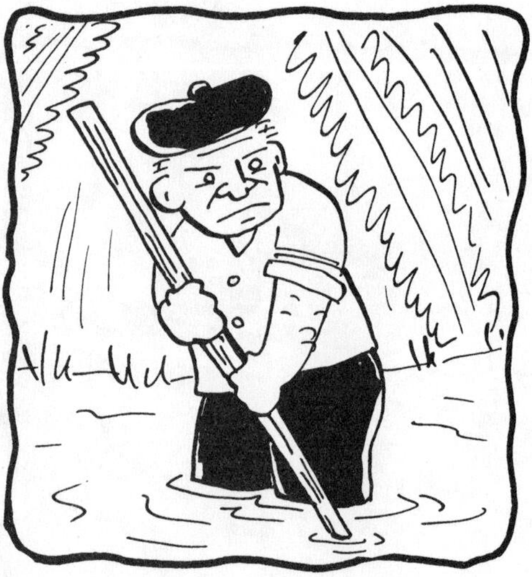

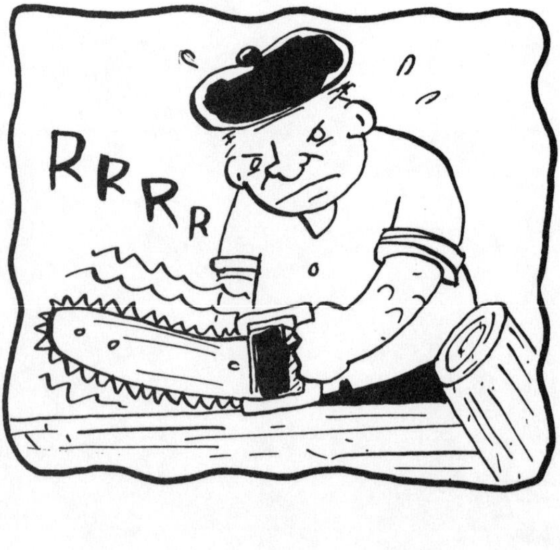
RRRRR

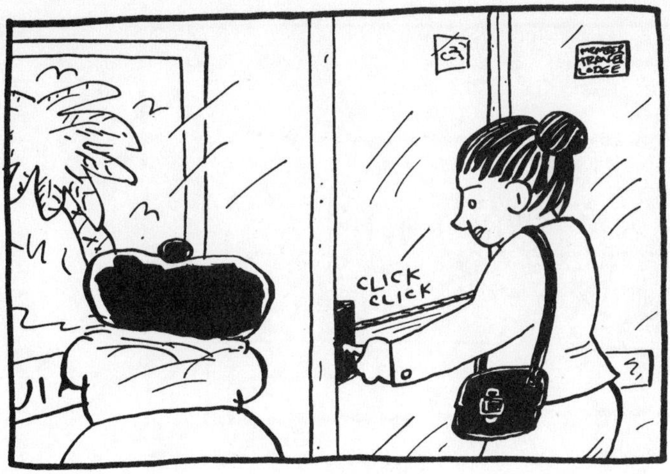
CLICK
CLICK

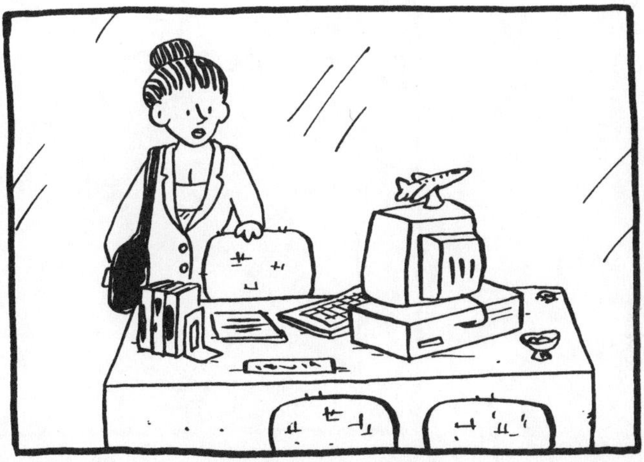

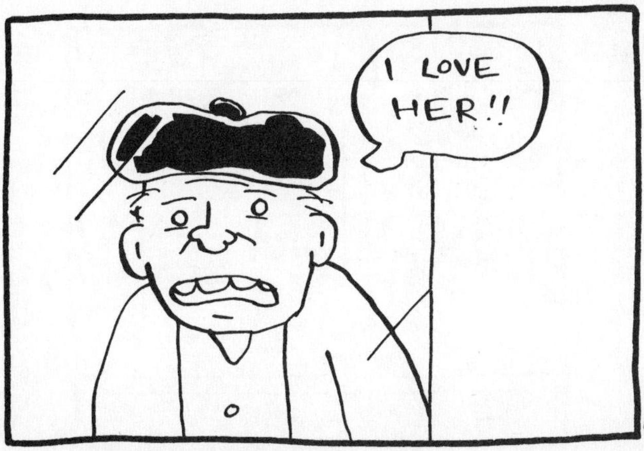
I LOVE HER!!

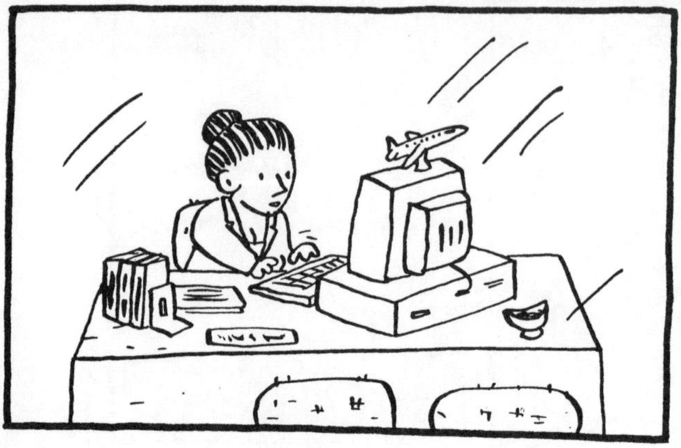

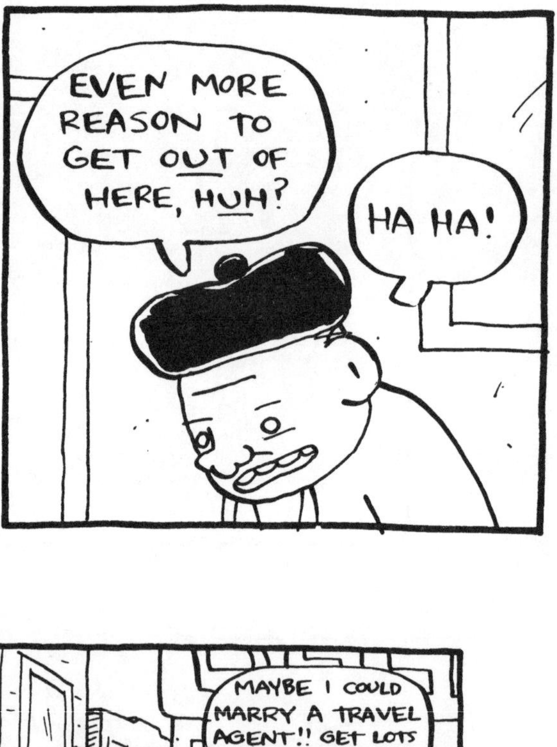
EVEN MORE REASON TO GET OUT OF HERE, HUH?
HA HA!

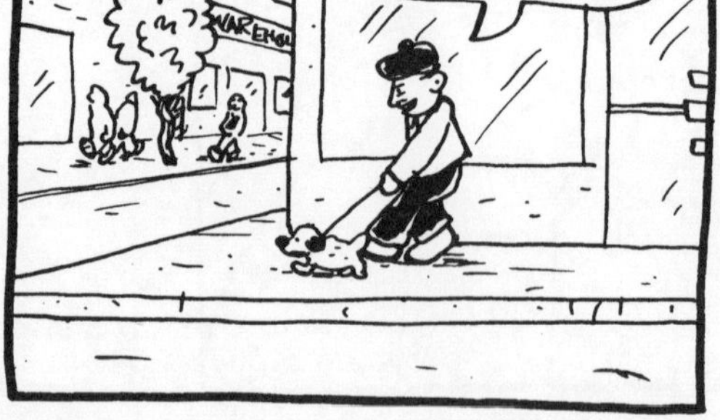
MAYBE I COULD MARRY A TRAVEL AGENT!! GET LOTS OF GOOD DEALS!

49

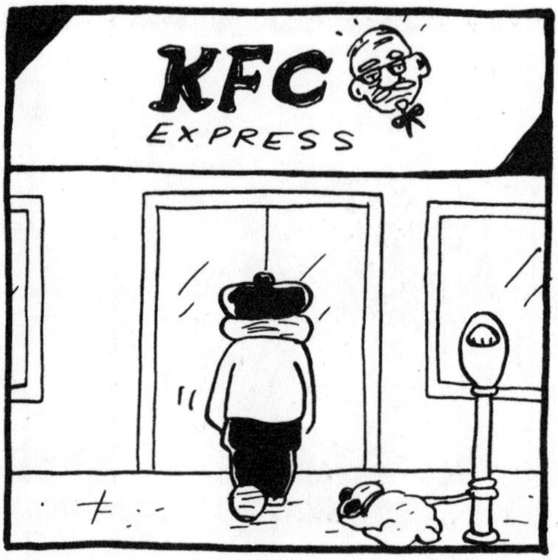
KFC
EXPRESS

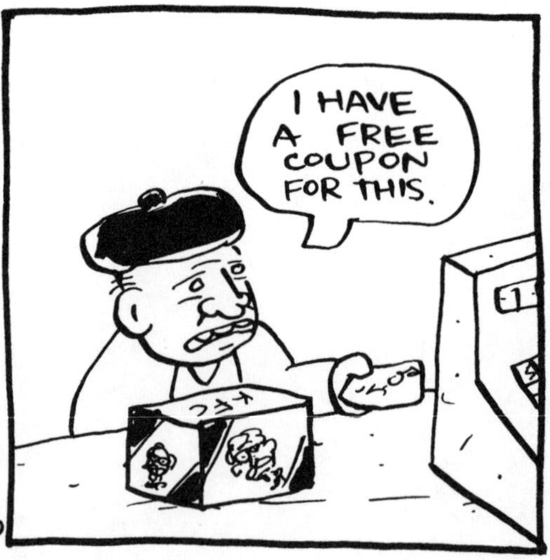
I HAVE A FREE COUPON FOR THIS.
KFC

51

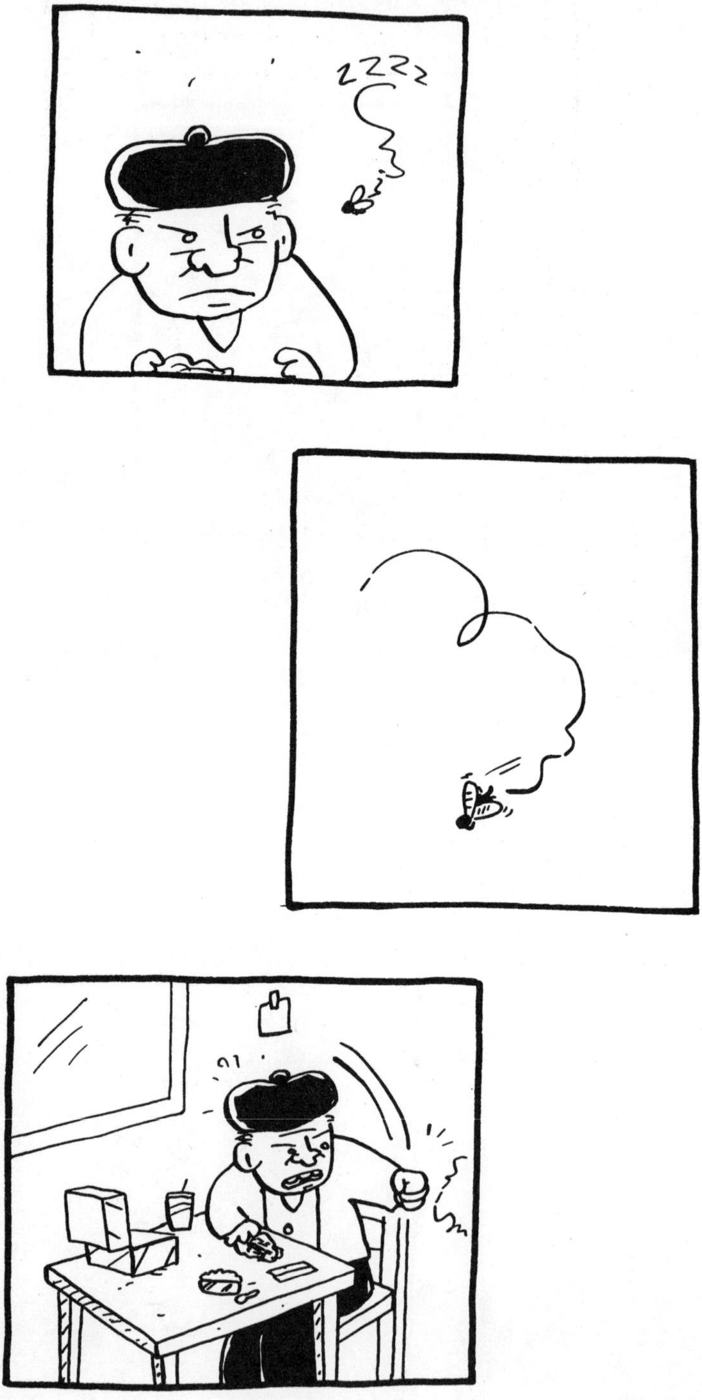
ZZZZ

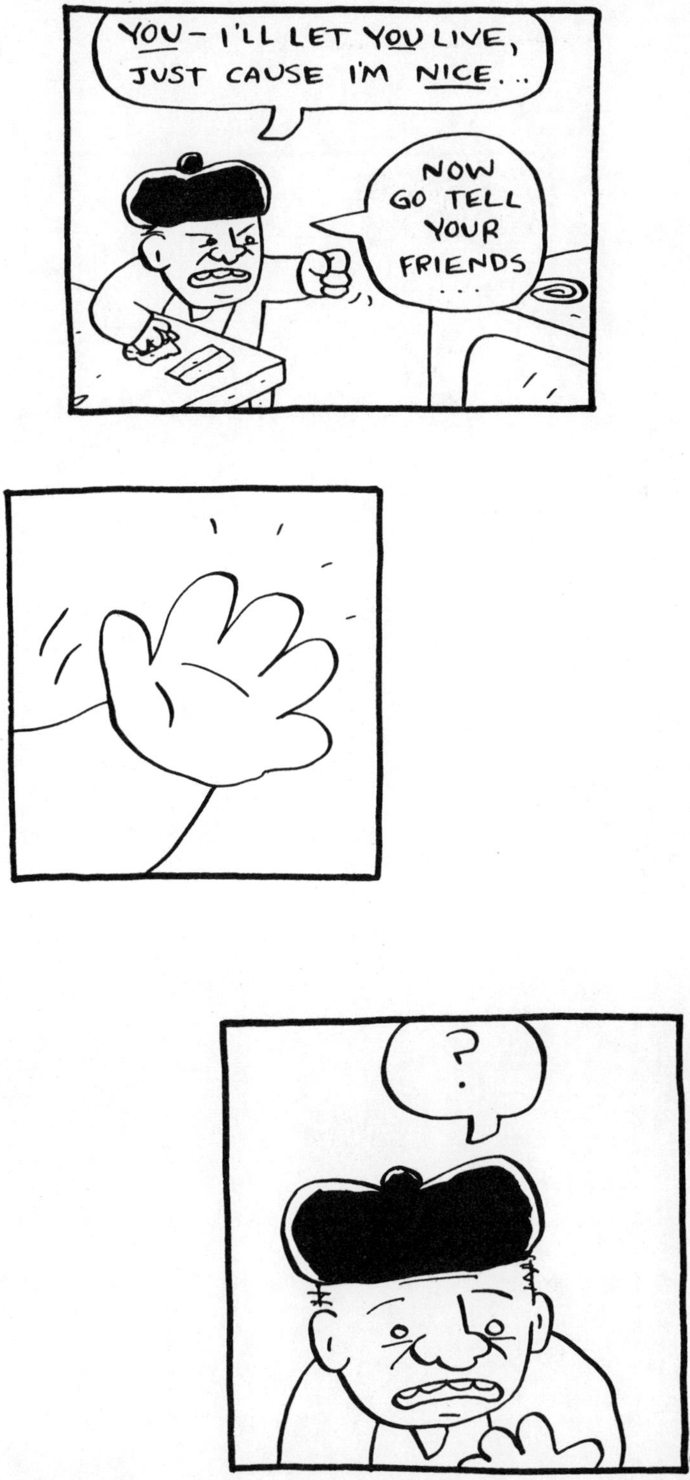
YOU- I'LL LET YOU LIVE, JUST CAUSE I'M NICE...
NOW GO TELL YOUR FRIENDS ...
?

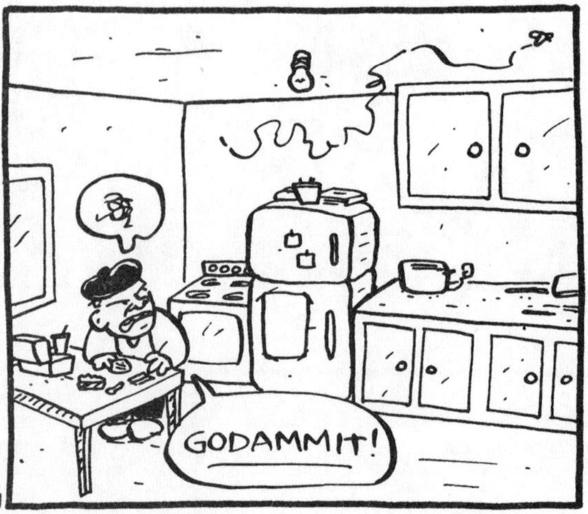
GODAMMIT!

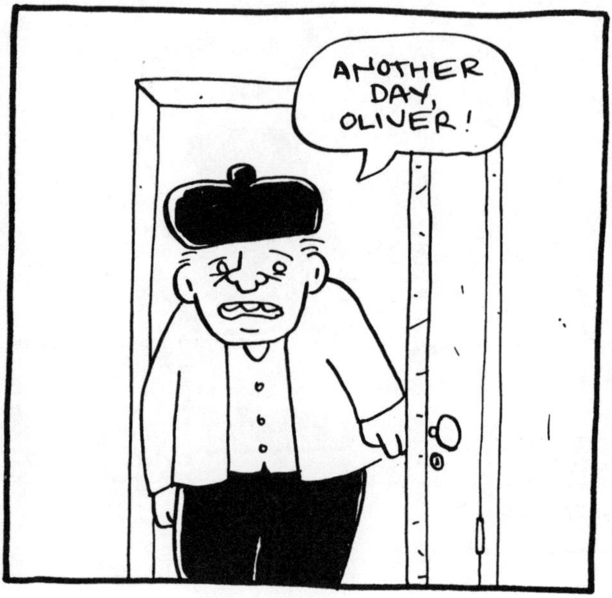
ANOTHER DAY, OLIVER!

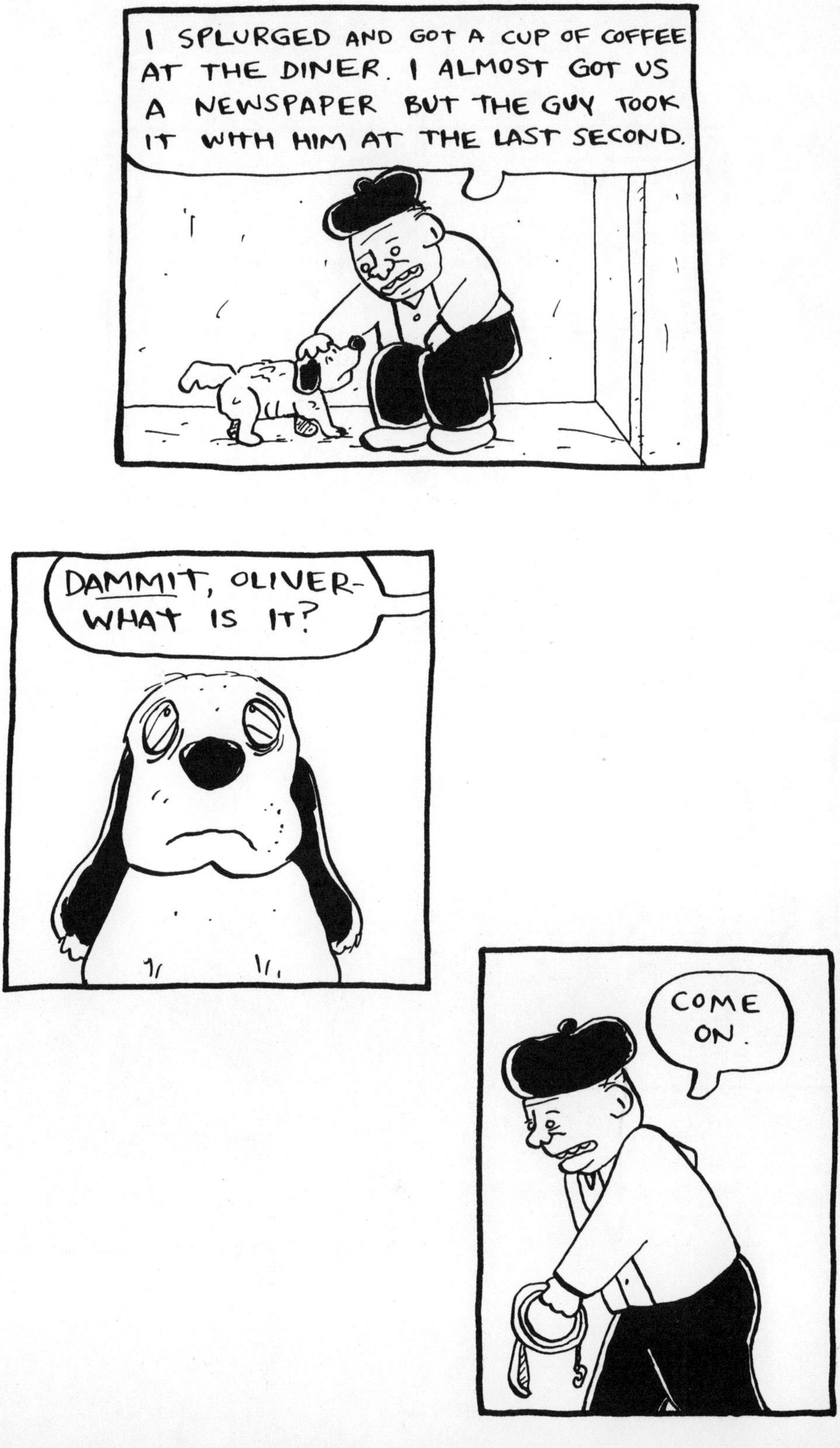
I SPLURGED AND GOT A CUP OF COFFEE AT THE DINER. I ALMOST GOT US A NEWSPAPER BUT THE GUY TOOK IT WITH HIM AT THE LAST SECOND.
DAMMIT, OLIVER- WHAT IS IT?
COME ON.

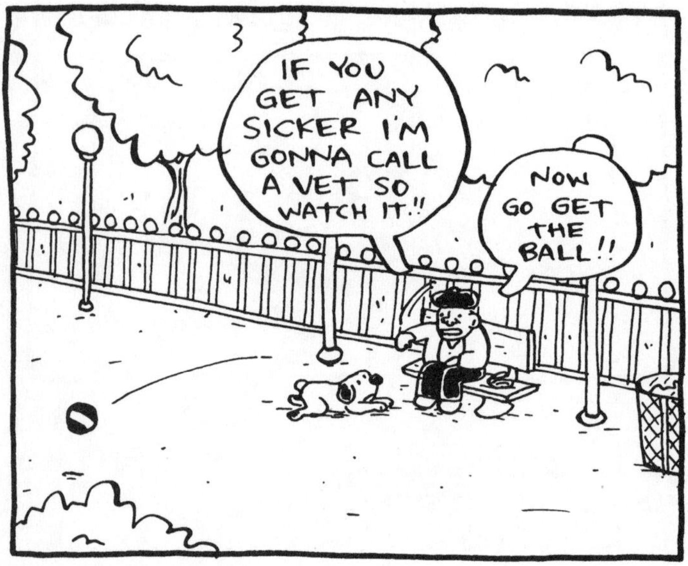
IF YOU GET ANY SICKER I'M GONNA CALL A VET SO WATCH IT!!
NOW GO GET THE BALL!!

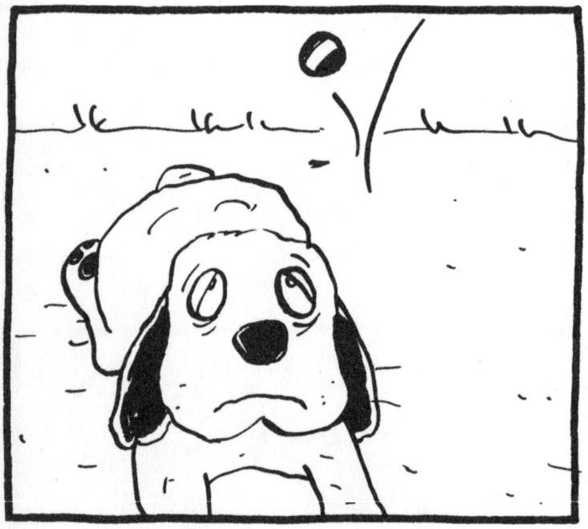

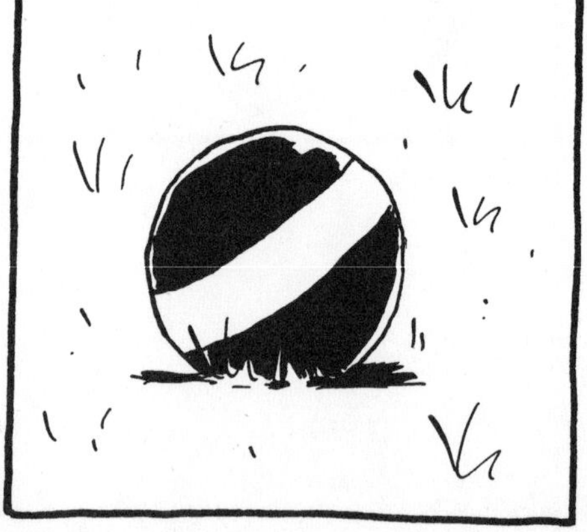

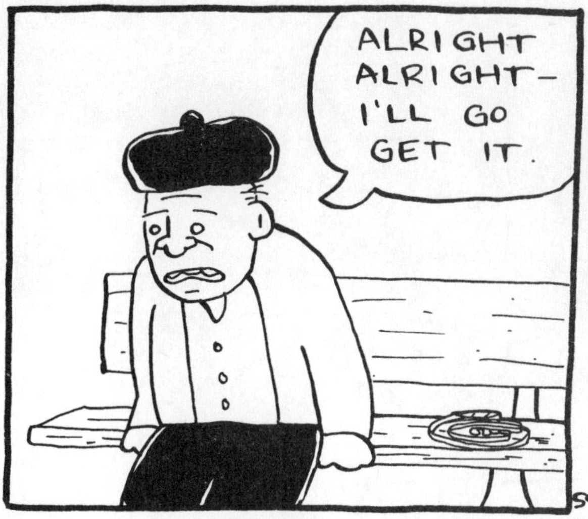
ALRIGHT ALRIGHT– I'LL GO GET IT.

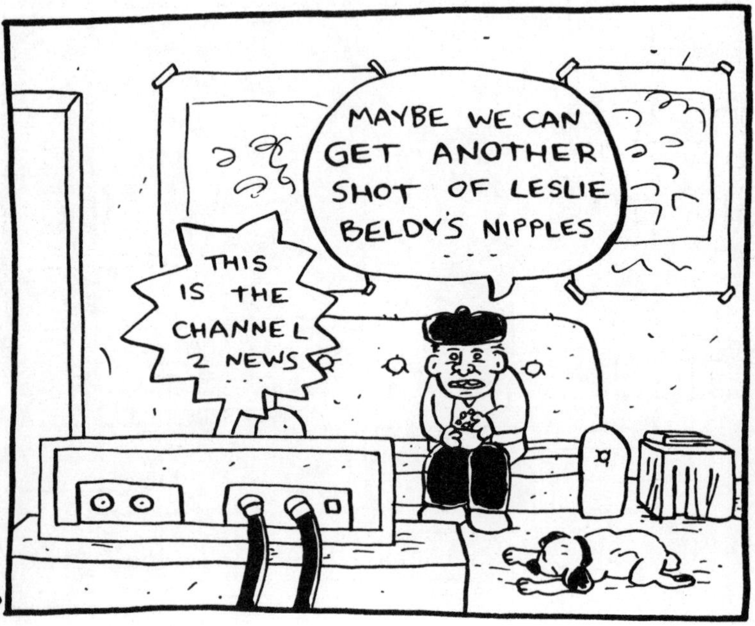
MAYBE WE CAN GET ANOTHER SHOT OF LESLIE BELDY'S NIPPLES . . .
THIS IS THE CHANNEL 2 NEWS . . .

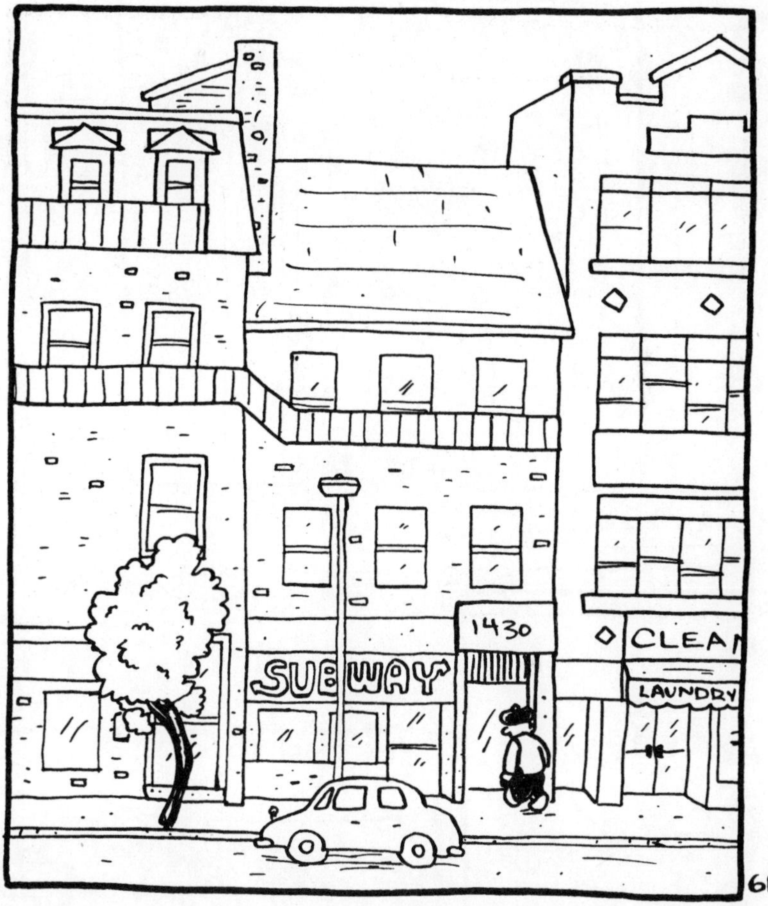
1430
SUBWAY
CLEA
LAUNDRY

A LETTER FROM MY SISTER...
WHAT - DID I MISS HER BIRTHDAY?

RRRRRPP

WHAT KIND OF LETTER IS THIS?
ear Barney,
Hows my dog? Ha ha.
Barney, I'm sicker, possibly
dying. In these sad times
I've been thinking back
to our childhood days. Do
you remember the woods
we played in? The tracks
we water tower we clim
strange, moldy living
ture we used to jum
stream and
tired

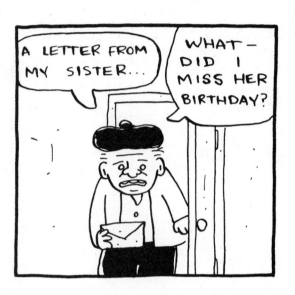

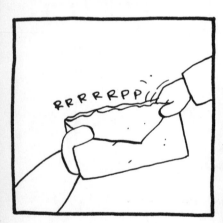

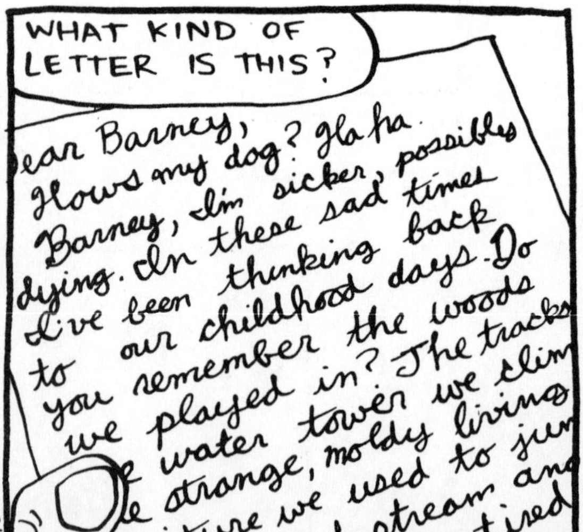

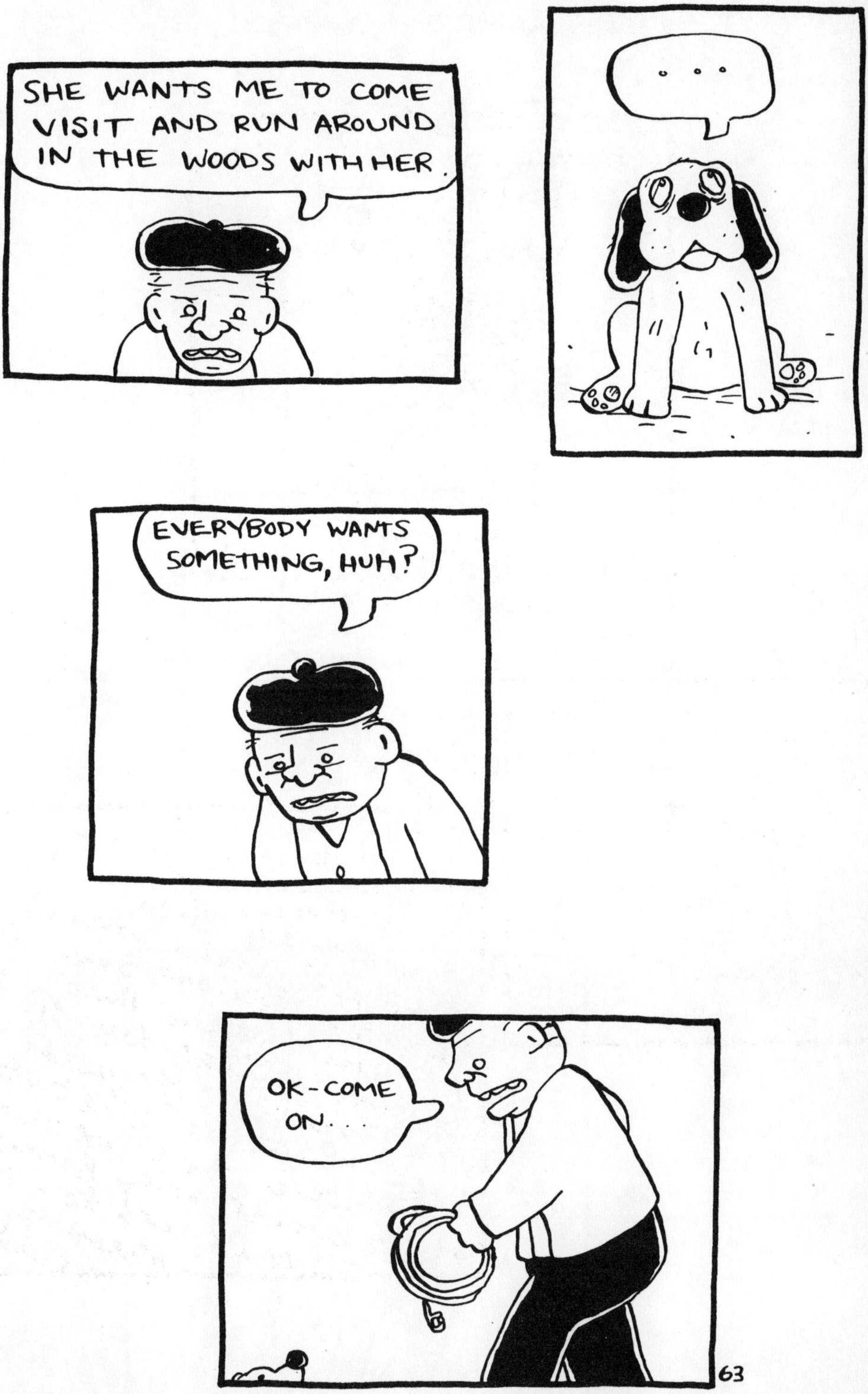
SHE WANTS ME TO COME VISIT AND RUN AROUND IN THE WOODS WITH HER.
. . .
EVERYBODY WANTS SOMETHING, HUH?
OK-COME ON...

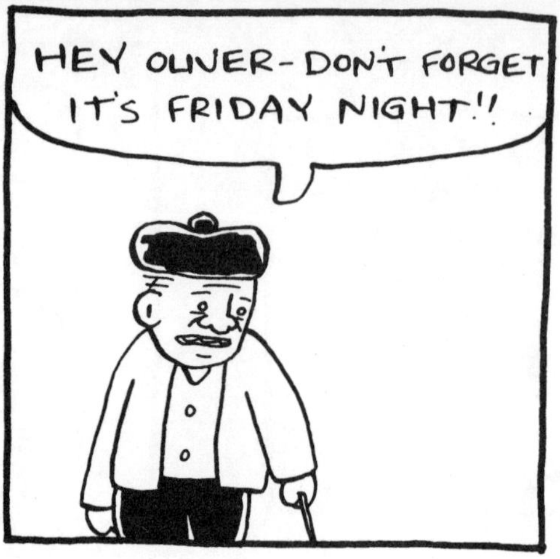
HEY OLIVER- DON'T FORGET IT'S FRIDAY NIGHT!!

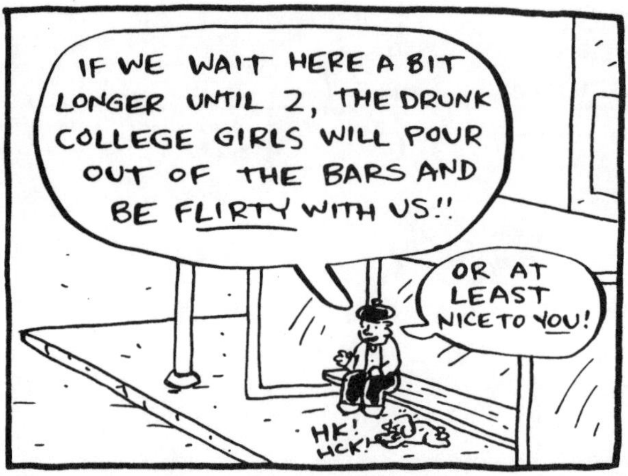
IF WE WAIT HERE A BIT LONGER UNTIL 2, THE DRUNK COLLEGE GIRLS WILL POUR OUT OF THE BARS AND BE FLIRTY WITH US!!
OR AT LEAST NICE TO YOU!
HK! HCK!

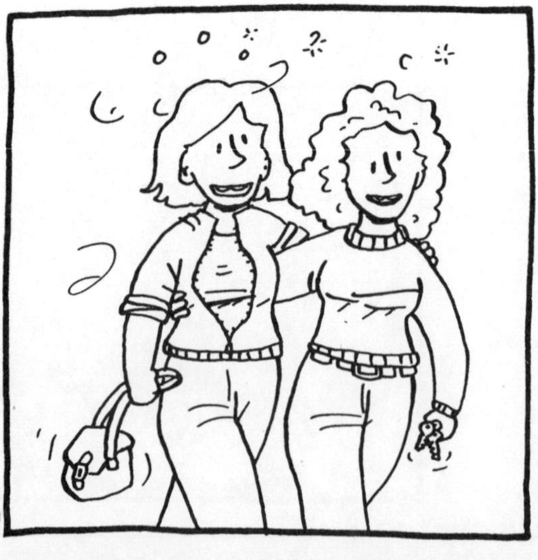

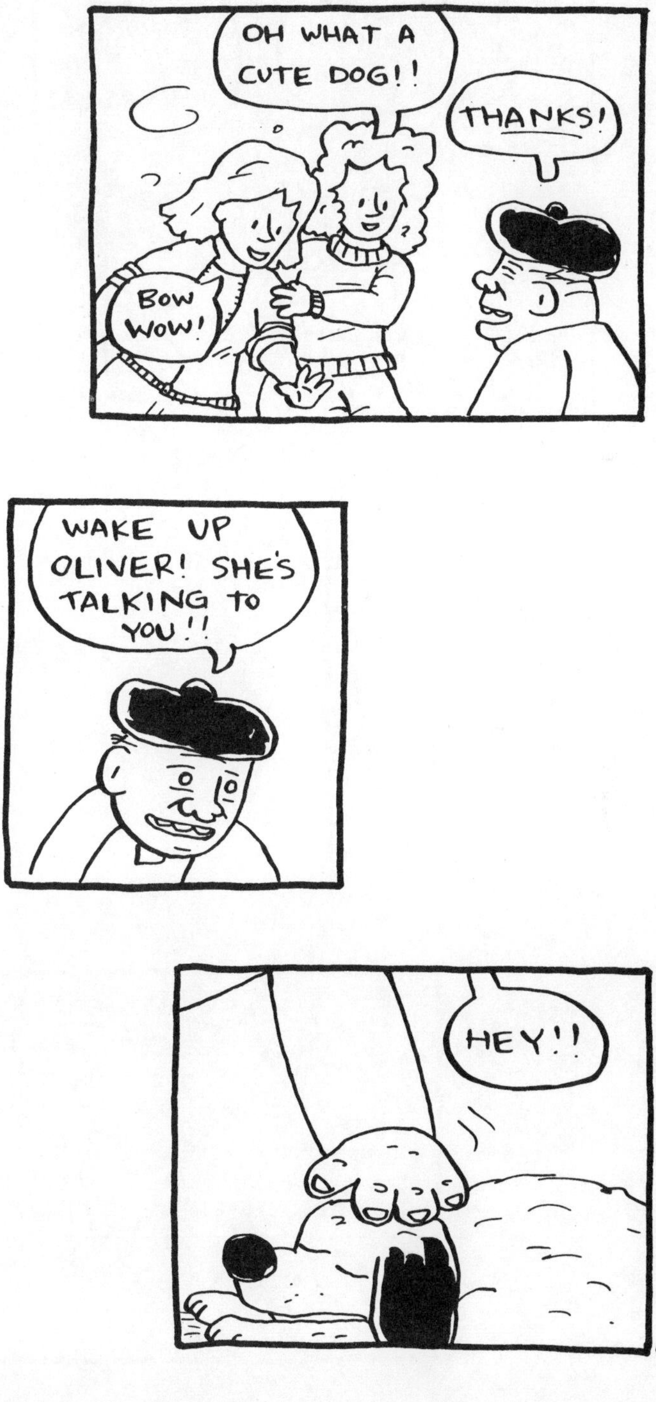
OH WHAT A CUTE DOG!!
THANKS!
BOW WOW!
WAKE UP OLIVER! SHE'S TALKING TO YOU!!
HEY!!

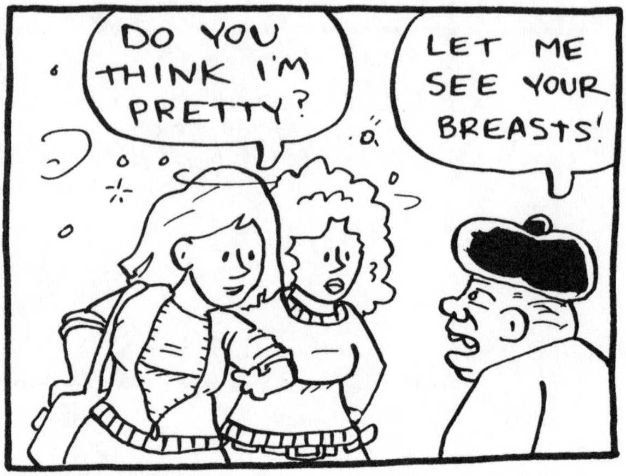
DO YOU THINK I'M PRETTY?
LET ME SEE YOUR BREASTS!

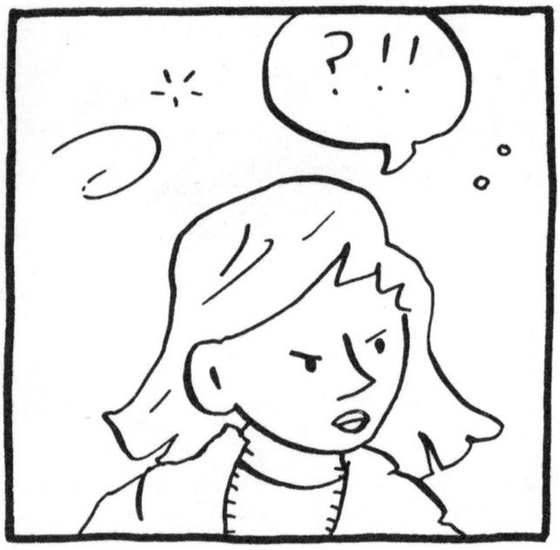
?!!

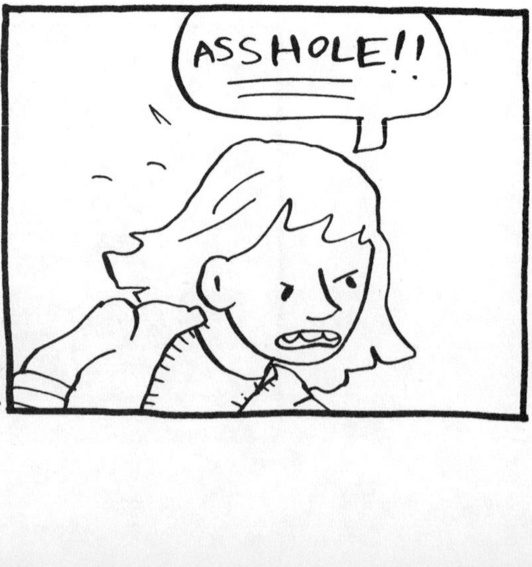
ASSHOLE!!

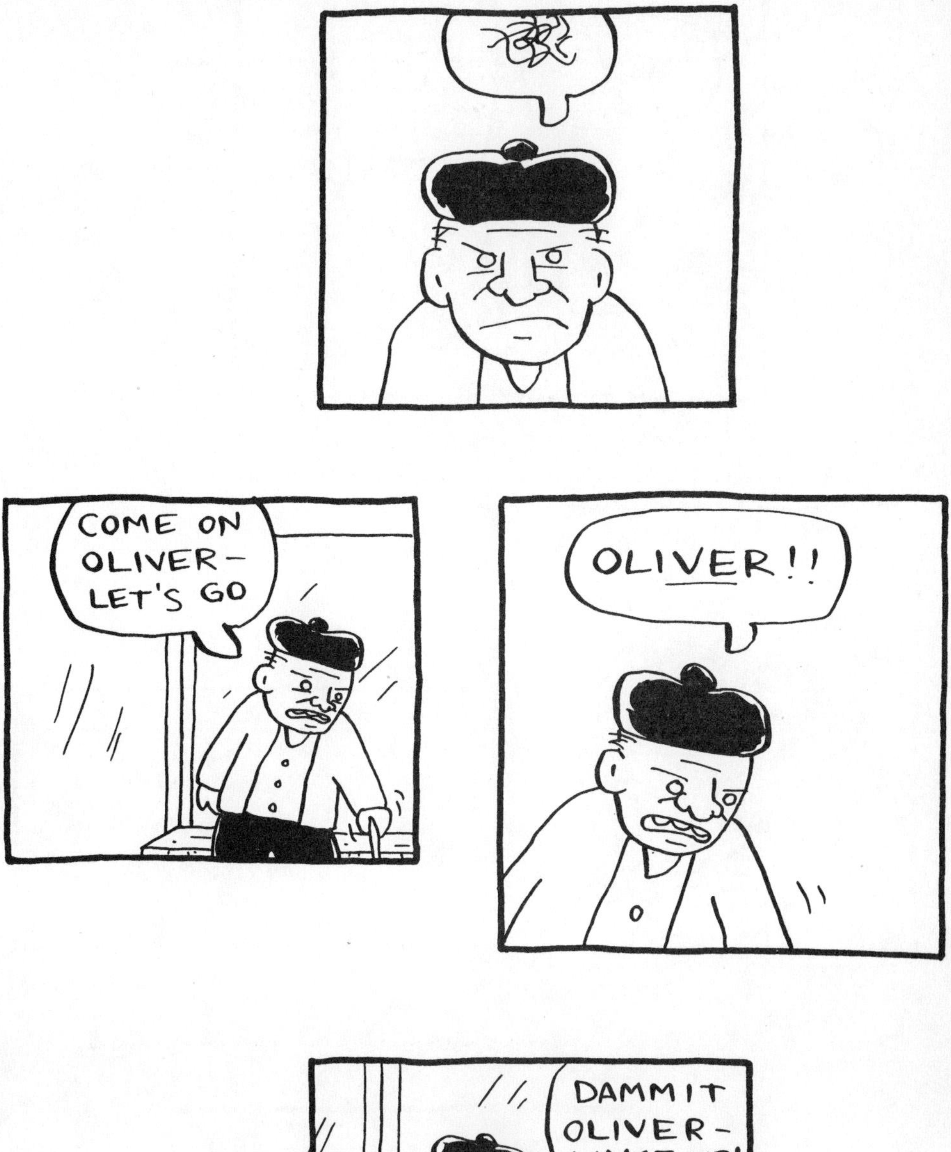
COME ON
OLIVER-
LET'S GO
OLIVER!!
DAMMIT
OLIVER-
WAKE UP!

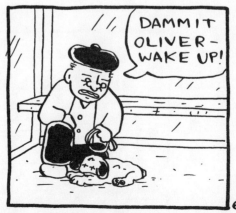

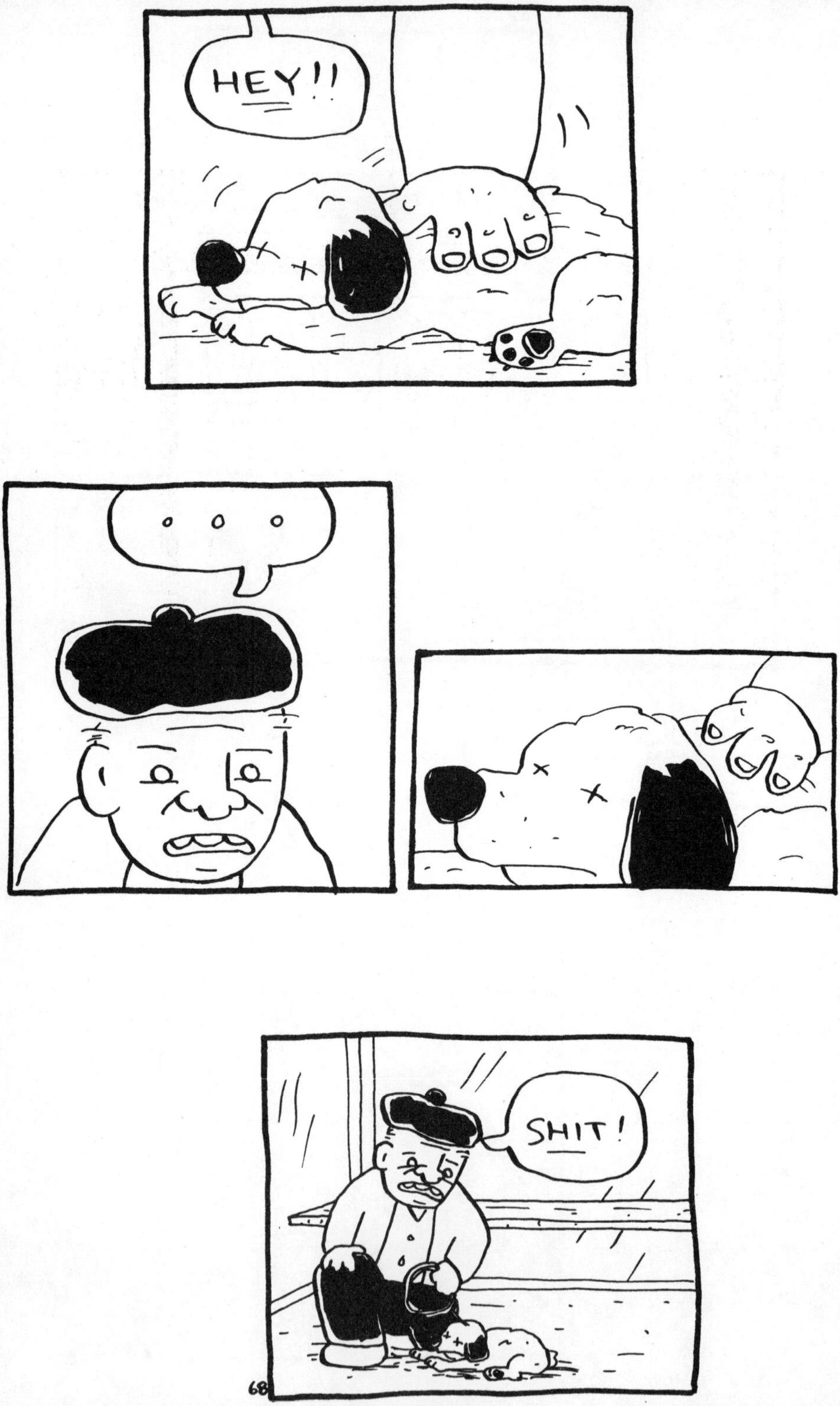
HEY!!
...
SHIT!

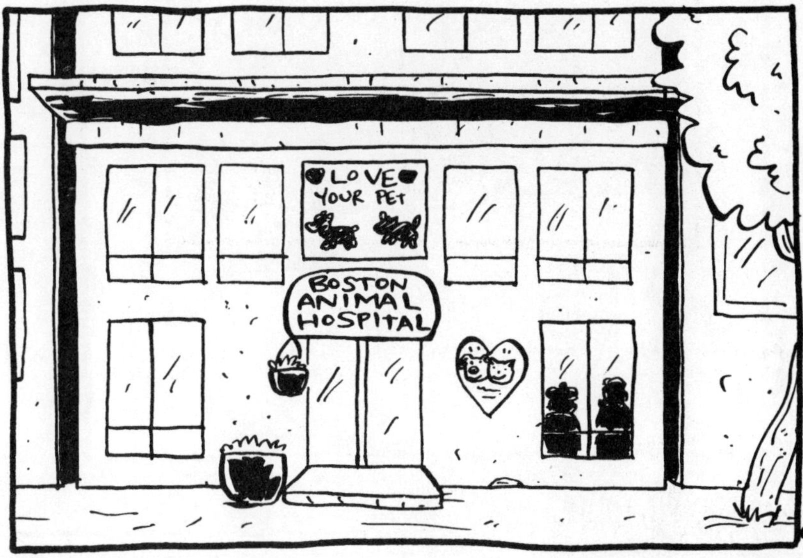
LOVE YOUR PET
BOSTON ANIMAL HOSPITAL

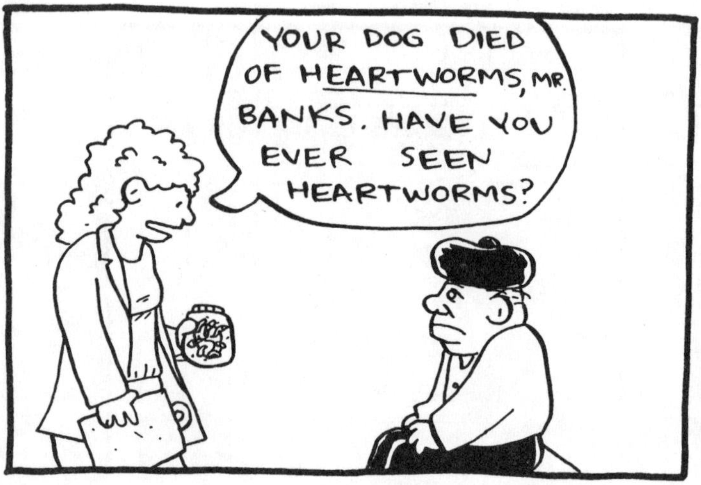
YOUR DOG DIED OF HEARTWORMS, MR. BANKS. HAVE YOU EVER SEEN HEARTWORMS?

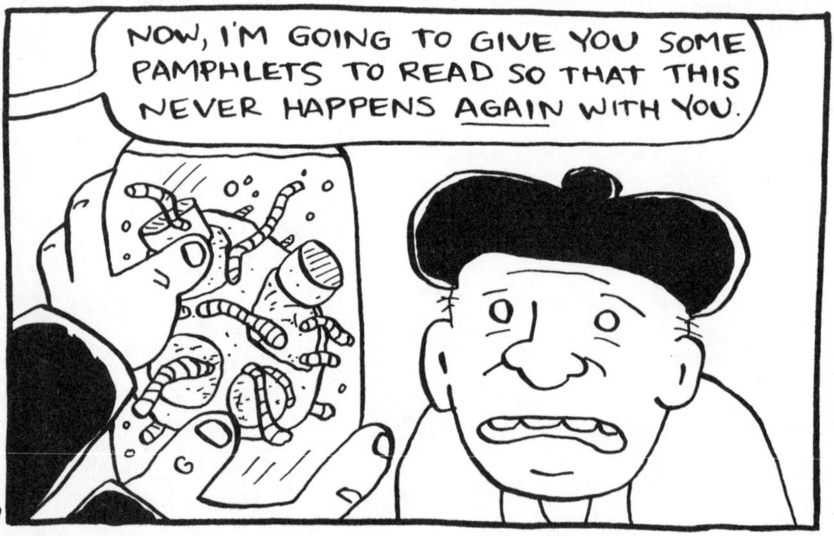
NOW, I'M GOING TO GIVE YOU SOME PAMPHLETS TO READ SO THAT THIS NEVER HAPPENS AGAIN WITH YOU.

71

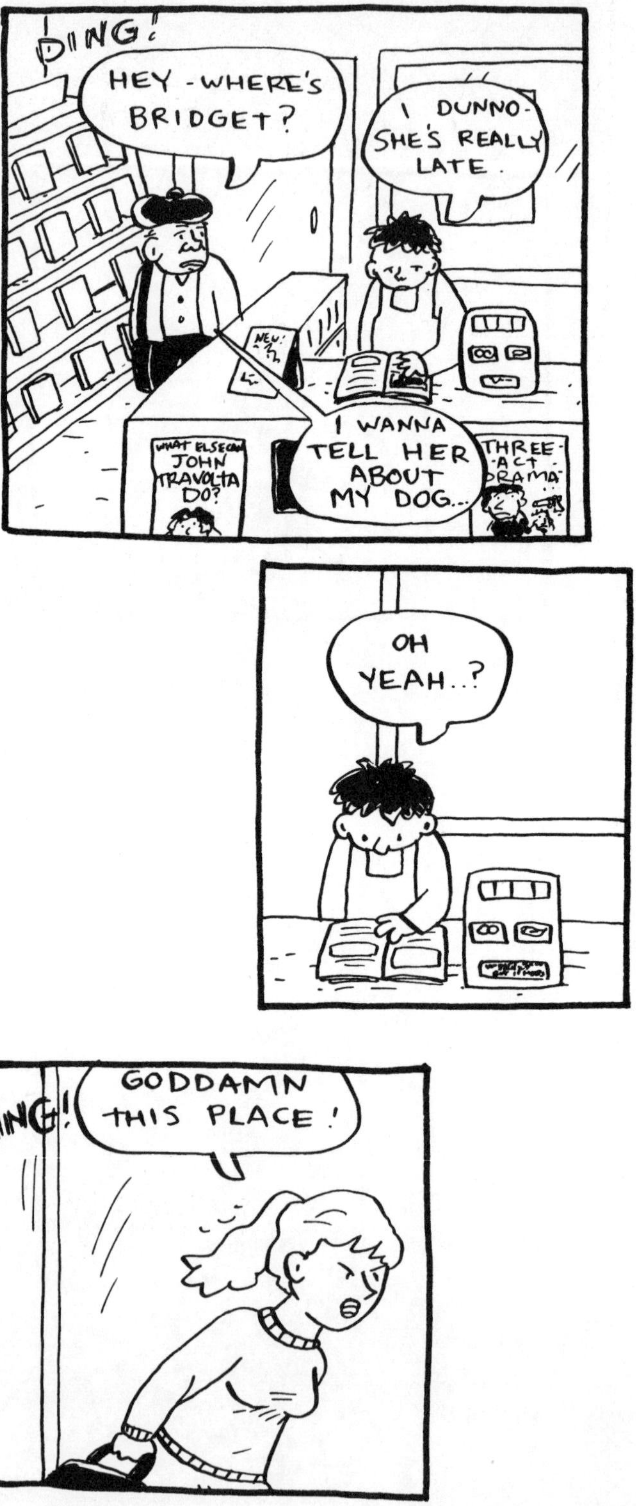
DING!
HEY - WHERE'S BRIDGET?
I DUNNO - SHE'S REALLY LATE.
I WANNA TELL HER ABOUT MY DOG...
NEW!
WHAT ELSE CAN JOHN TRAVOLTA DO?
THREE-ACT DRAMA
OH YEAH..?
DING!
GODDAMN THIS PLACE!

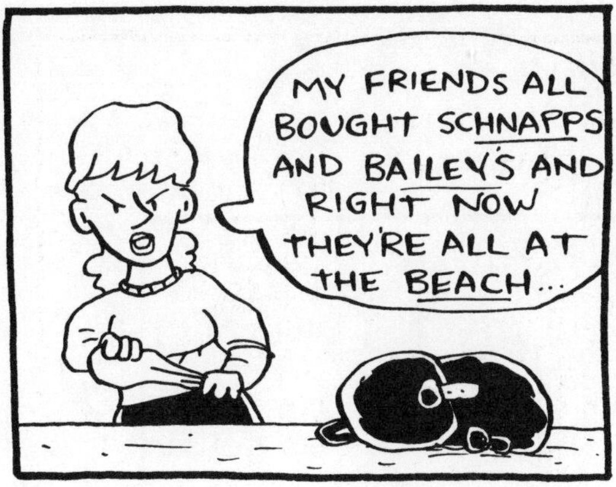
MY FRIENDS ALL BOUGHT SCHNAPPS AND BAILEY'S AND RIGHT NOW THEY'RE ALL AT THE BEACH...

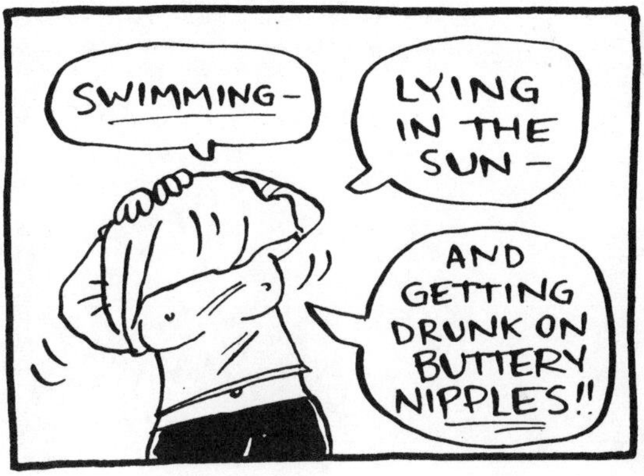
SWIMMING-
LYING IN THE SUN-
AND GETTING DRUNK ON BUTTERY NIPPLES!!

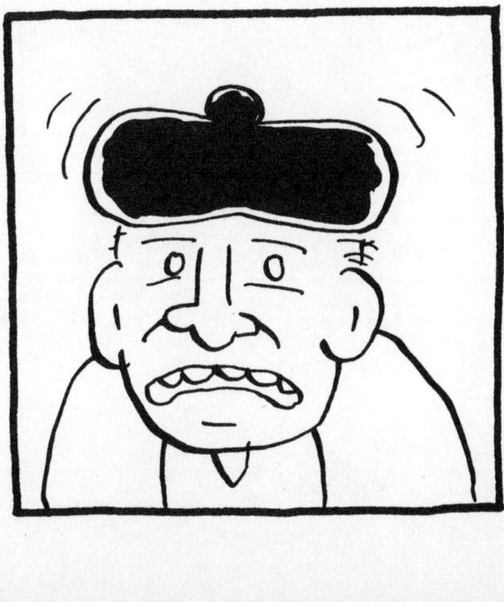

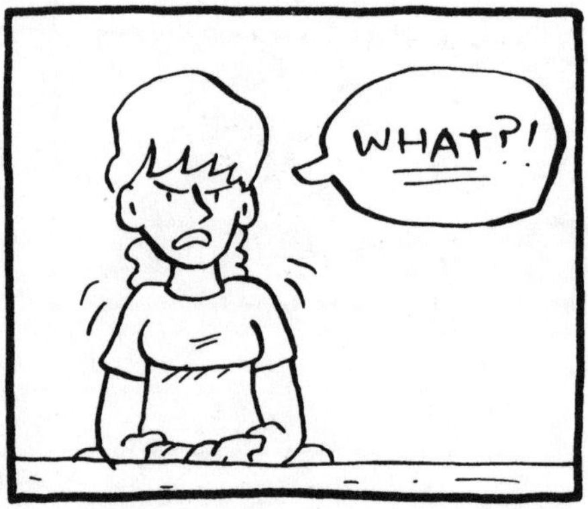
WHAT?!

74

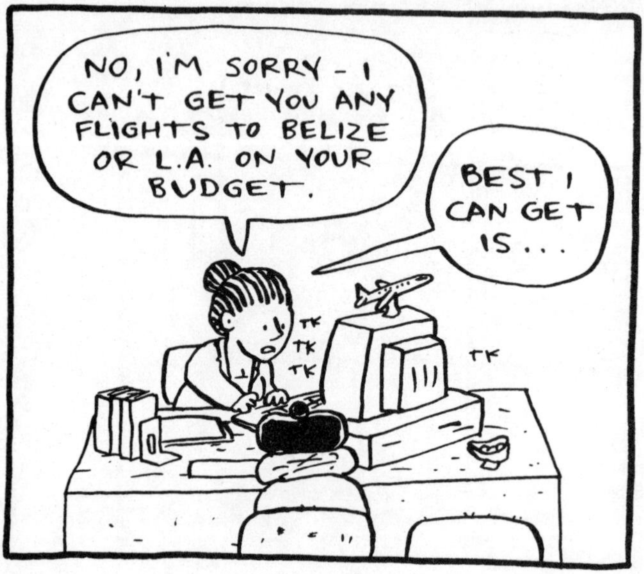
NO, I'M SORRY - I CAN'T GET YOU ANY FLIGHTS TO BELIZE OR L.A. ON YOUR BUDGET.
BEST I CAN GET IS . . .
TK
TK
TK
TK

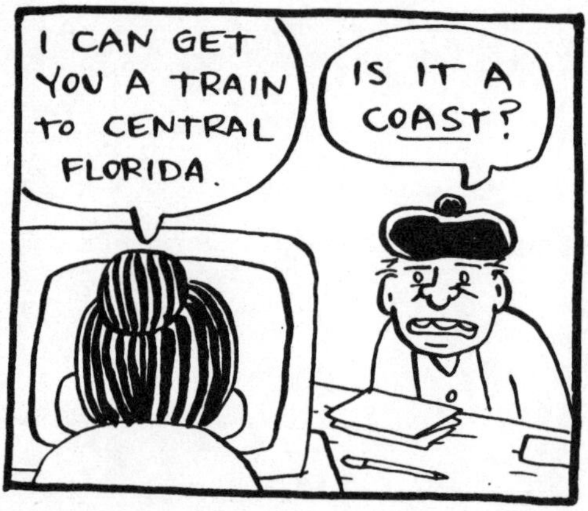
I CAN GET YOU A TRAIN TO CENTRAL FLORIDA.
IS IT A COAST?

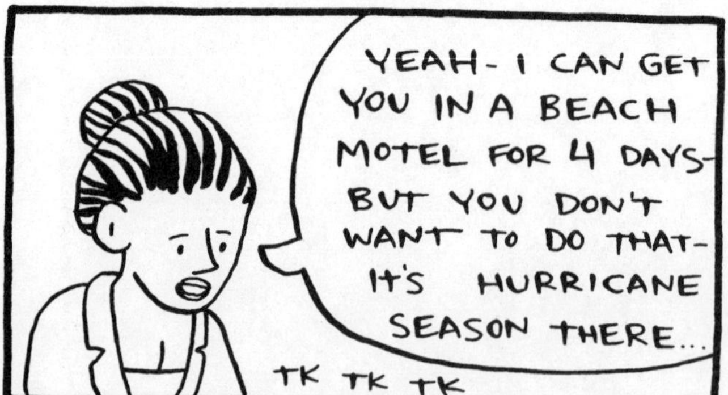
YEAH - I CAN GET YOU IN A BEACH MOTEL FOR 4 DAYS - BUT YOU DON'T WANT TO DO THAT - IT'S HURRICANE SEASON THERE...
TK TK TK

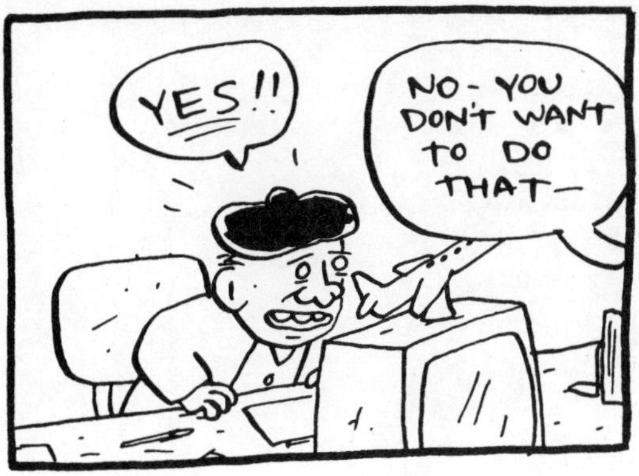
YES!!
NO - YOU DON'T WANT TO DO THAT-

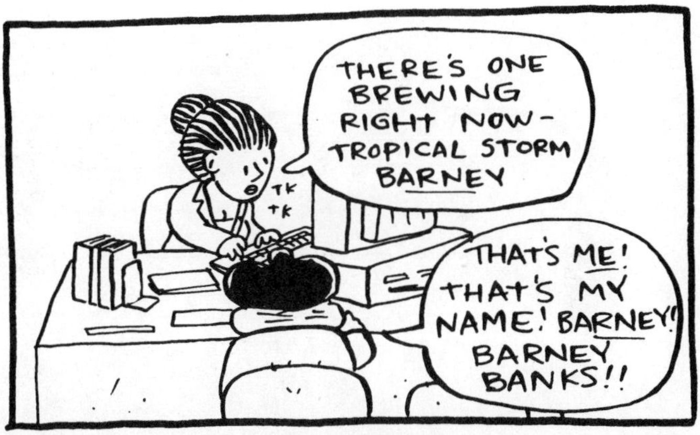
THERE'S ONE BREWING RIGHT NOW- TROPICAL STORM BARNEY
TK TK
THAT'S ME! THAT'S MY NAME! BARNEY! BARNEY BANKS!!

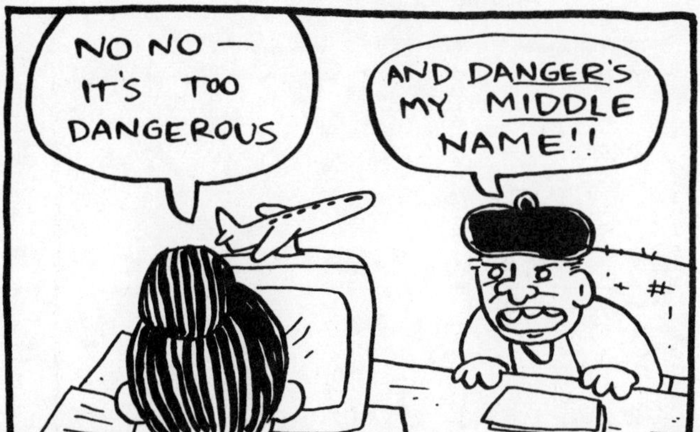
NO NO - IT'S TOO DANGEROUS
AND DANGER'S MY MIDDLE NAME!!

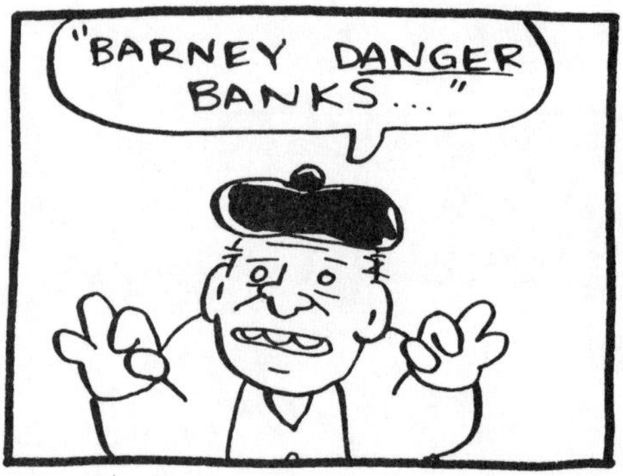
"BARNEY DANGER BANKS..."

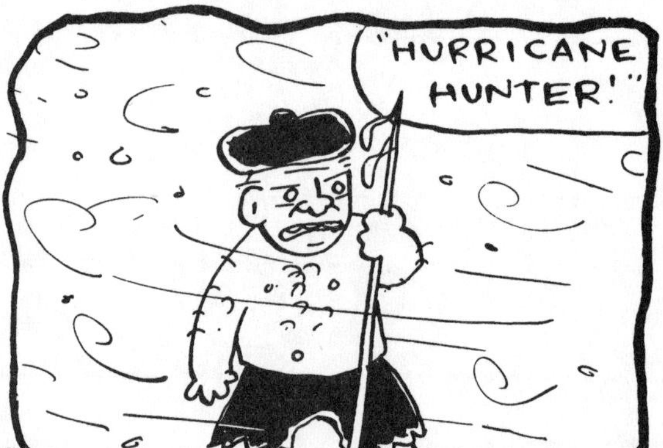
"HURRICANE HUNTER!"

79

PART II

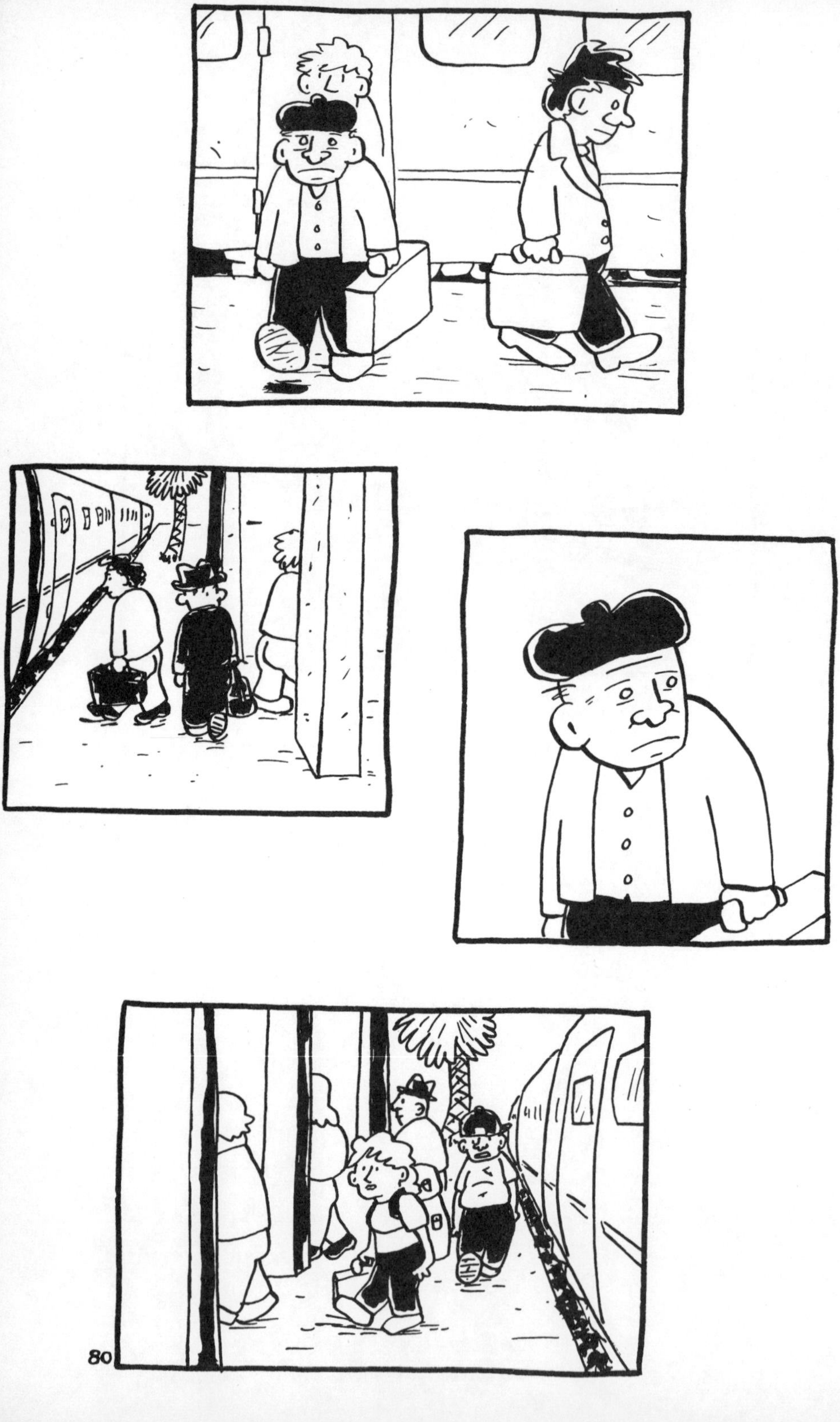

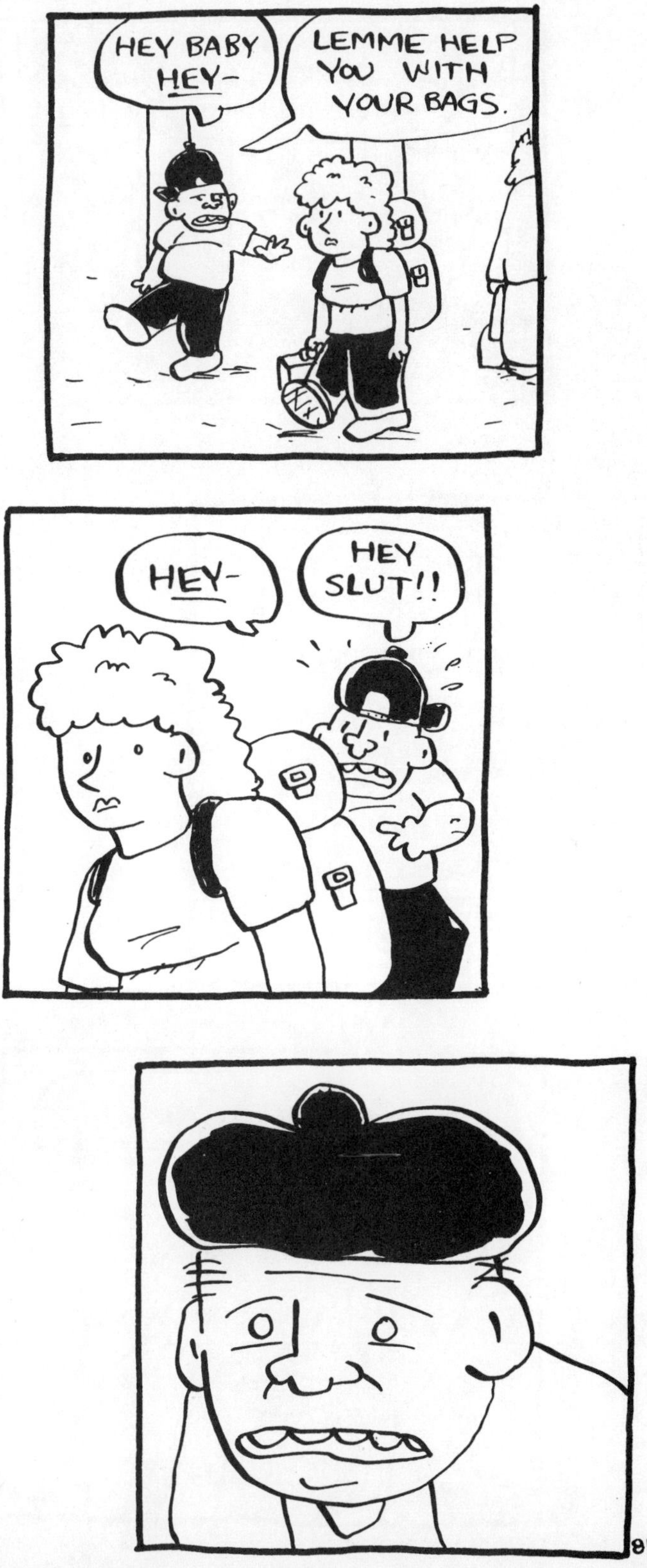
HEY BABY
HEY-
LEMME HELP YOU WITH YOUR BAGS.
HEY-
HEY SLUT!!

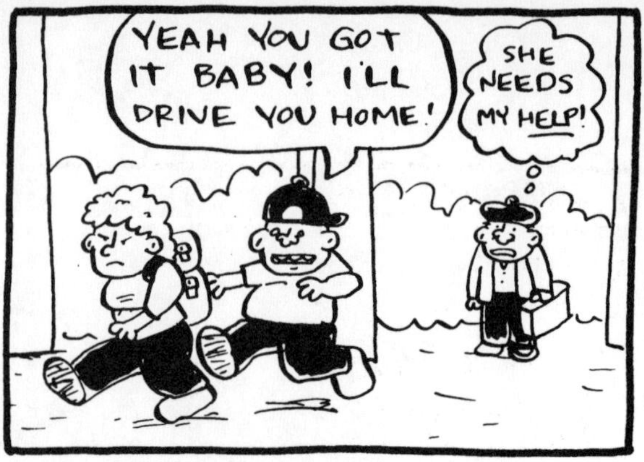
YEAH YOU GOT IT BABY! I'LL DRIVE YOU HOME!
SHE NEEDS MY HELP!

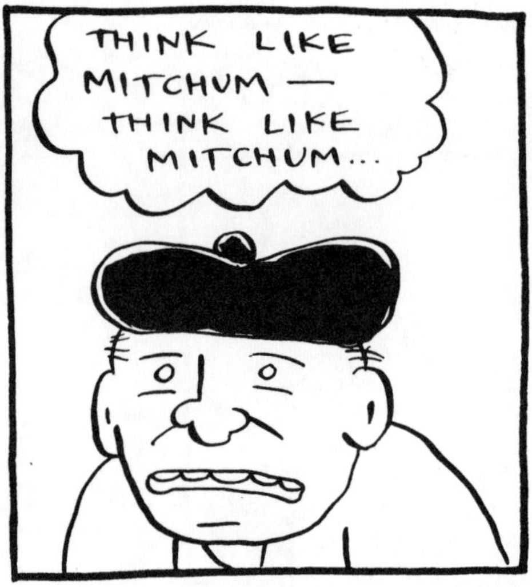
THINK LIKE MITCHUM — THINK LIKE MITCHUM...

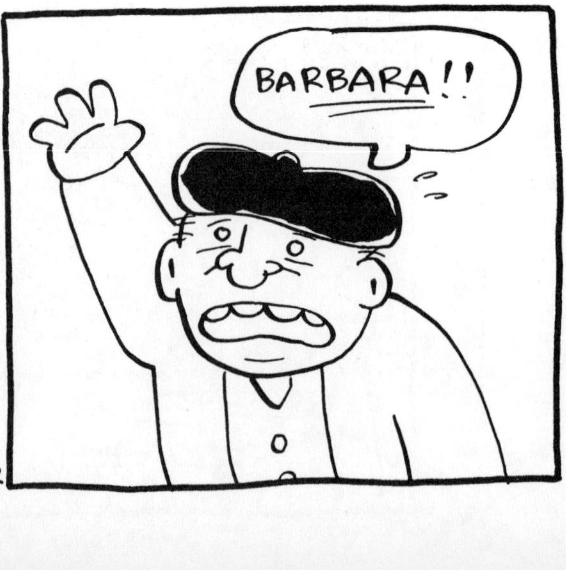
BARBARA!!

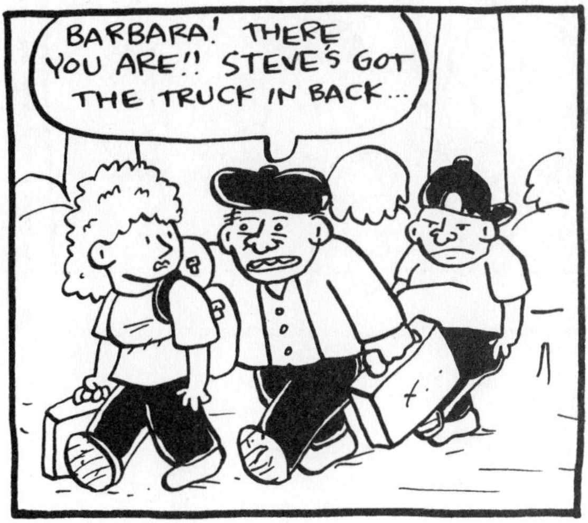
BARBARA! THERE YOU ARE!! STEVE'S GOT THE TRUCK IN BACK...

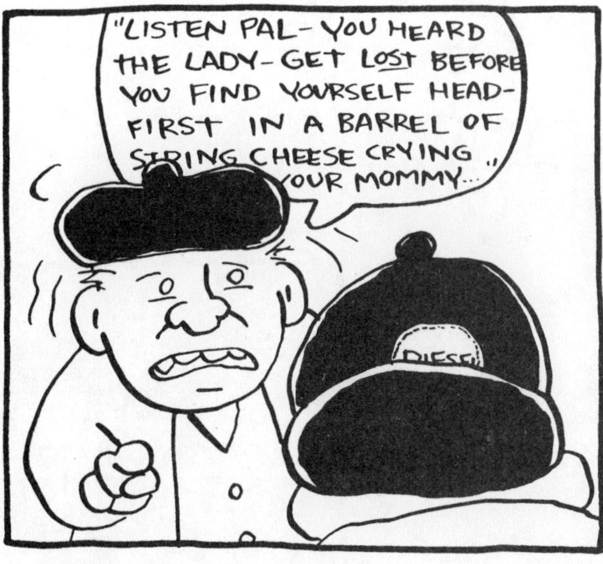
"LISTEN PAL- YOU HEARD THE LADY- GET LOST BEFORE YOU FIND YOURSELF HEAD-FIRST IN A BARREL OF STRING CHEESE CRYING YOUR MOMMY..."

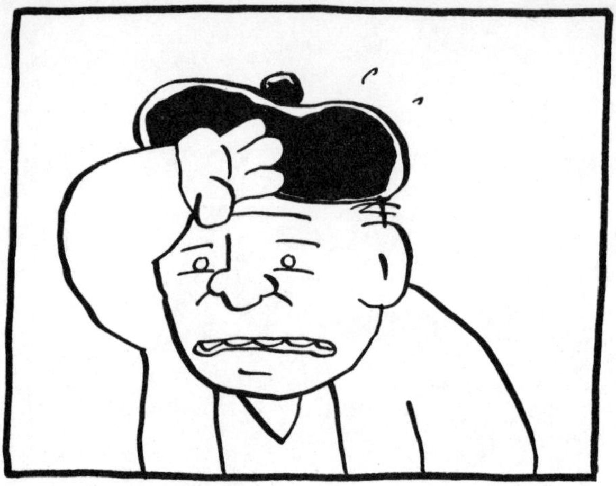

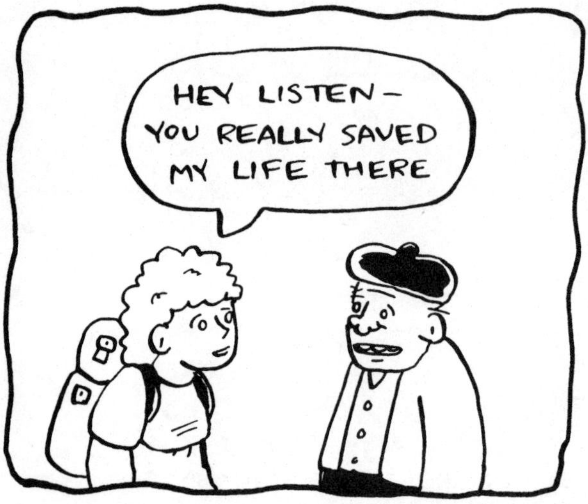
HEY LISTEN–
YOU REALLY SAVED
MY LIFE THERE

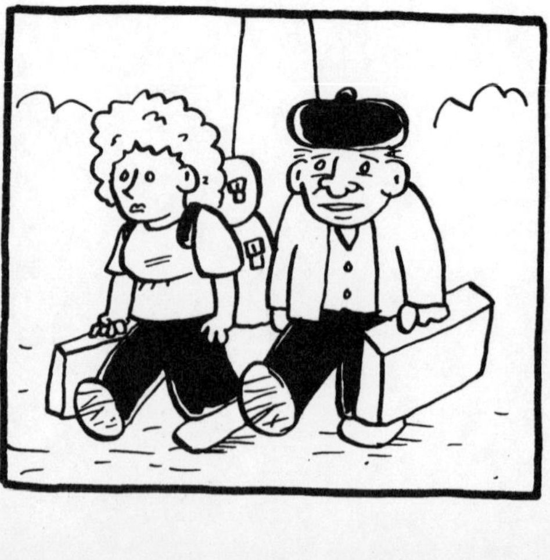

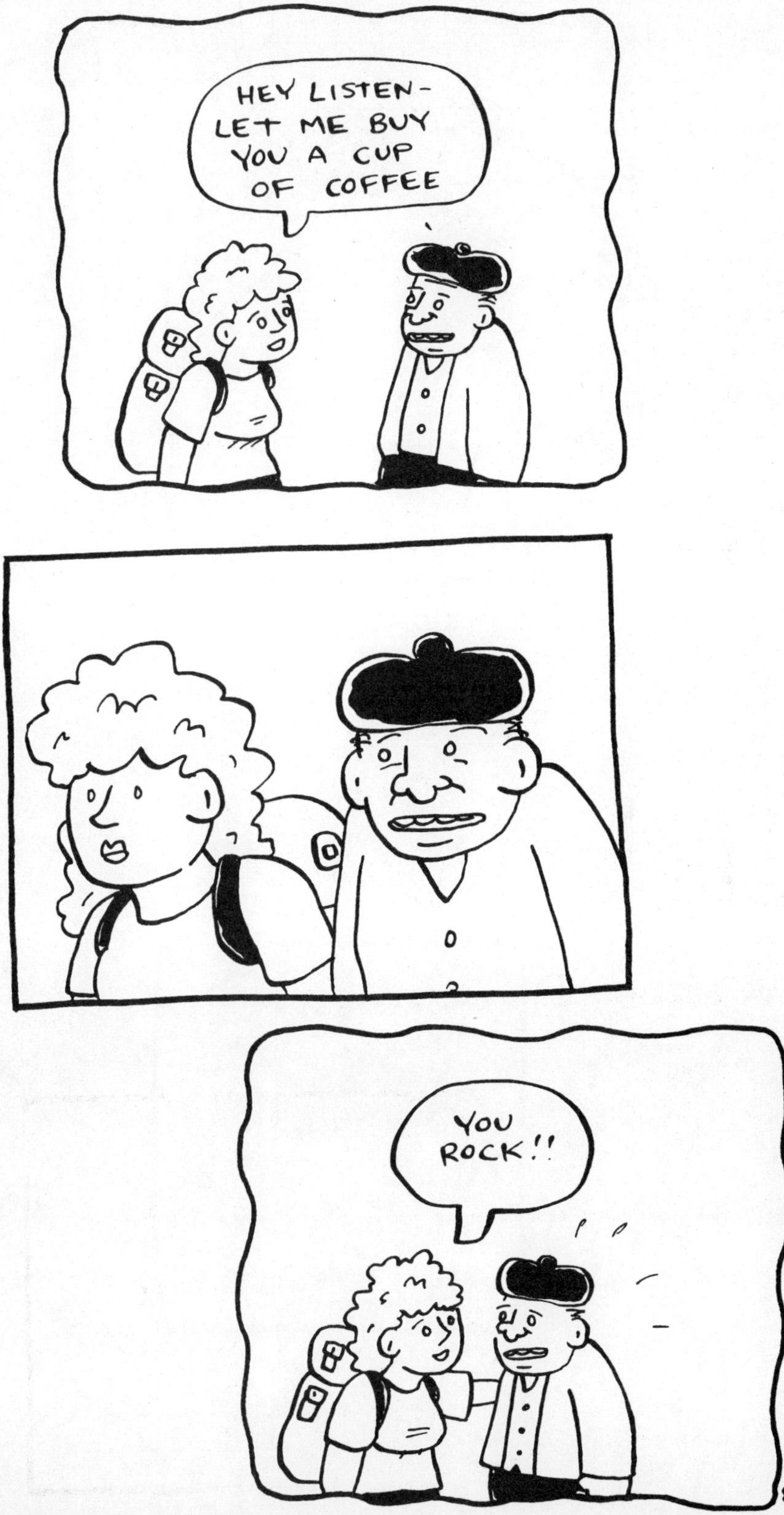
HEY LISTEN-
LET ME BUY
YOU A CUP
OF COFFEE
YOU
ROCK!!

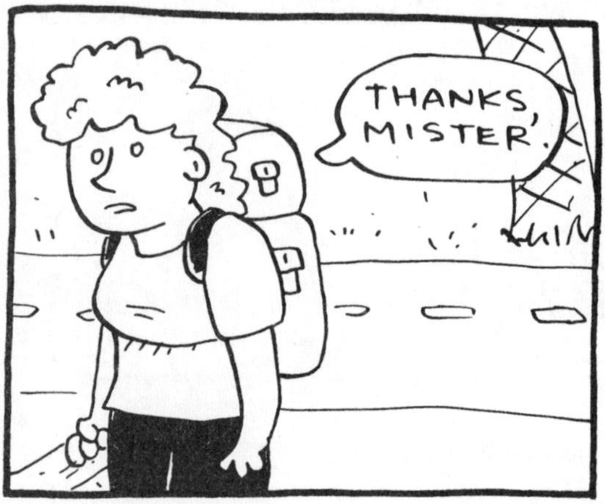
THANKS, MISTER.

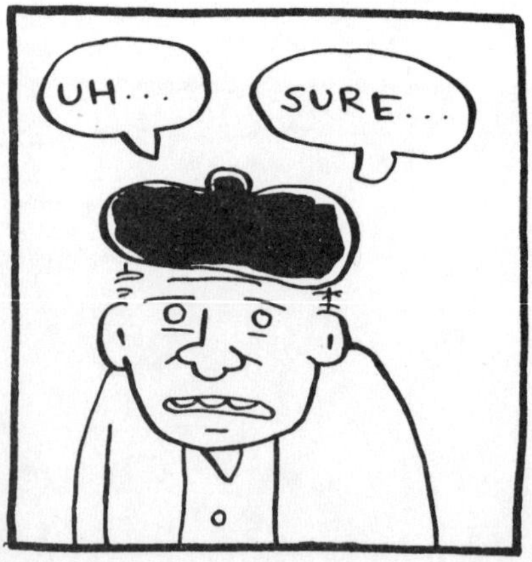
UH...
SURE...

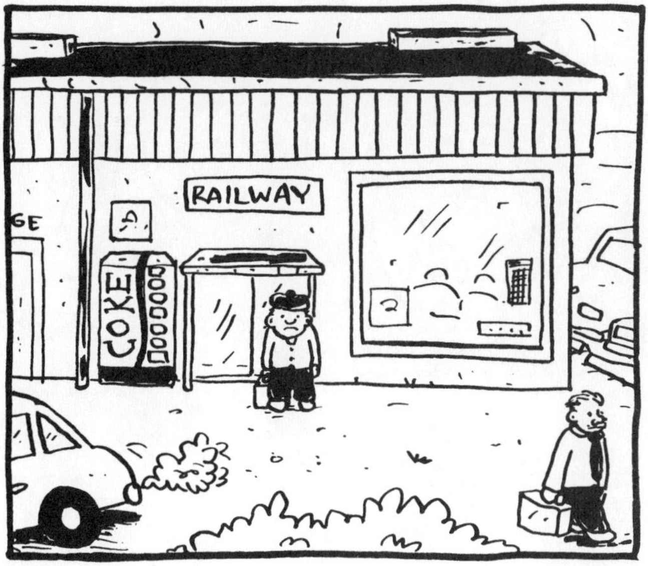
RAILWAY
COKE

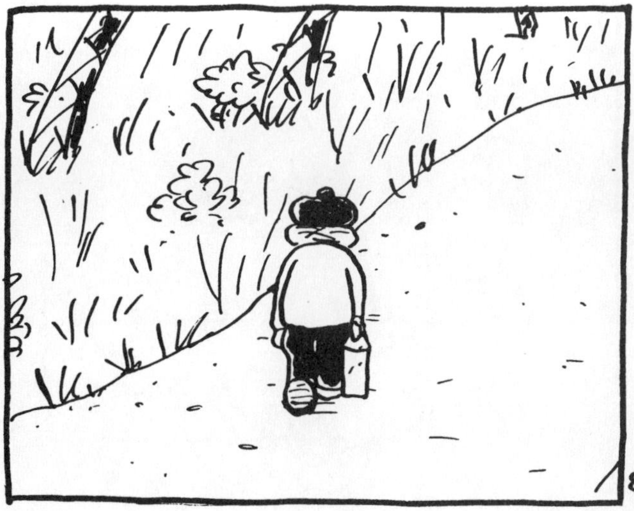

88

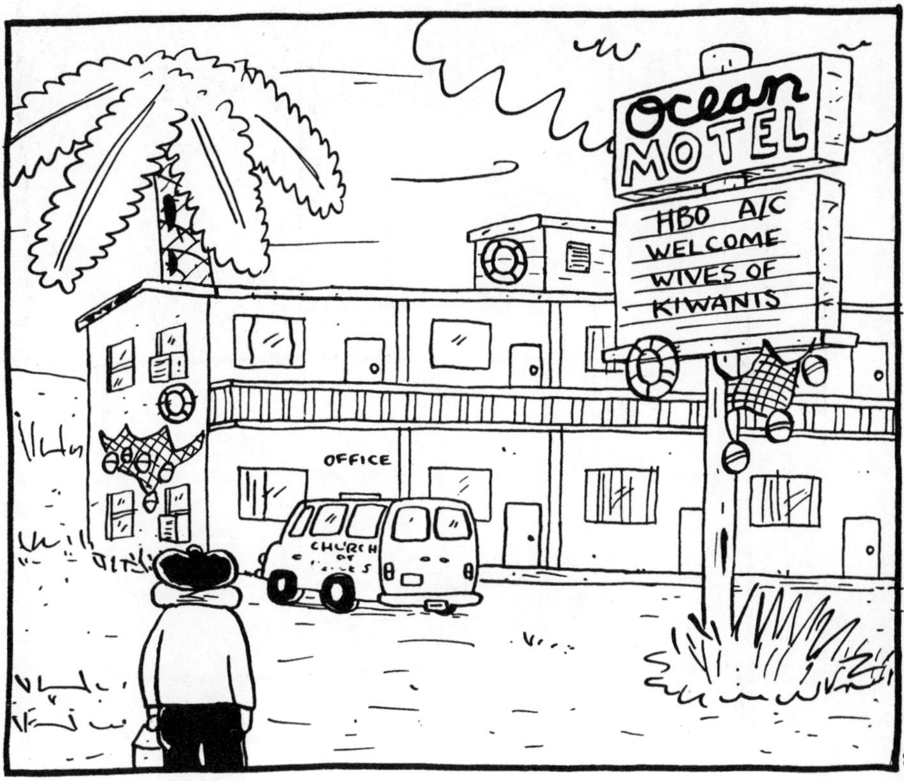
Ocean
MOTEL
HBO A/C
WELCOME
WIVES OF
KIWANIS
OFFICE
CHURCH

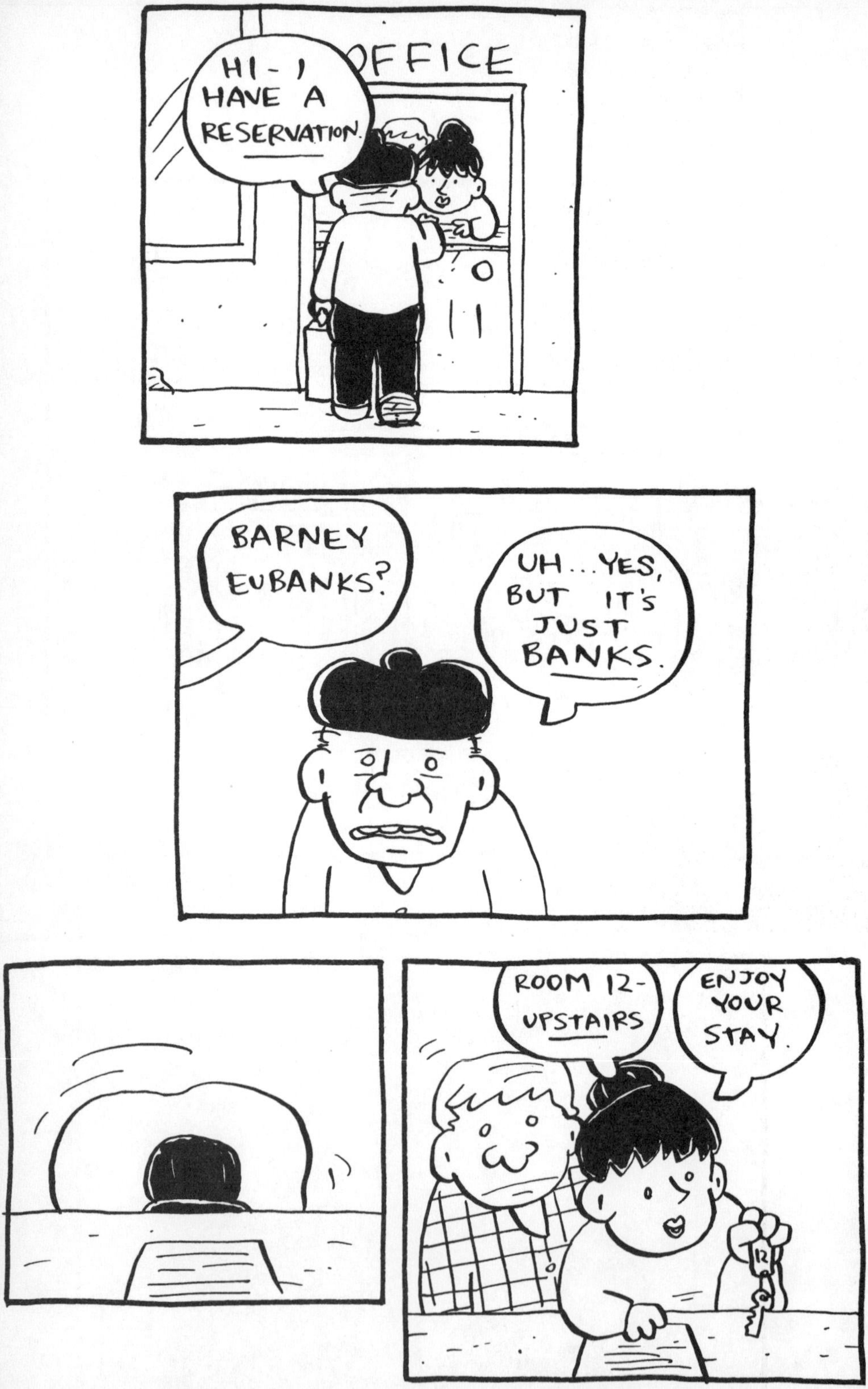
OFFICE
HI- I HAVE A RESERVATION.
BARNEY EUBANKS?
UH... YES, BUT IT'S JUST BANKS.
ROOM 12- UPSTAIRS
ENJOY YOUR STAY.
12

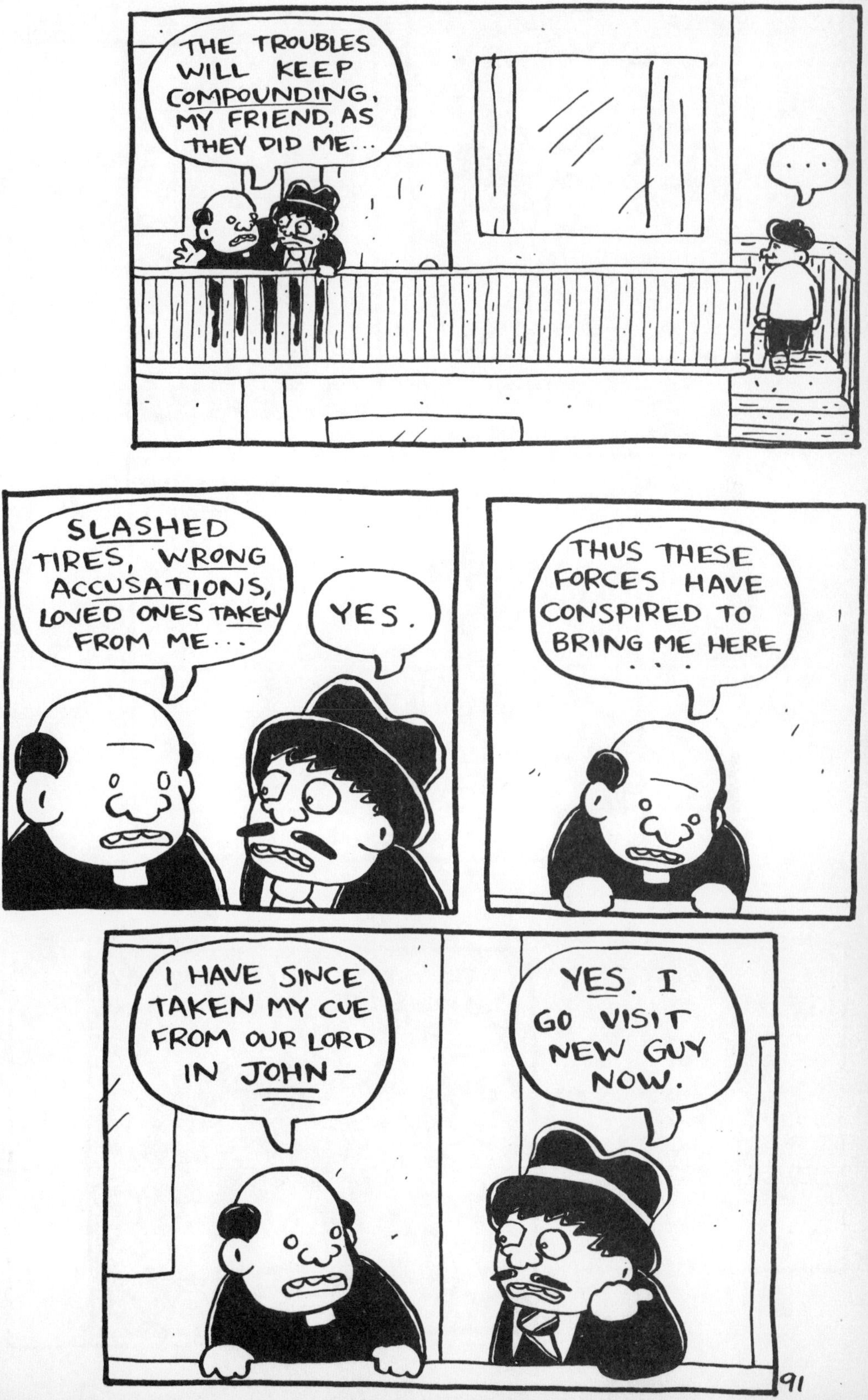
THE TROUBLES WILL KEEP COMPOUNDING, MY FRIEND, AS THEY DID ME...
...
SLASHED TIRES, WRONG ACCUSATIONS, LOVED ONES TAKEN FROM ME...
YES.
THUS THESE FORCES HAVE CONSPIRED TO BRING ME HERE...
I HAVE SINCE TAKEN MY CUE FROM OUR LORD IN JOHN–
YES. I GO VISIT NEW GUY NOW.

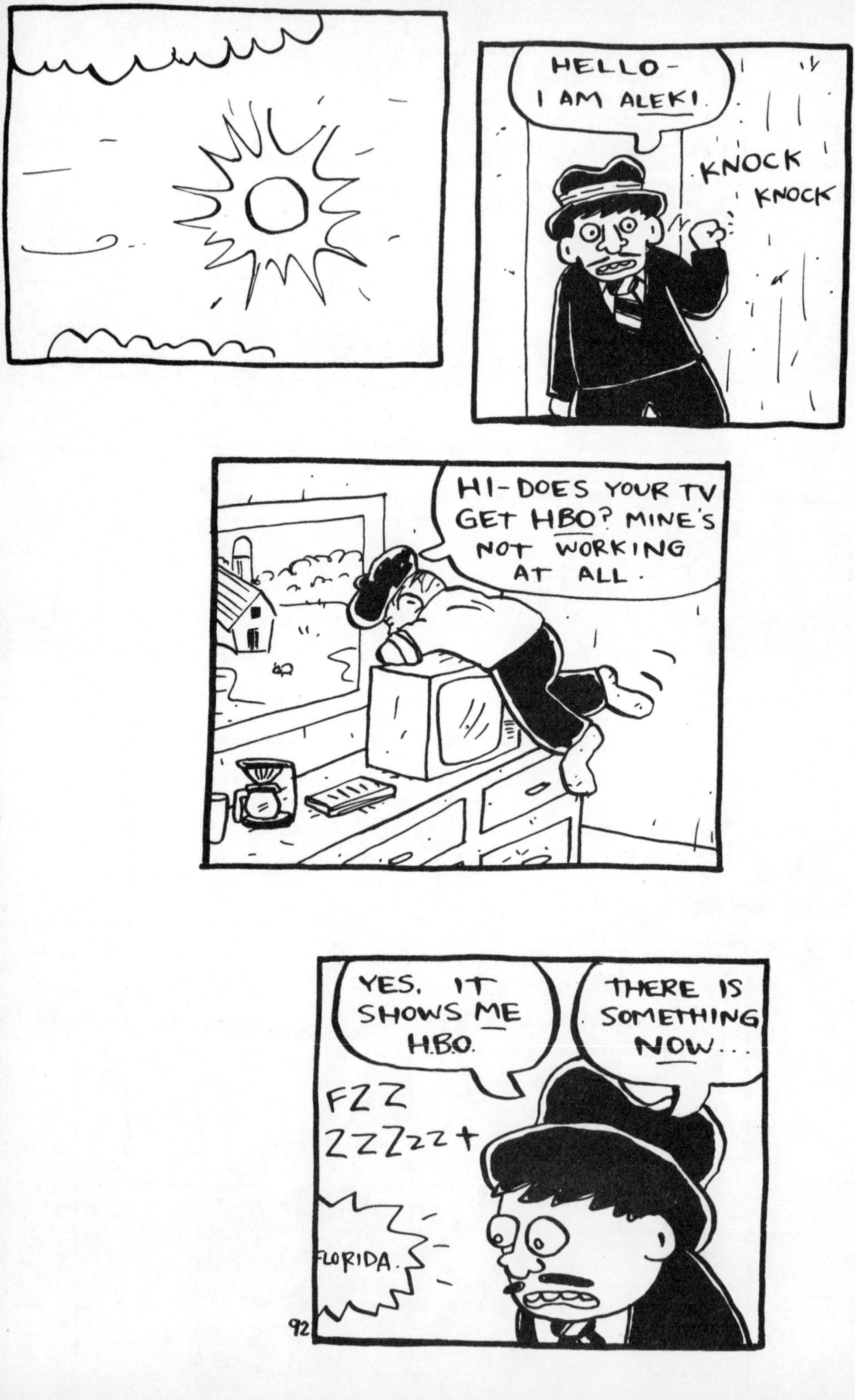
HELLO- I AM ALEKI.
KNOCK KNOCK
HI-DOES YOUR TV GET HBO? MINE'S NOT WORKING AT ALL.
YES. IT SHOWS ME H.B.O.
THERE IS SOMETHING NOW...
FZZ ZZZzz+
FLORIDA.
92

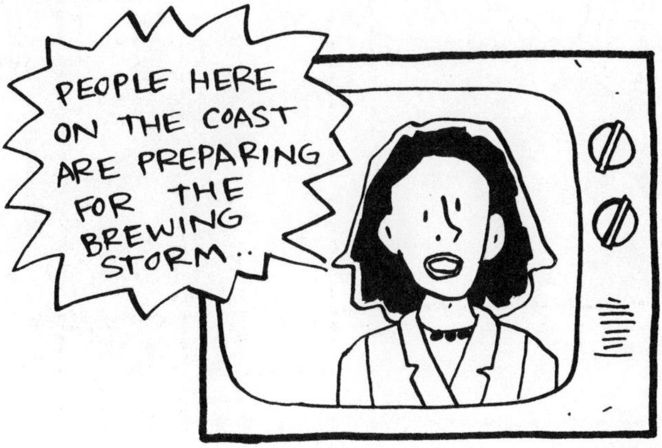
PEOPLE HERE ON THE COAST ARE PREPARING FOR THE BREWING STORM..

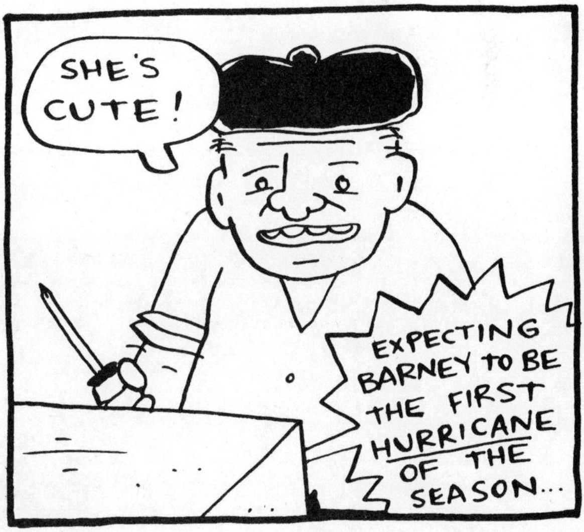
SHE'S CUTE!
EXPECTING BARNEY TO BE THE FIRST HURRICANE OF THE SEASON...

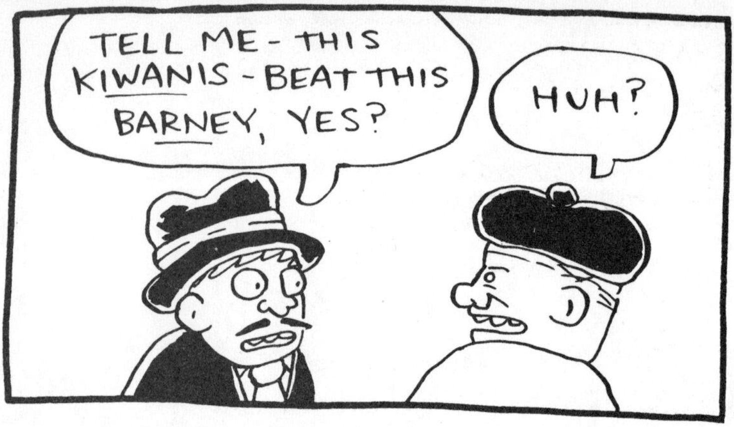
TELL ME - THIS KIWANIS - BEAT THIS BARNEY, YES?
HUH?

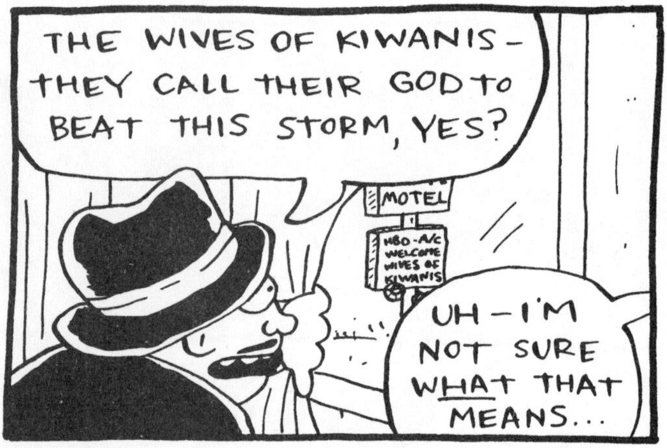
THE WIVES OF KIWANIS - THEY CALL THEIR GOD TO BEAT THIS STORM, YES?
MOTEL
HBO - A/C WELCOME WIVES OF KIWANIS
UH - I'M NOT SURE WHAT THAT MEANS...

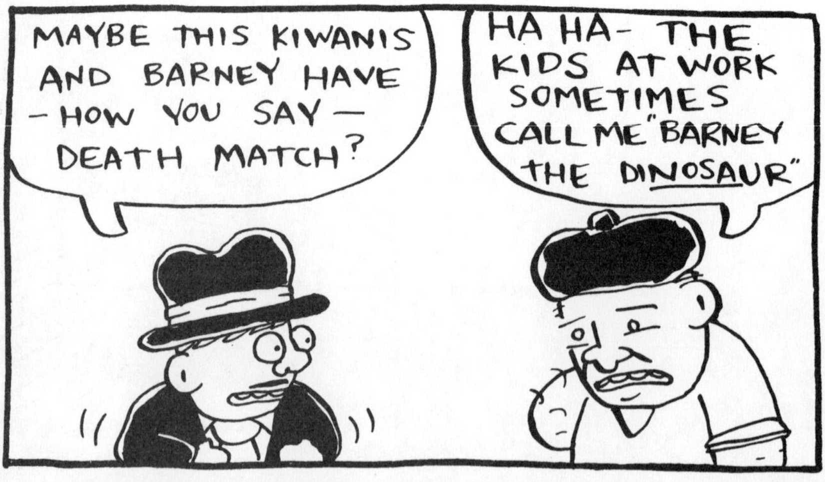
MAYBE THIS KIWANIS AND BARNEY HAVE - HOW YOU SAY - DEATH MATCH?
HA HA - THE KIDS AT WORK SOMETIMES CALL ME "BARNEY THE DINOSAUR"

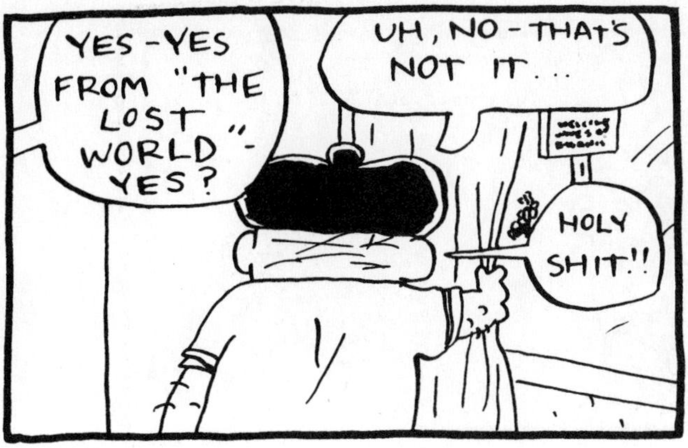
YES-YES FROM "THE LOST WORLD"- YES?
UH, NO-THAT'S NOT IT...
HOLY SHIT!!

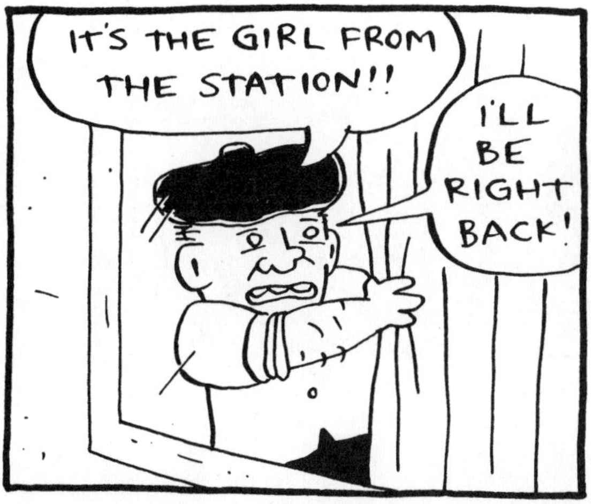
IT'S THE GIRL FROM THE STATION!!
I'LL BE RIGHT BACK!

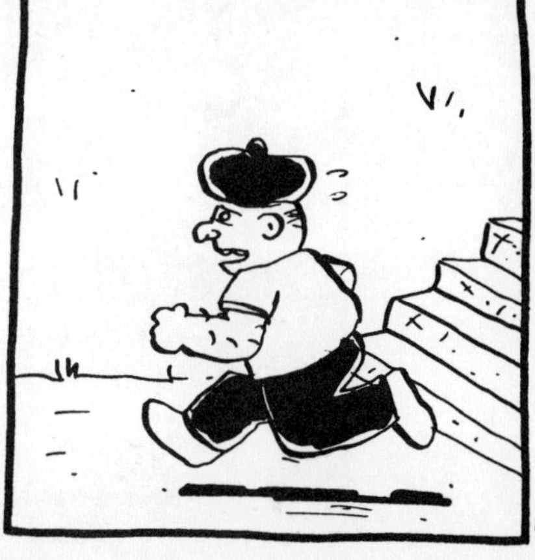

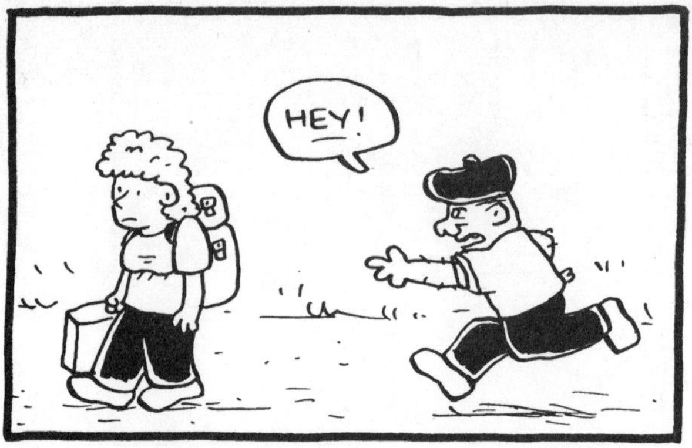
HEY!

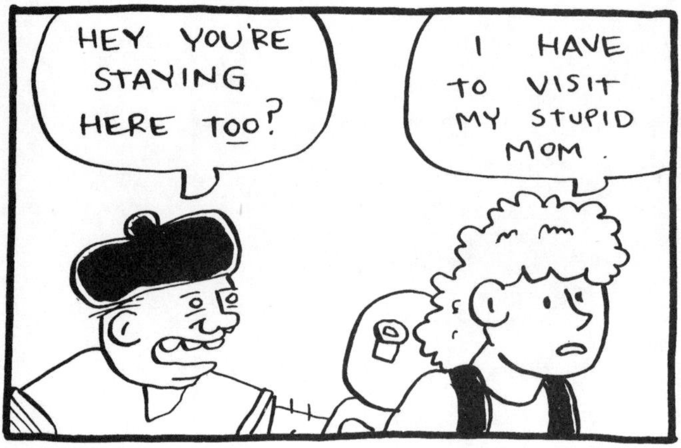
HEY YOU'RE STAYING HERE TOO?
I HAVE TO VISIT MY STUPID MOM.

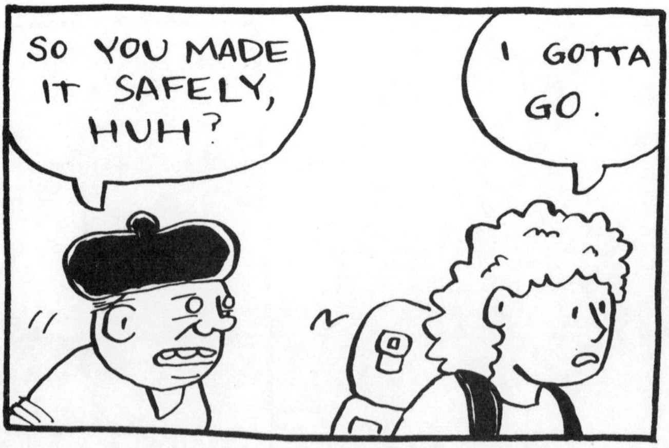
SO YOU MADE IT SAFELY, HUH?
I GOTTA GO.

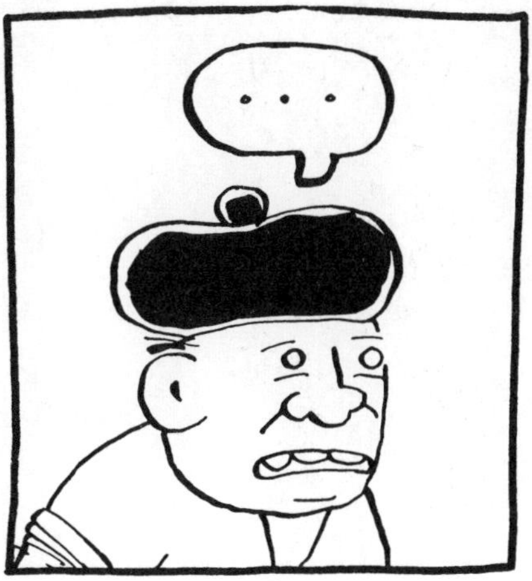
. . .

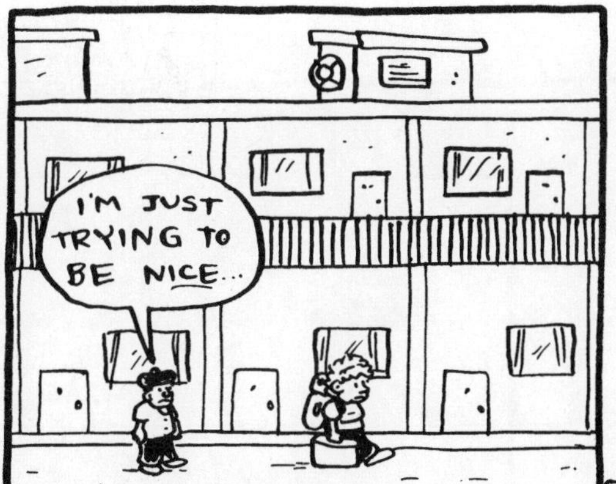
I'M JUST TRYING TO BE NICE...

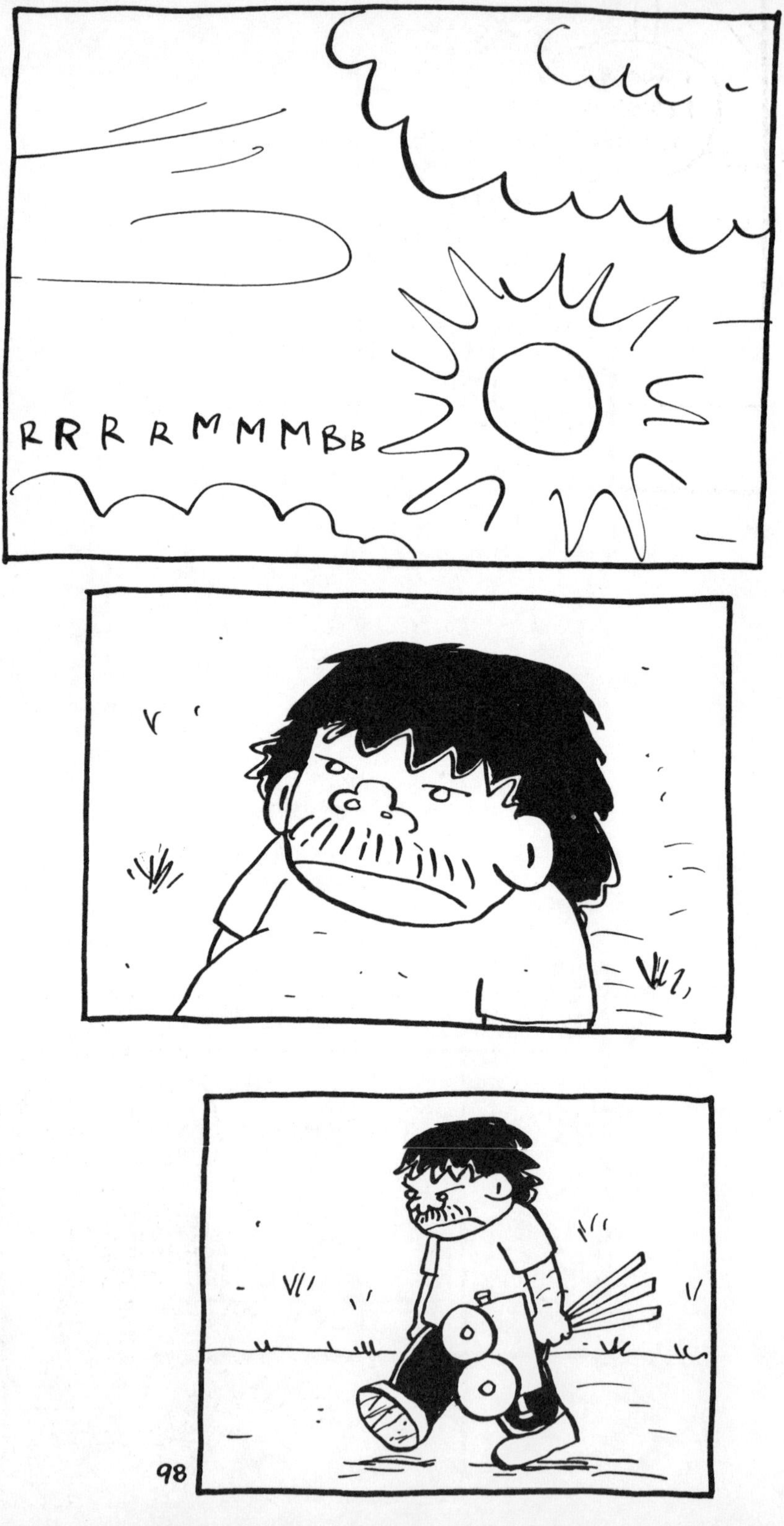
RRRRMMMMBB

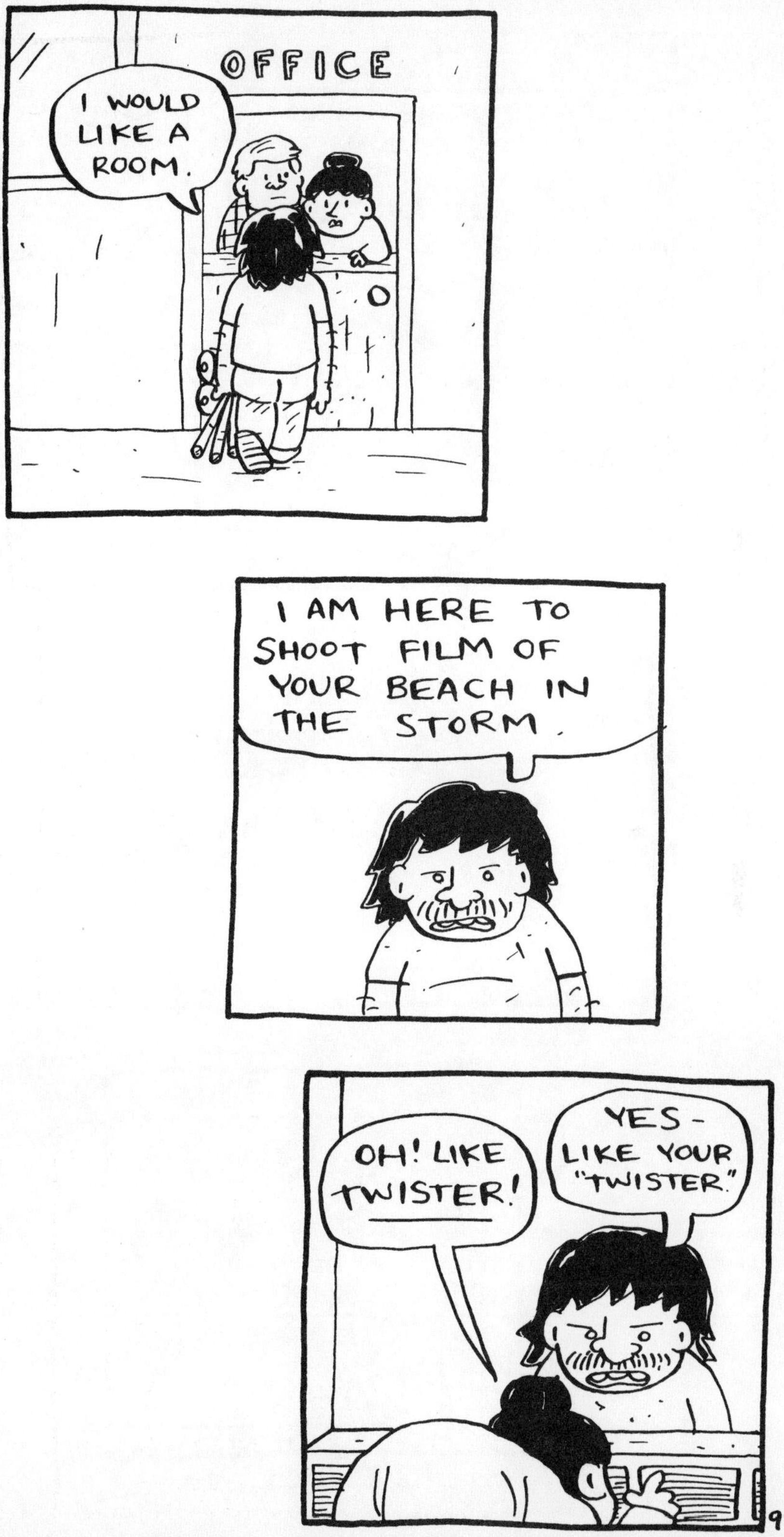
OFFICE
I WOULD LIKE A ROOM.
I AM HERE TO SHOOT FILM OF YOUR BEACH IN THE STORM.
OH! LIKE TWISTER!
YES - LIKE YOUR "TWISTER."

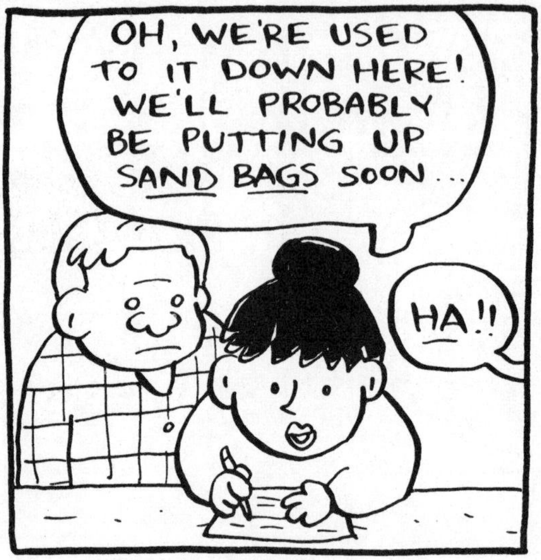
OH, WE'RE USED TO IT DOWN HERE! WE'LL PROBABLY BE PUTTING UP SAND BAGS SOON...
HA!!

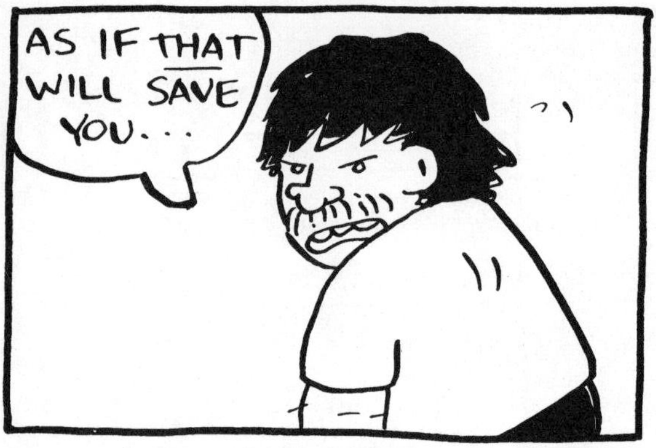
AS IF THAT WILL SAVE YOU...

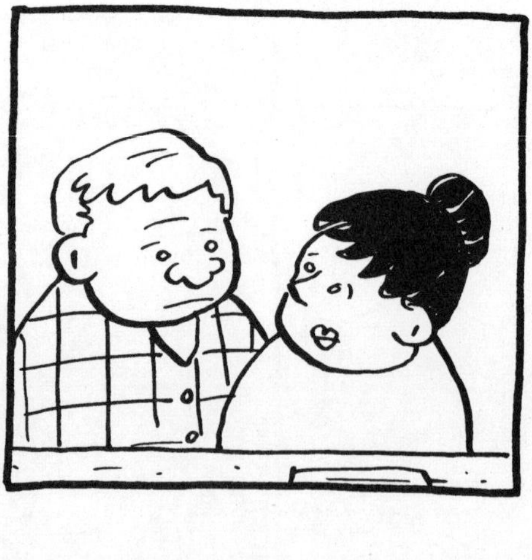

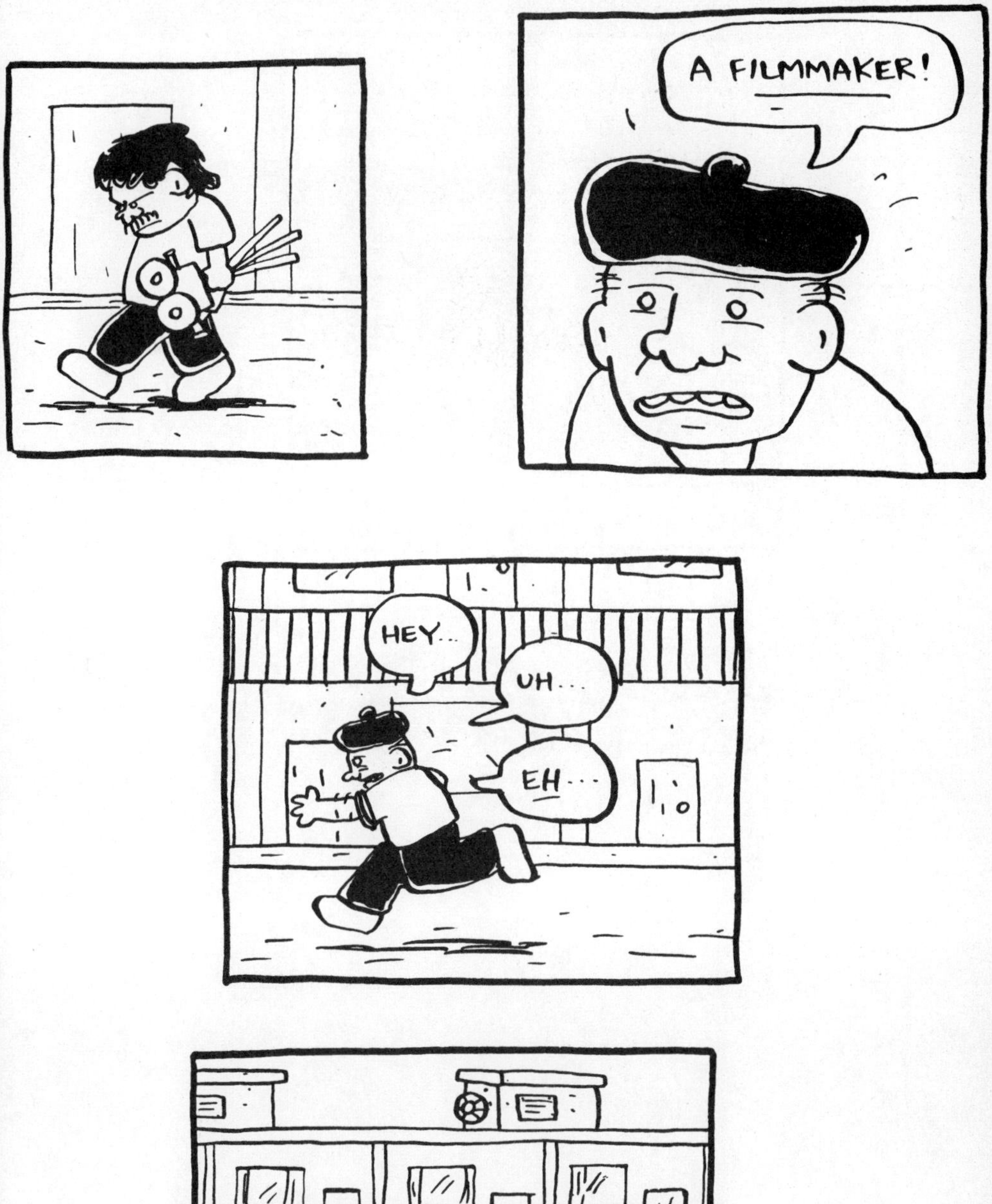
A FILMMAKER!
HEY...
UH...
EH...
. . .

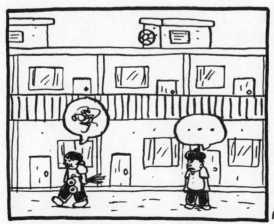

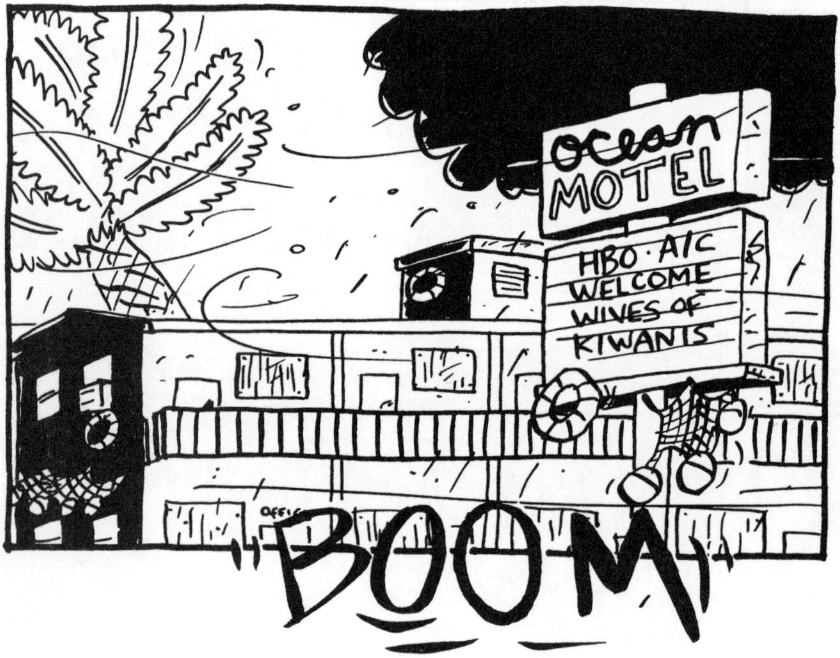
ocean
MOTEL
HBO · A/C
WELCOME
WIVES OF
KIWANIS
BOOM

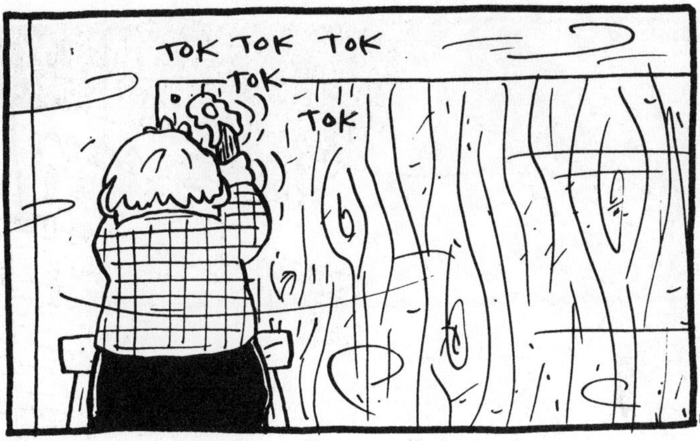
TOK TOK TOK
TOK
TOK

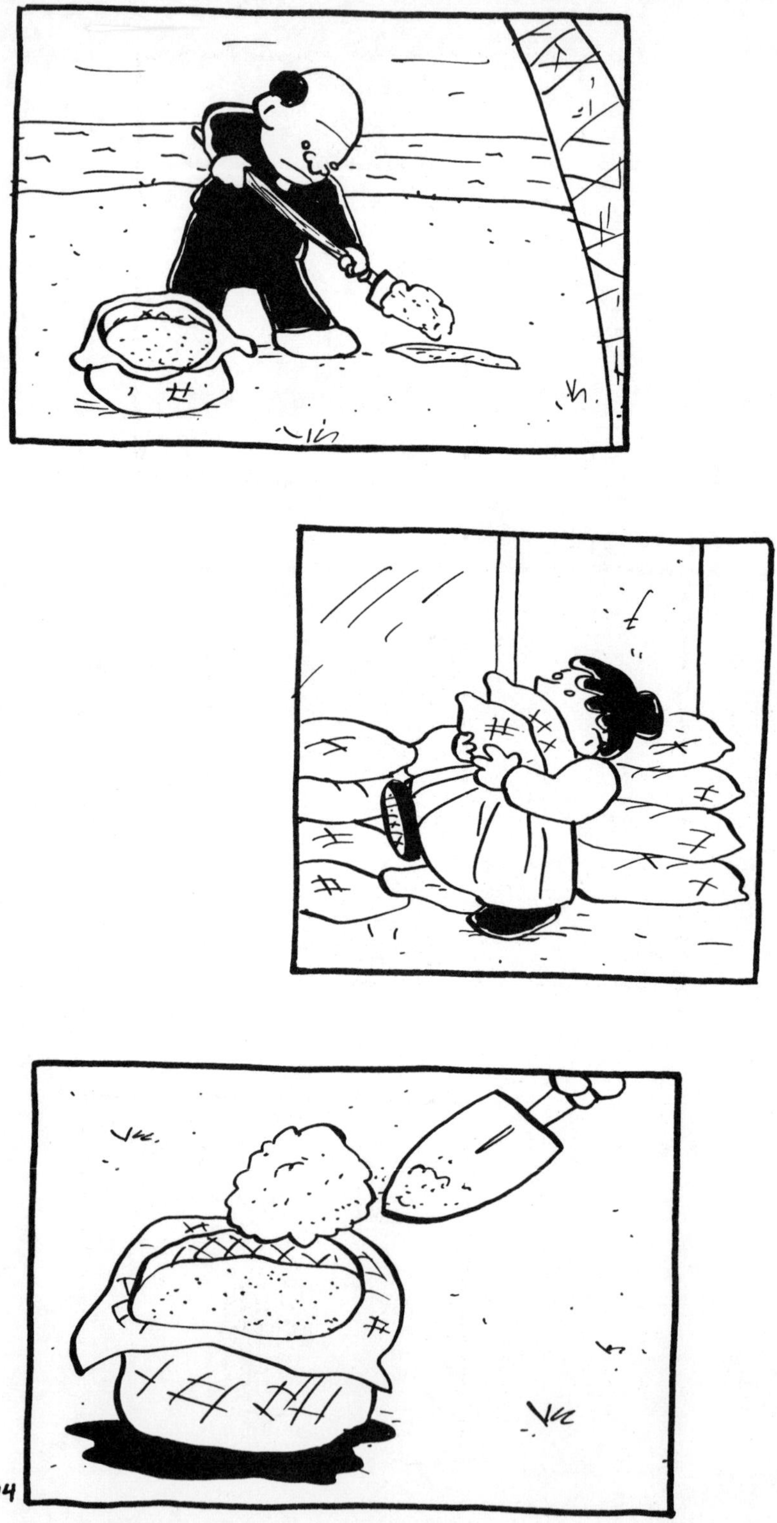

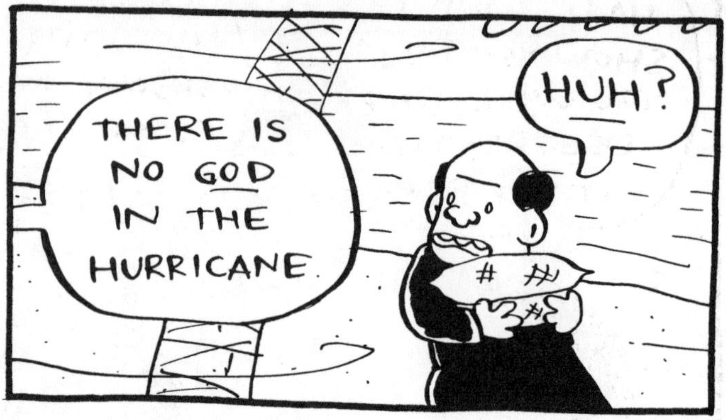
THERE IS NO GOD IN THE HURRICANE.
HUH?

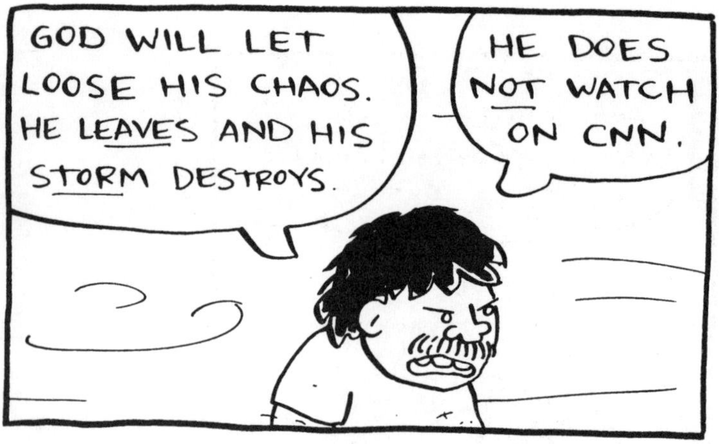
GOD WILL LET LOOSE HIS CHAOS. HE LEAVES AND HIS STORM DESTROYS.
HE DOES NOT WATCH ON CNN.

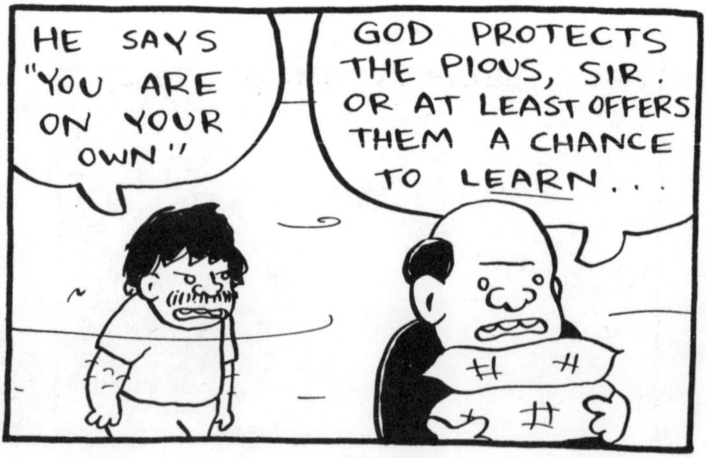
HE SAYS "YOU ARE ON YOUR OWN"
GOD PROTECTS THE PIOUS, SIR. OR AT LEAST OFFERS THEM A CHANCE TO LEARN...

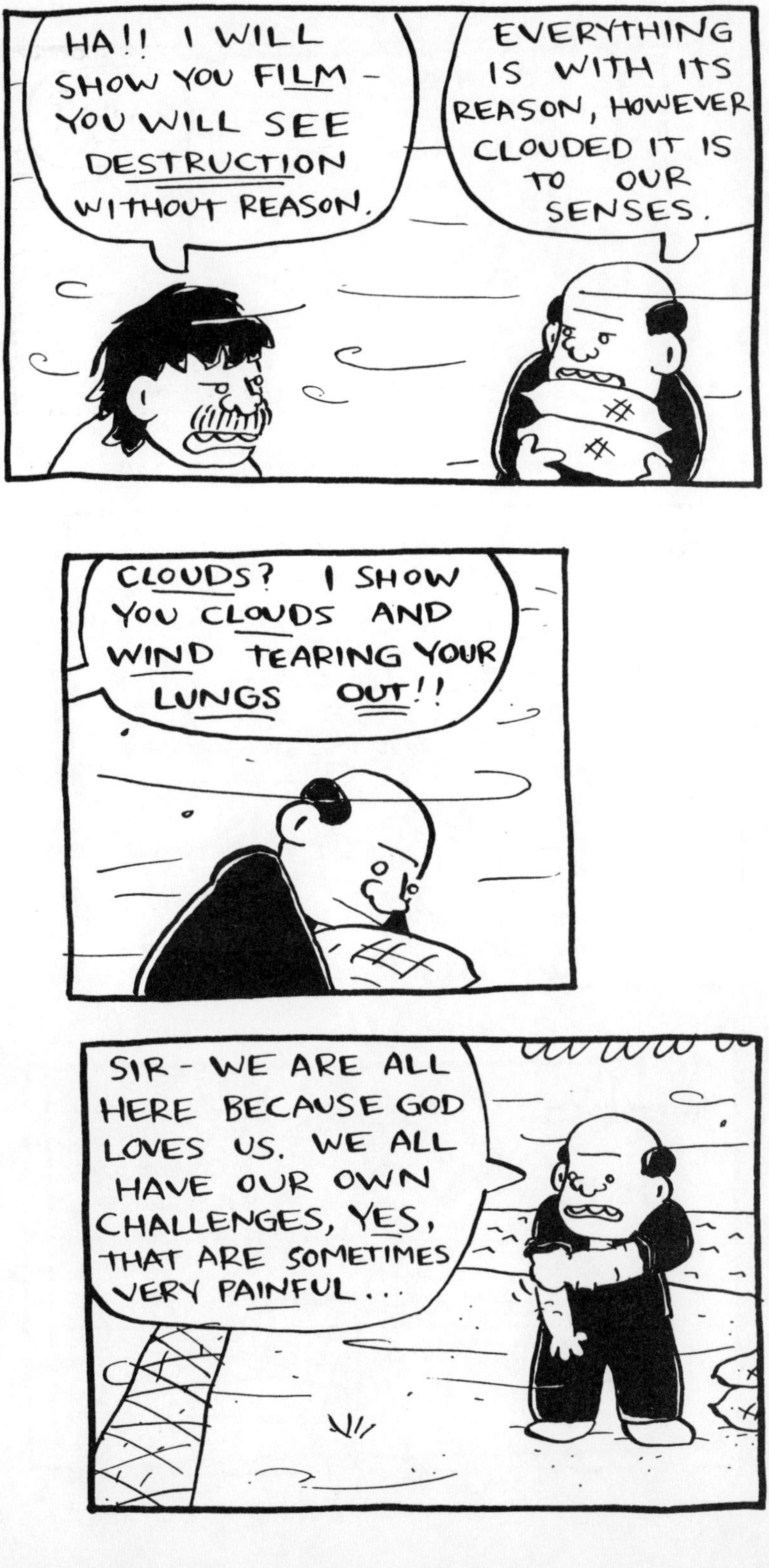
HA!! I WILL SHOW YOU FILM - YOU WILL SEE DESTRUCTION WITHOUT REASON.
EVERYTHING IS WITH ITS REASON, HOWEVER CLOUDED IT IS TO OUR SENSES.
CLOUDS? I SHOW YOU CLOUDS AND WIND TEARING YOUR LUNGS OUT!!
SIR - WE ARE ALL HERE BECAUSE GOD LOVES US. WE ALL HAVE OUR OWN CHALLENGES, YES, THAT ARE SOMETIMES VERY PAINFUL...

THIS GOOD. I GET ON FILM.
WHIRRR

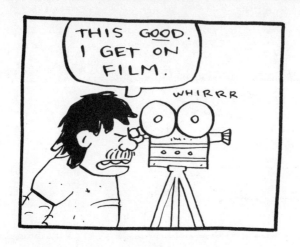

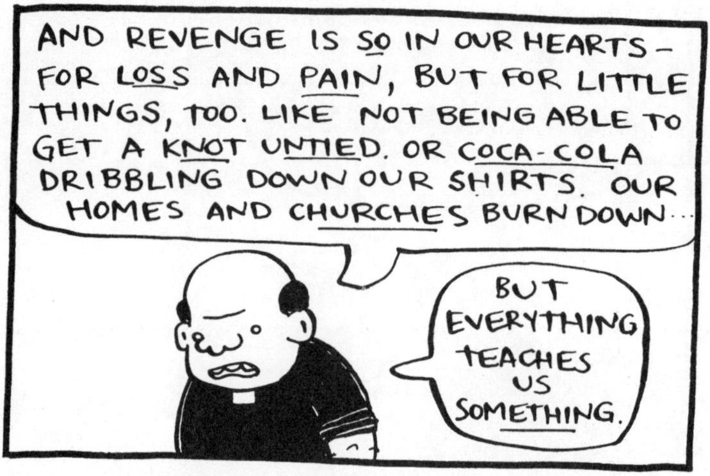

AND REVENGE IS SO IN OUR HEARTS– FOR LOSS AND PAIN, BUT FOR LITTLE THINGS, TOO. LIKE NOT BEING ABLE TO GET A KNOT UNTIED. OR COCA-COLA DRIBBLING DOWN OUR SHIRTS. OUR HOMES AND CHURCHES BURN DOWN...
BUT EVERYTHING TEACHES US SOMETHING.

DEATH? FAMINE?
POVERTY?
RRR
NEGLECT?

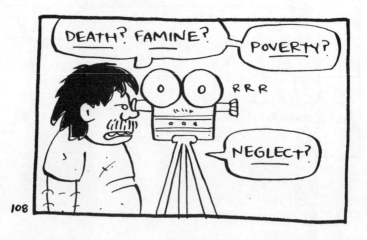

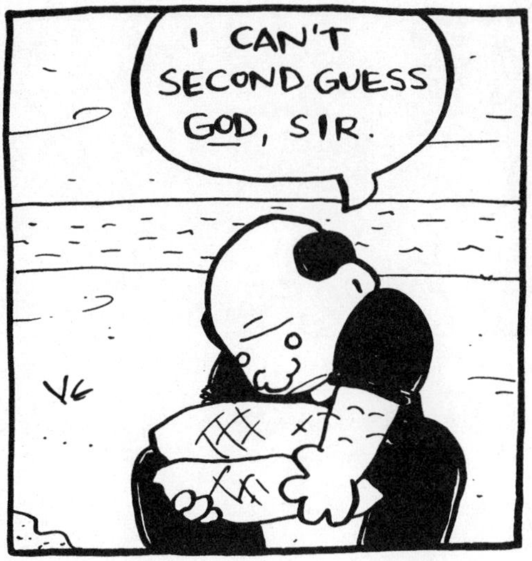
I CAN'T SECOND GUESS GOD, SIR.

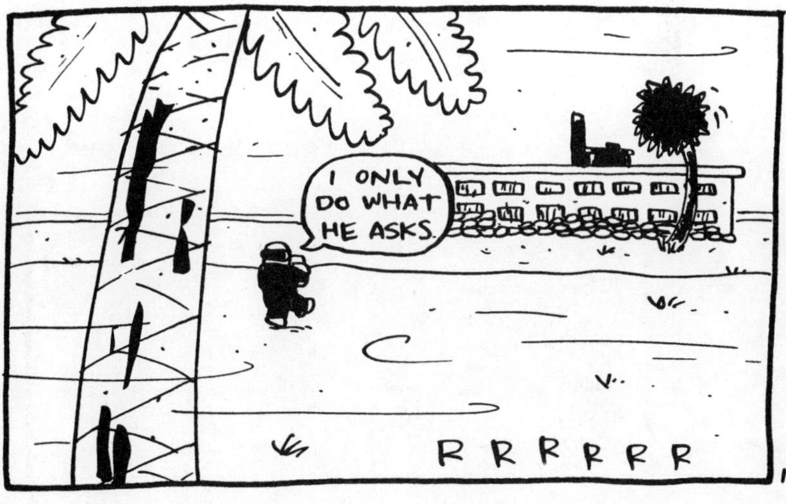
I ONLY DO WHAT HE ASKS.
R R R R R R

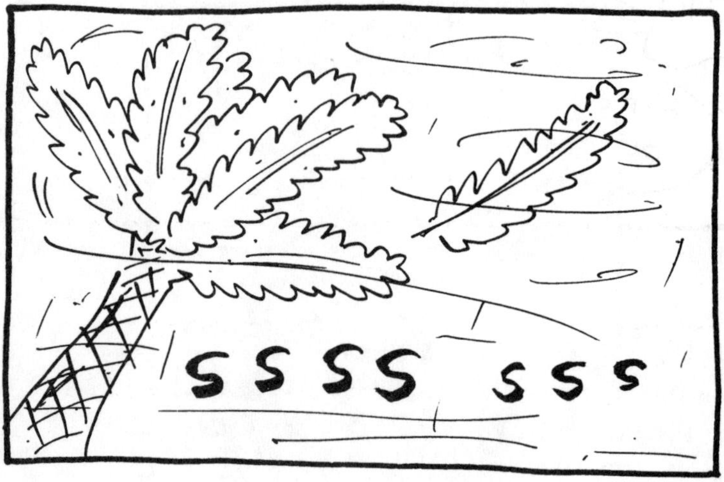
SSSS sss

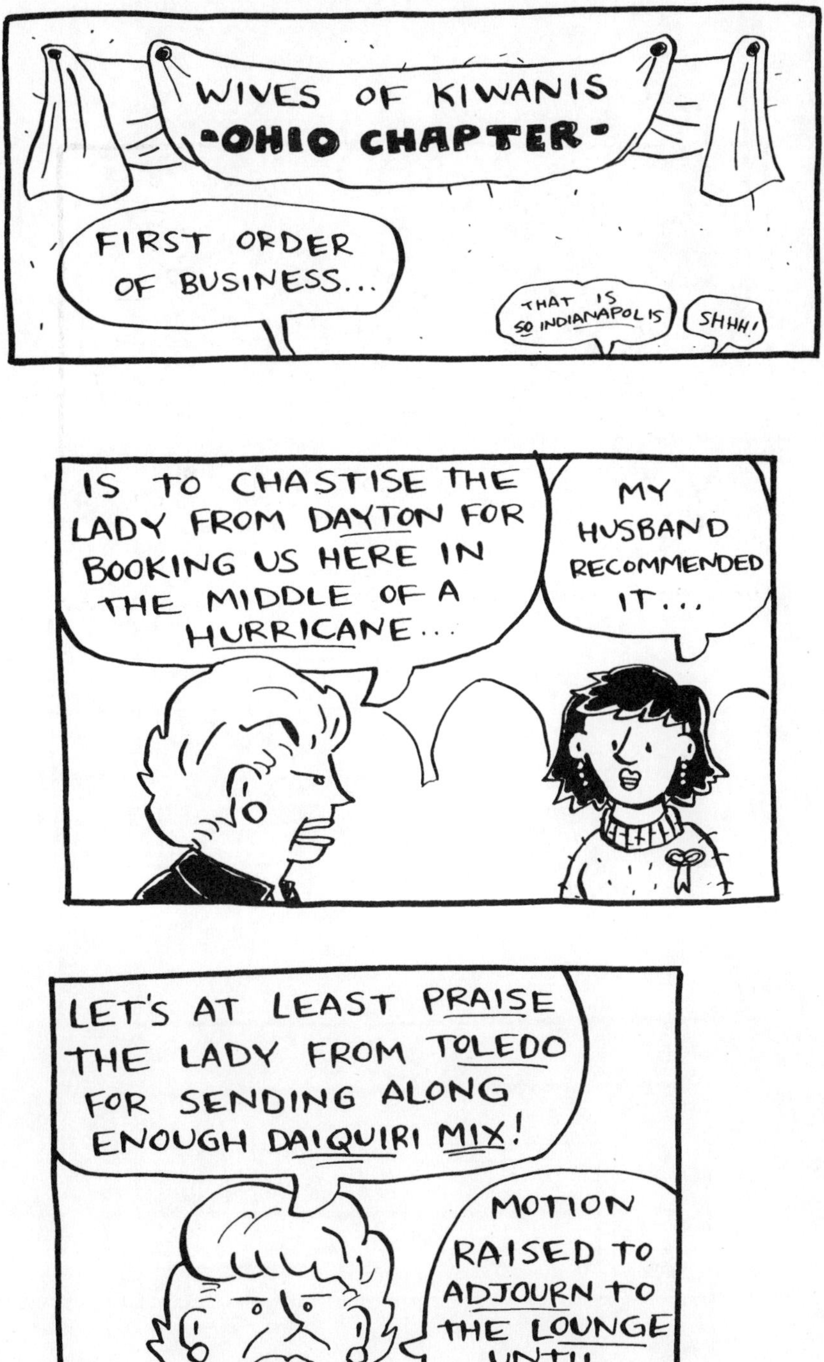
WIVES OF KIWANIS
-OHIO CHAPTER-
FIRST ORDER OF BUSINESS...
THAT IS SO INDIANAPOLIS
SHHH!
IS TO CHASTISE THE LADY FROM DAYTON FOR BOOKING US HERE IN THE MIDDLE OF A HURRICANE...
MY HUSBAND RECOMMENDED IT...
LET'S AT LEAST PRAISE THE LADY FROM TOLEDO FOR SENDING ALONG ENOUGH DAIQUIRI MIX!
MOTION RAISED TO ADJOURN TO THE LOUNGE UNTIL TUESDAY- HANDS?

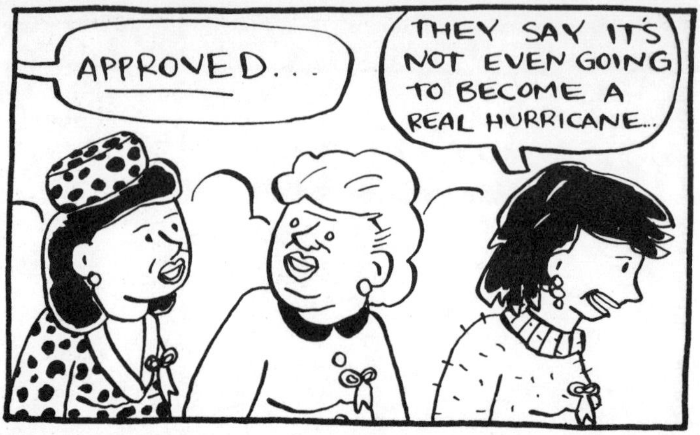
APPROVED...
THEY SAY IT'S NOT EVEN GOING TO BECOME A REAL HURRICANE...

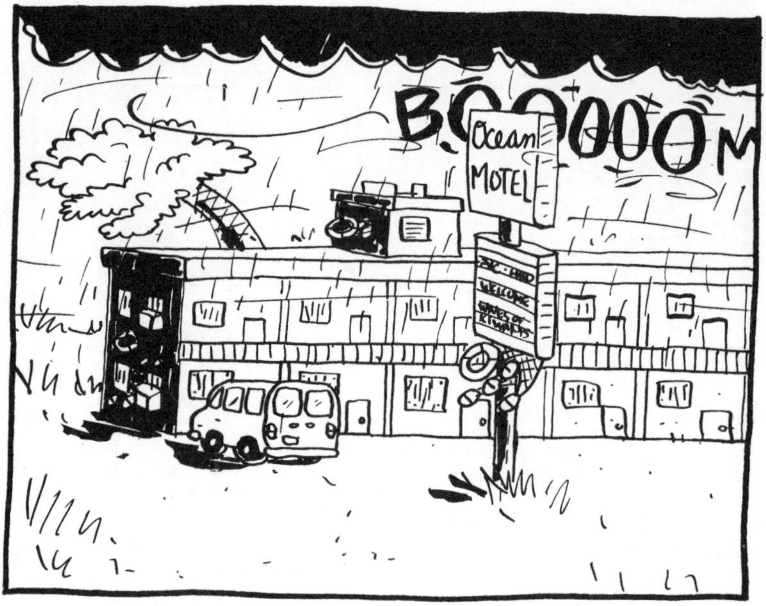
BOOOOOM
Ocean MOTEL
WELCOME

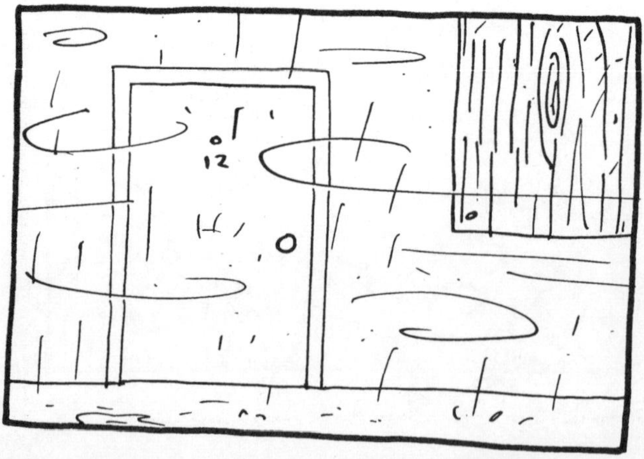
12

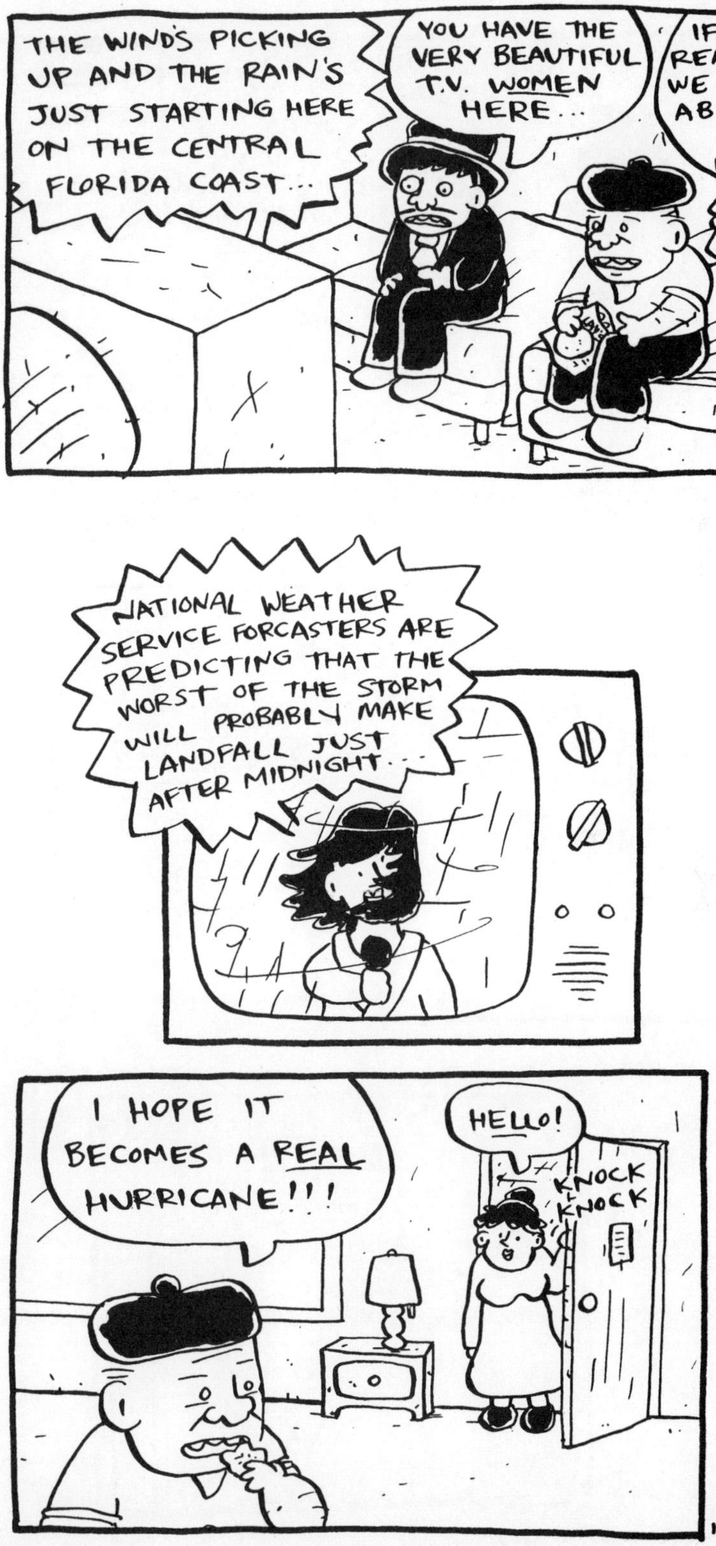
THE WIND'S PICKING UP AND THE RAIN'S JUST STARTING HERE ON THE CENTRAL FLORIDA COAST...
YOU HAVE THE VERY BEAUTIFUL T.V. WOMEN HERE...
IF IT GETS REALLY WET WE MIGHT BE ABLE TO SEE HER NIPPLES...
NATIONAL WEATHER SERVICE FORCASTERS ARE PREDICTING THAT THE WORST OF THE STORM WILL PROBABLY MAKE LANDFALL JUST AFTER MIDNIGHT...
I HOPE IT BECOMES A REAL HURRICANE!!!
HELLO!
KNOCK KNOCK

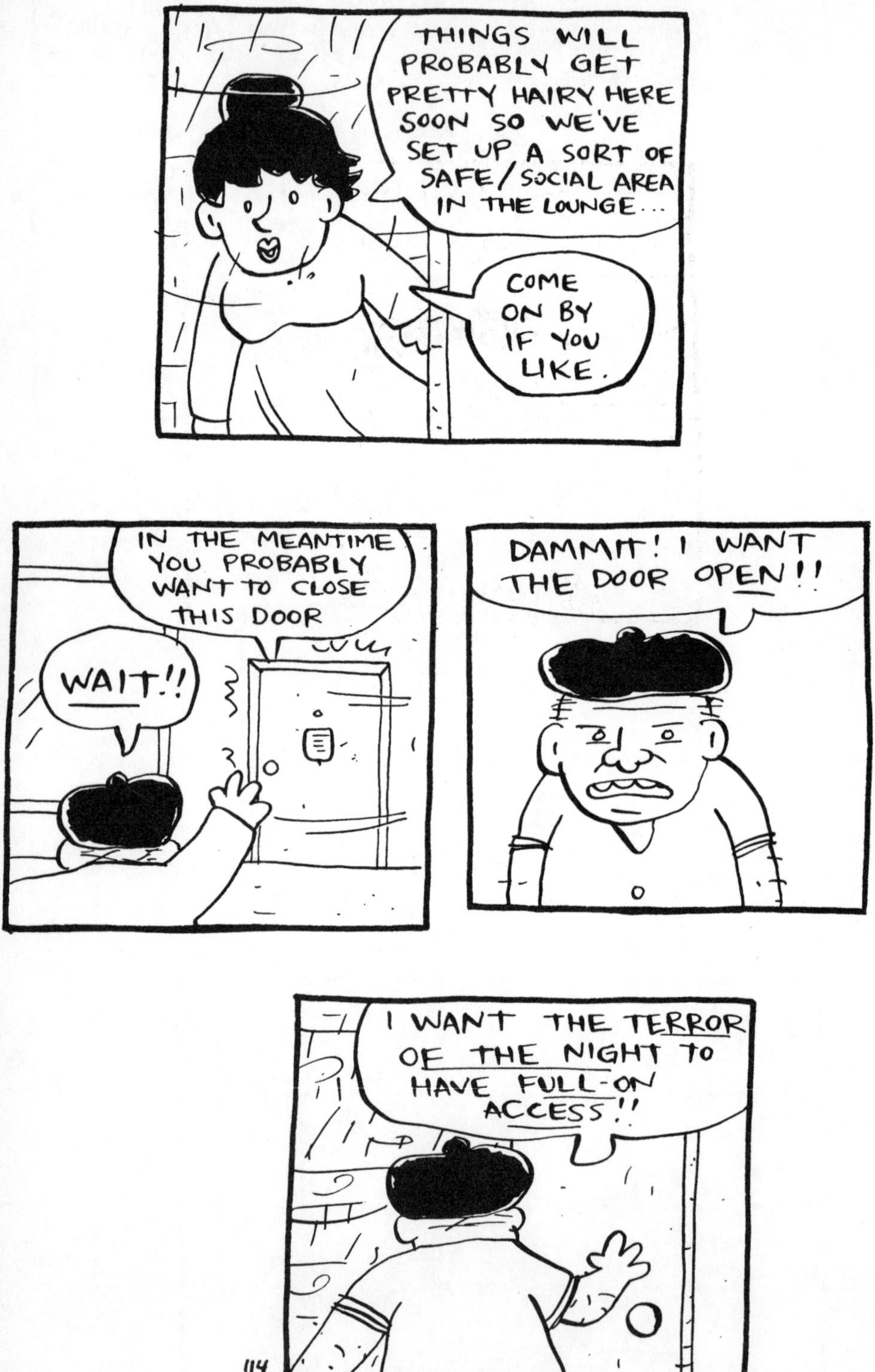
THINGS WILL PROBABLY GET PRETTY HAIRY HERE SOON SO WE'VE SET UP A SORT OF SAFE/SOCIAL AREA IN THE LOUNGE...
COME ON BY IF YOU LIKE.
IN THE MEANTIME YOU PROBABLY WANT TO CLOSE THIS DOOR
WAIT!!
DAMMIT! I WANT THE DOOR OPEN!!
I WANT THE TERROR OF THE NIGHT TO HAVE FULL-ON ACCESS!!

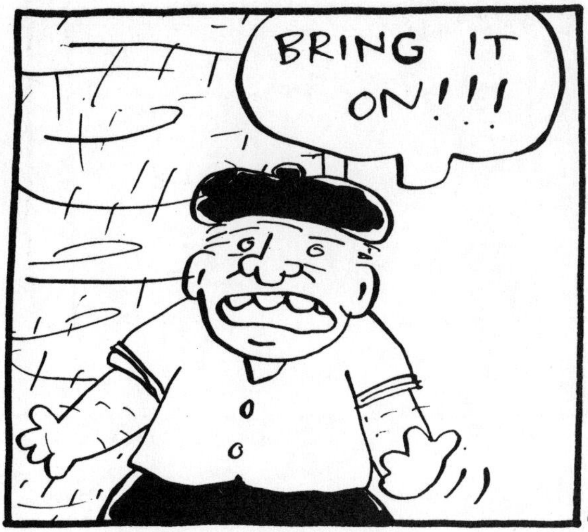
BRING IT ON!!!

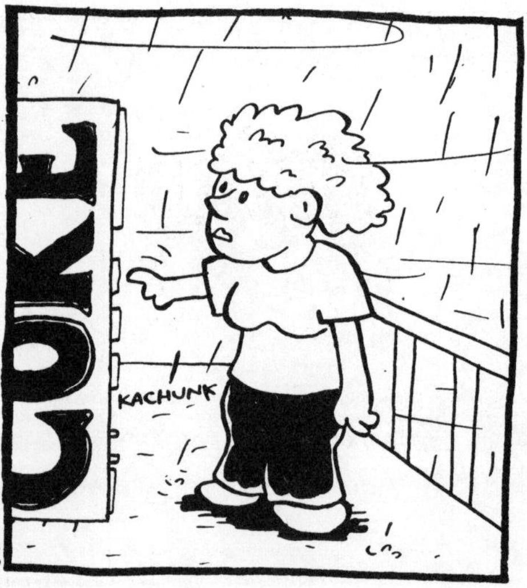
COKE
KACHUNK

117

118

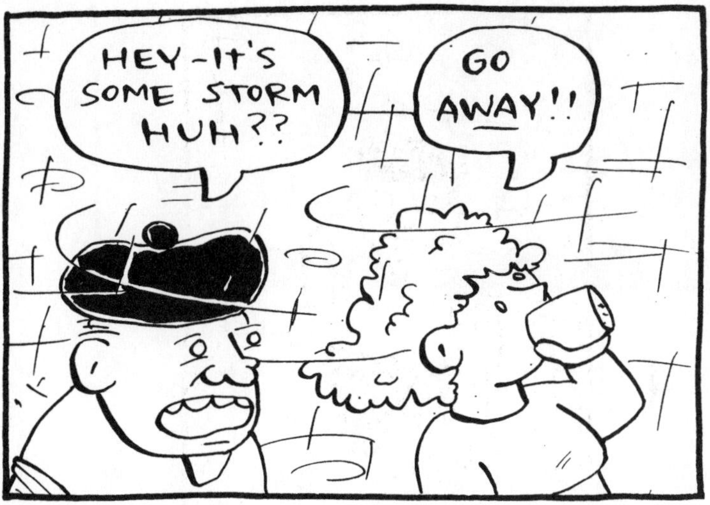
HEY-IT'S SOME STORM HUH??
GO AWAY!!

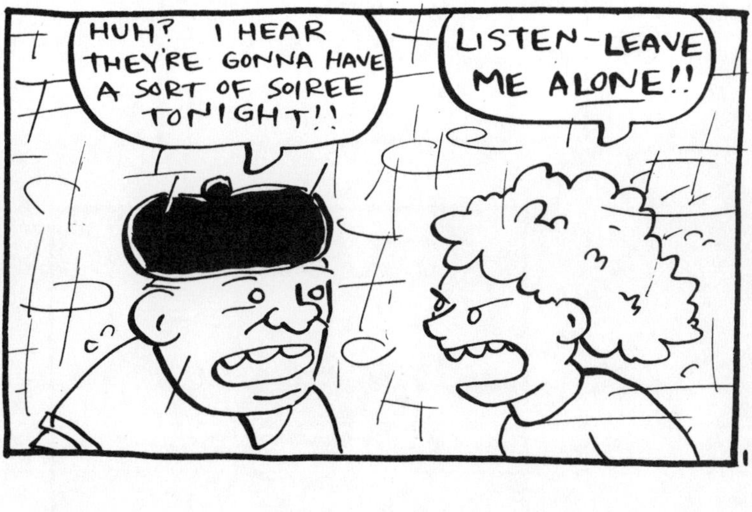
HUH? I HEAR THEY'RE GONNA HAVE A SORT OF SOIREE TONIGHT!!
LISTEN-LEAVE ME ALONE!!

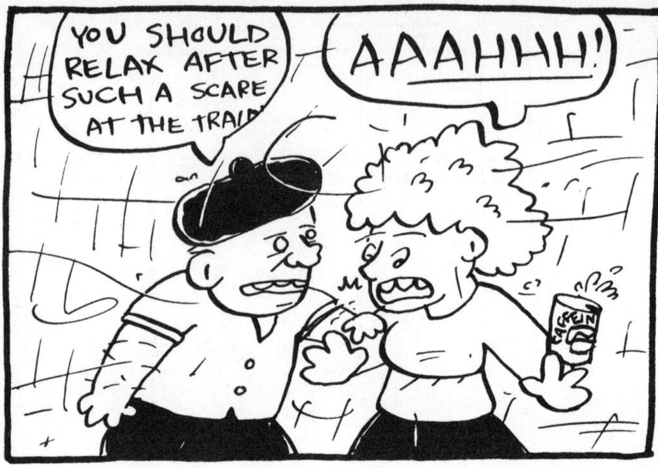
YOU SHOULD RELAX AFTER SUCH A SCARE AT THE TRAI
AAAHHH!

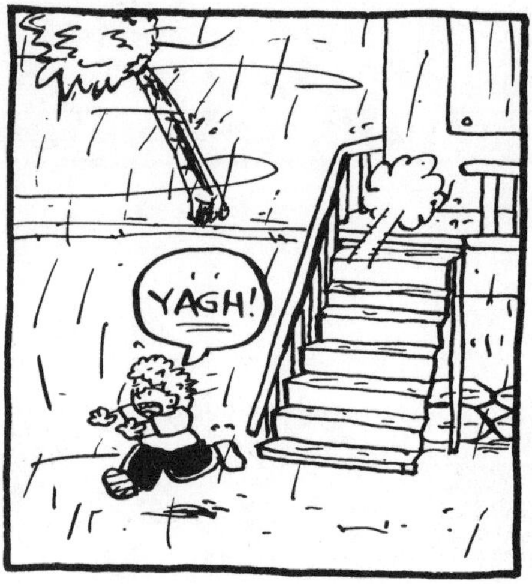
YAGH!

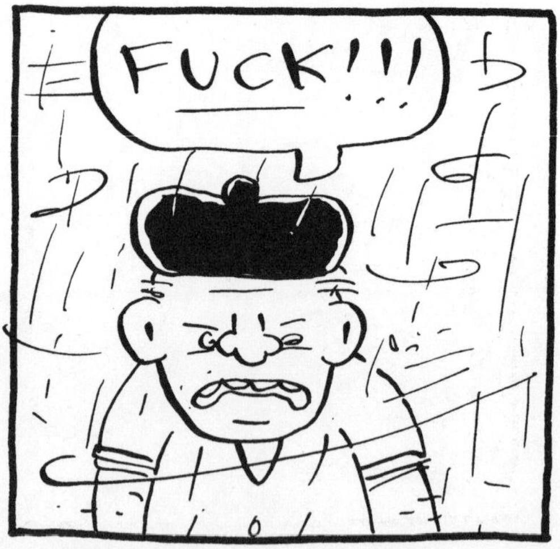
FUCK!!!

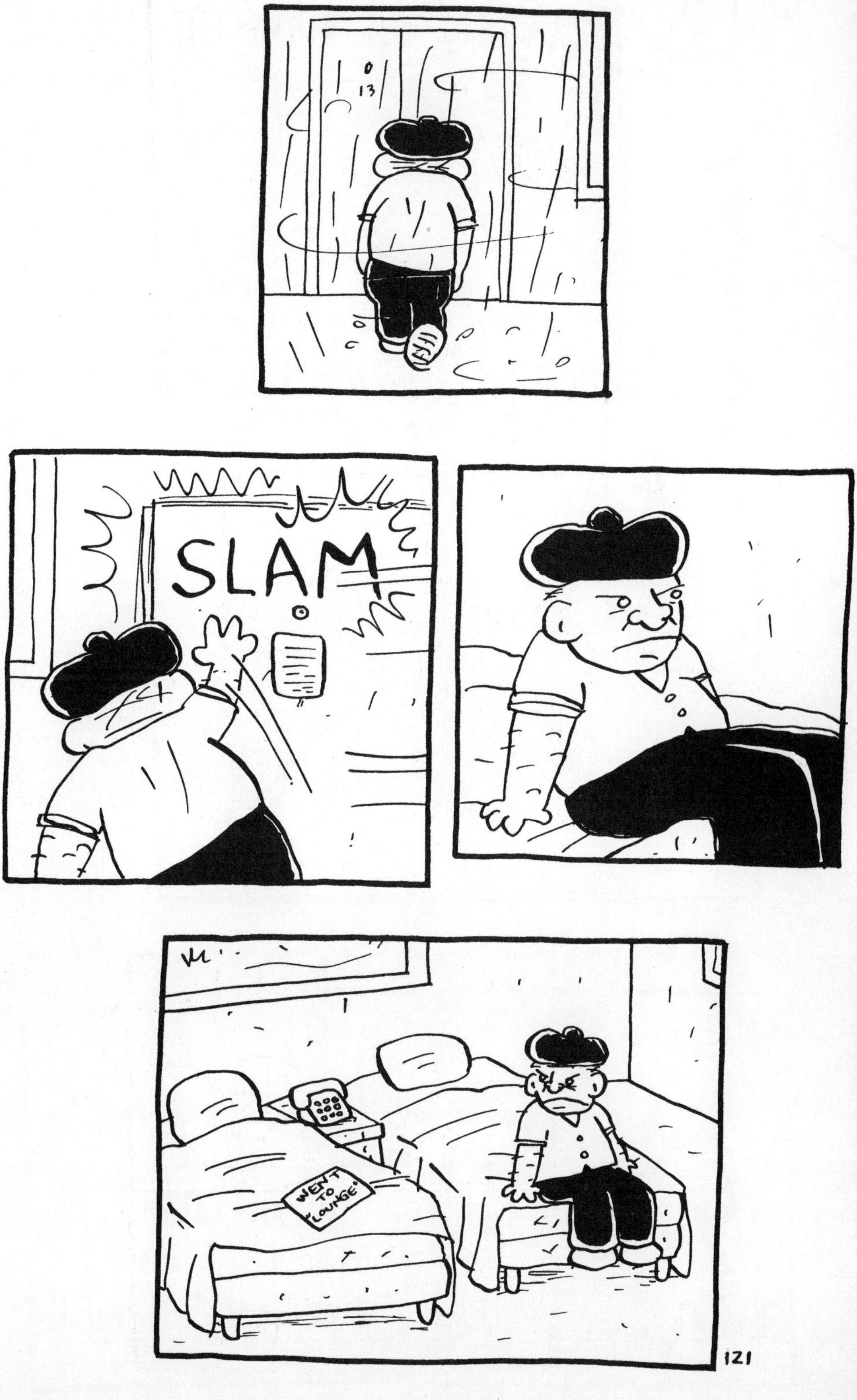
13
SLAM
WENT TO LOUNGE

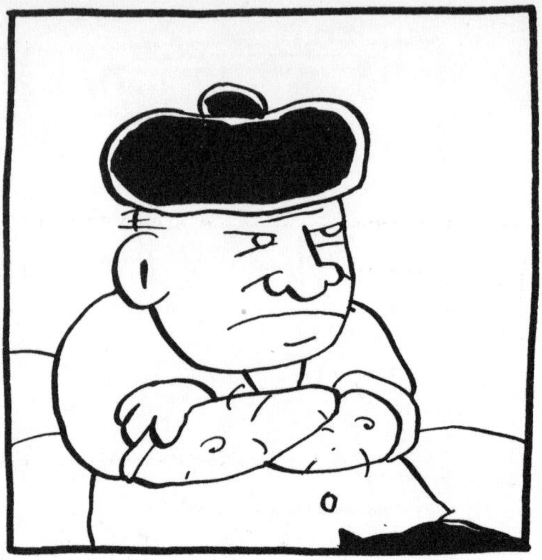

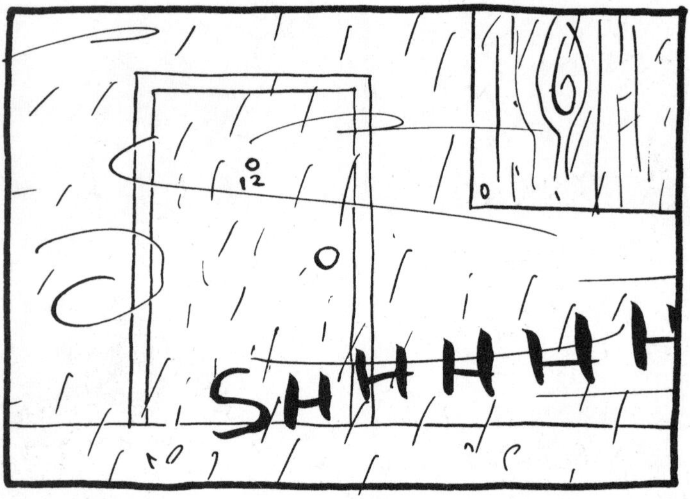
12
SHHHHH

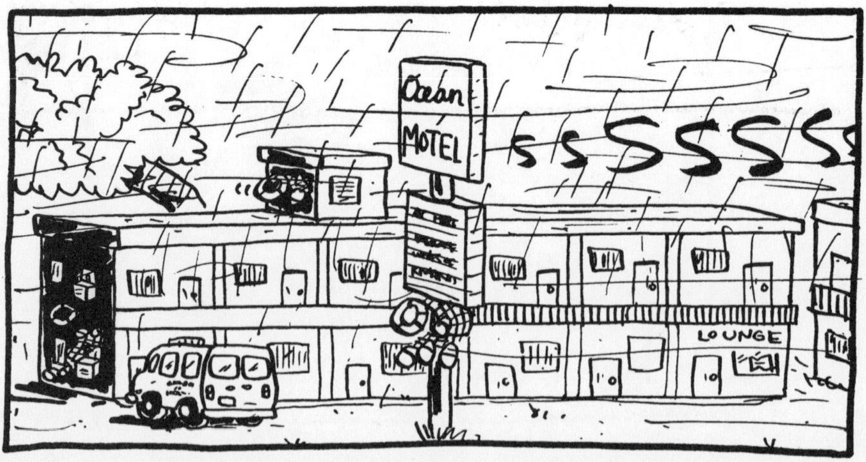
Ocean
MOTEL
ssSSSSS
LOUNGE

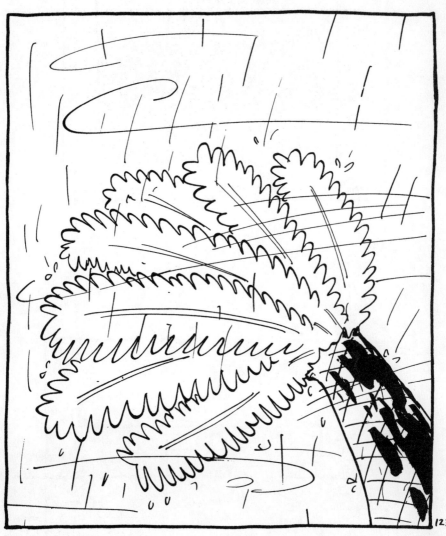

123

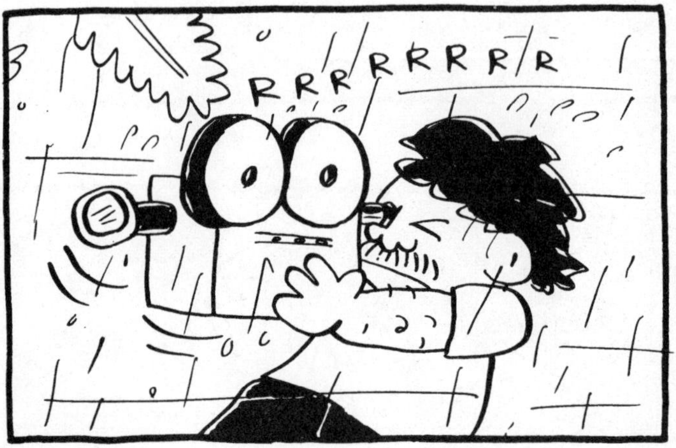
RRRRRRRR/R

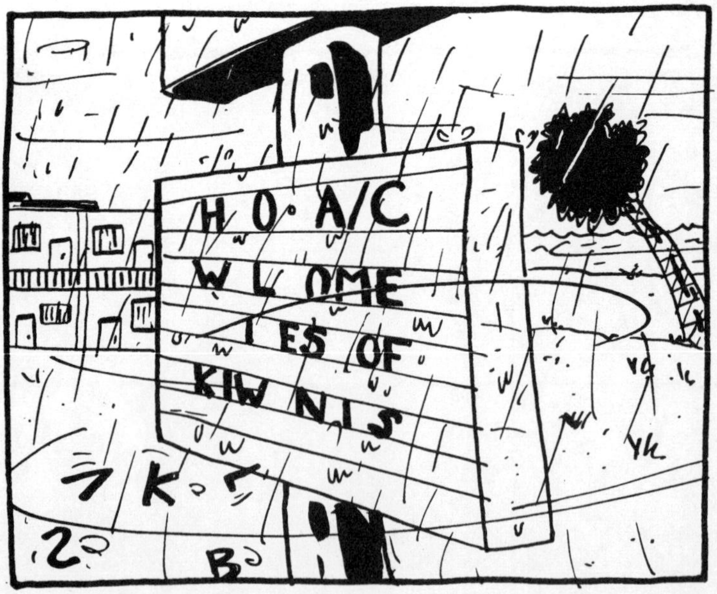
H O A/C
W L OME
I ES OF
KIW N I S

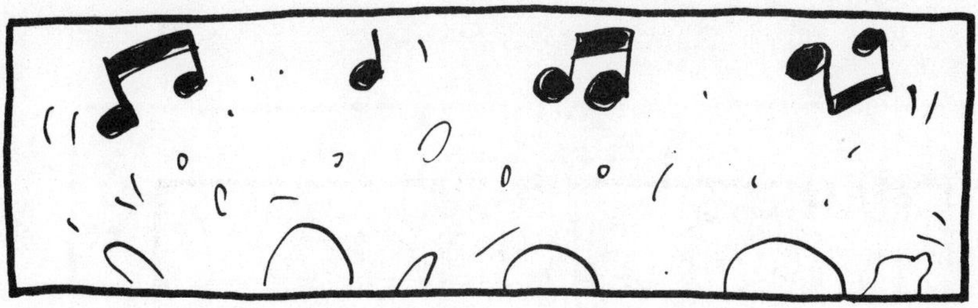

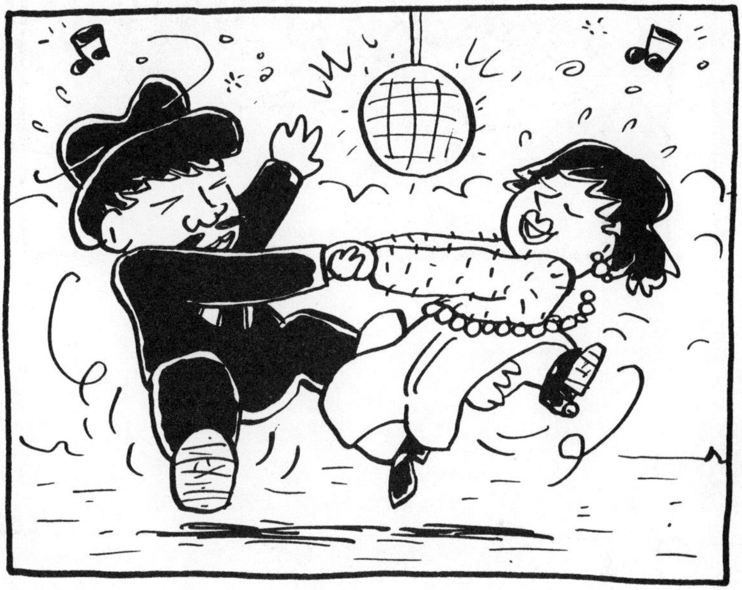

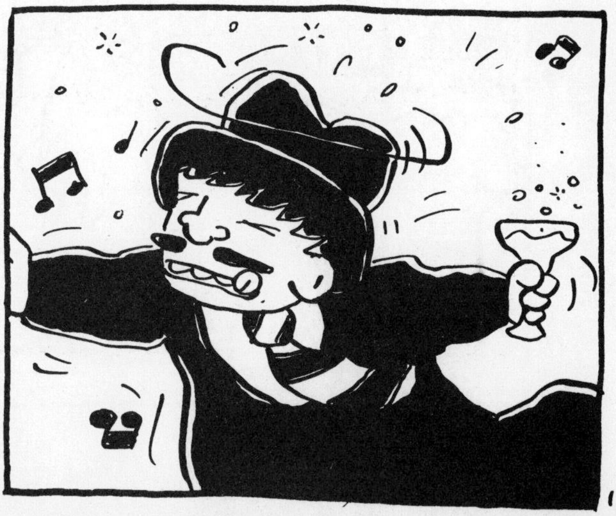

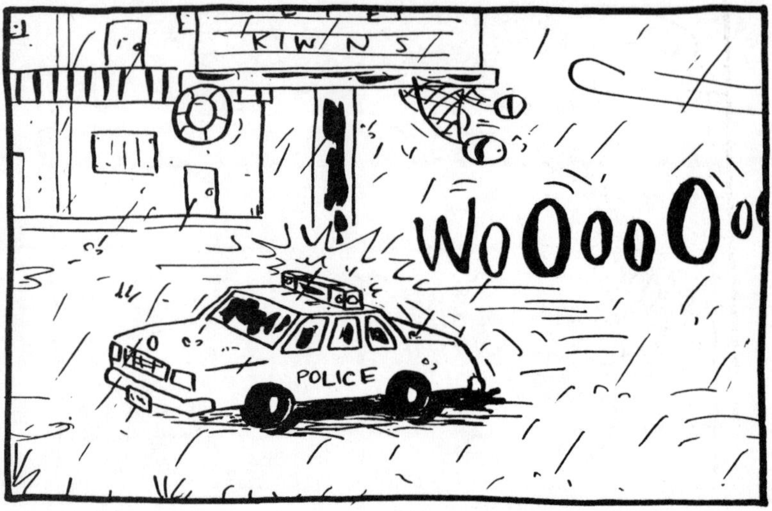
KIWNS
POLICE
WOOOOOO

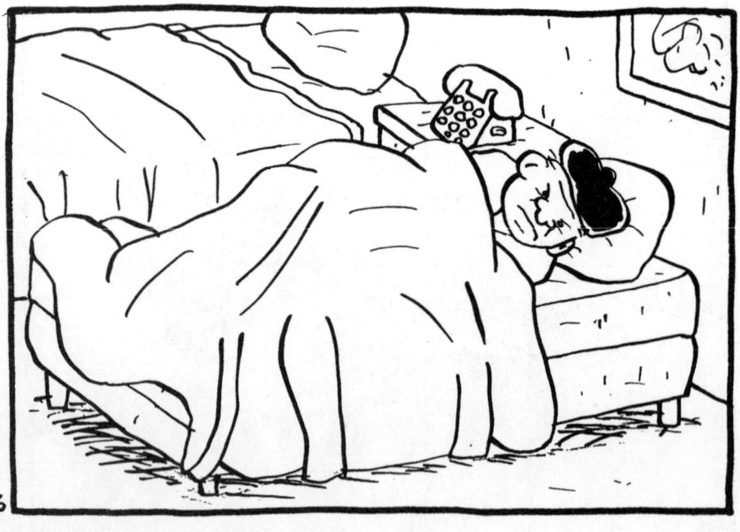

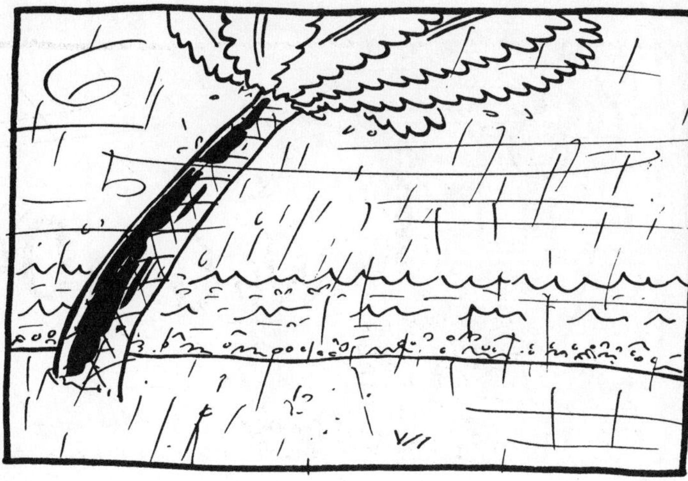

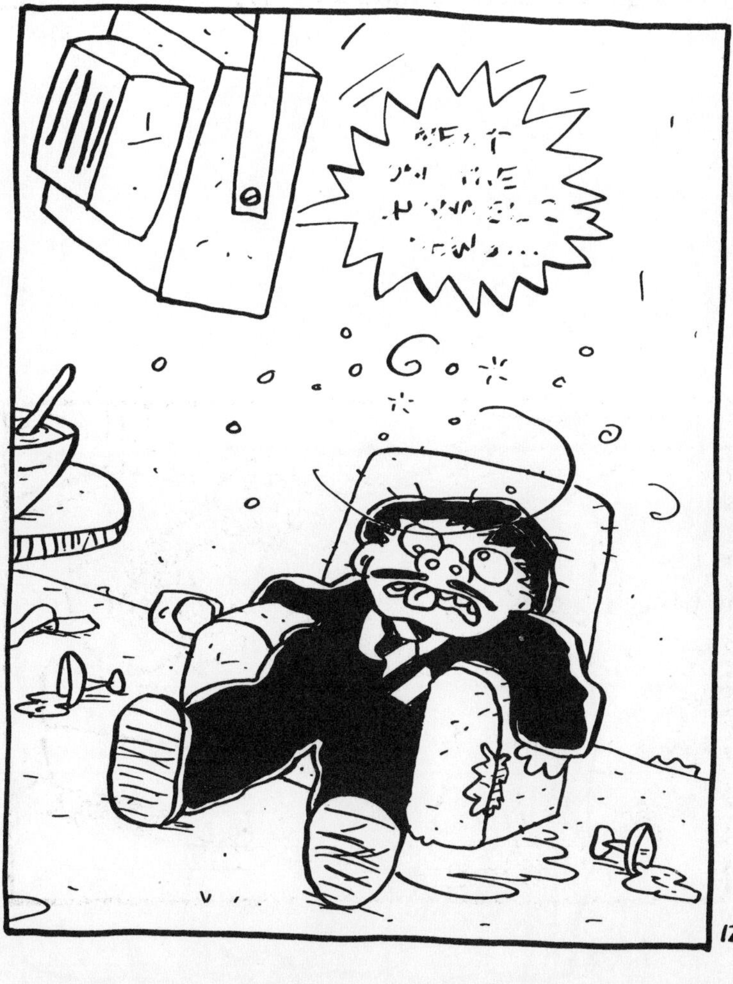

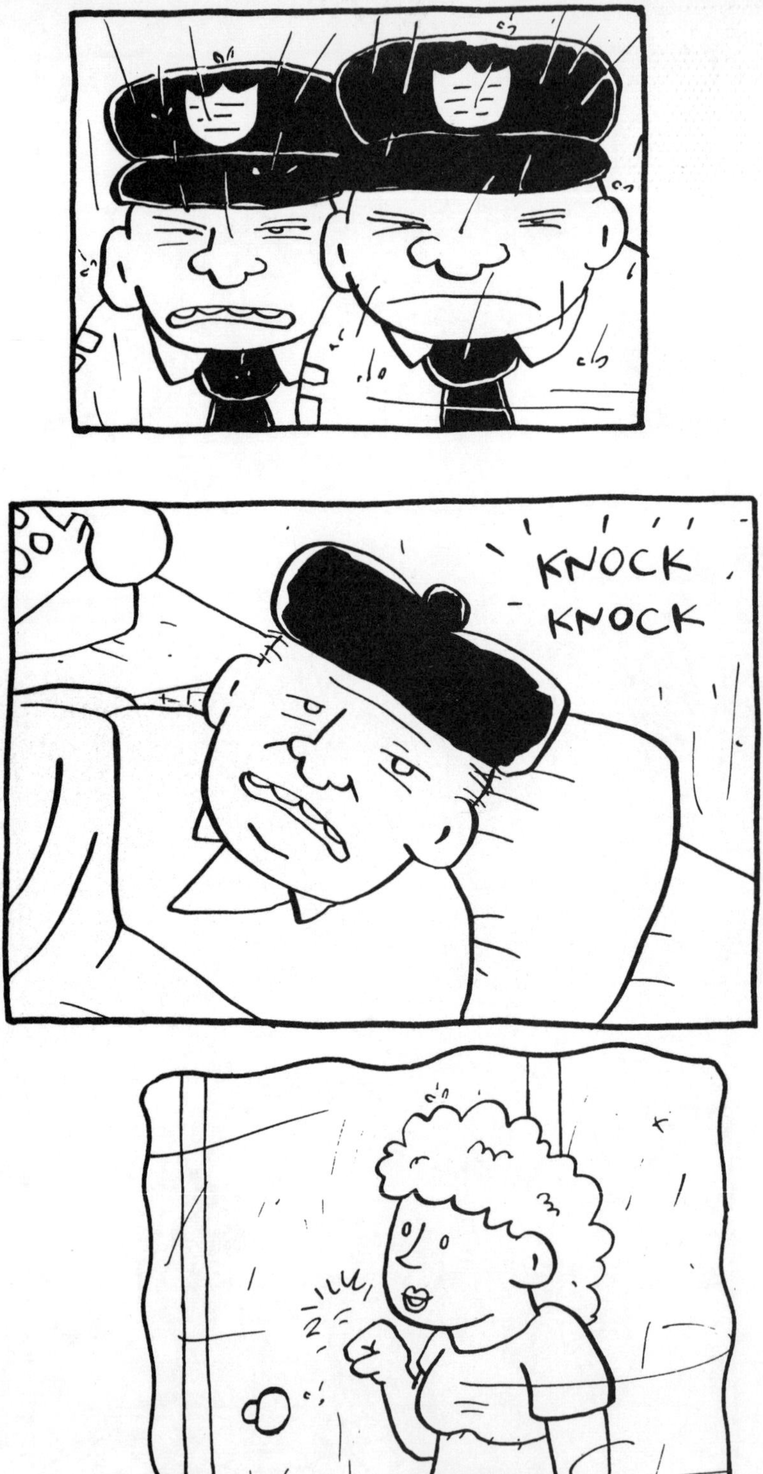
KNOCK
KNOCK

MR. BARNEY EUBANKS?
IT'S JUST BANKS - YES?
DO YOU KNOW THIS GIRL SIR??
YEAH HEY- THAT'S THE GIRL I MET AT THE TRAIN - SHE'S STAYING HERE - IS SHE OK..?

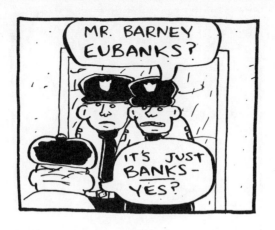

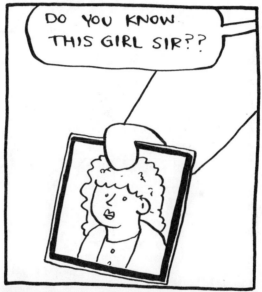

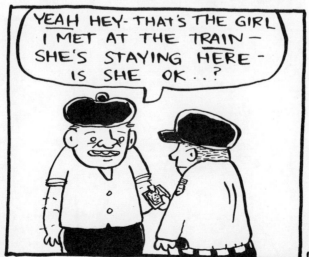

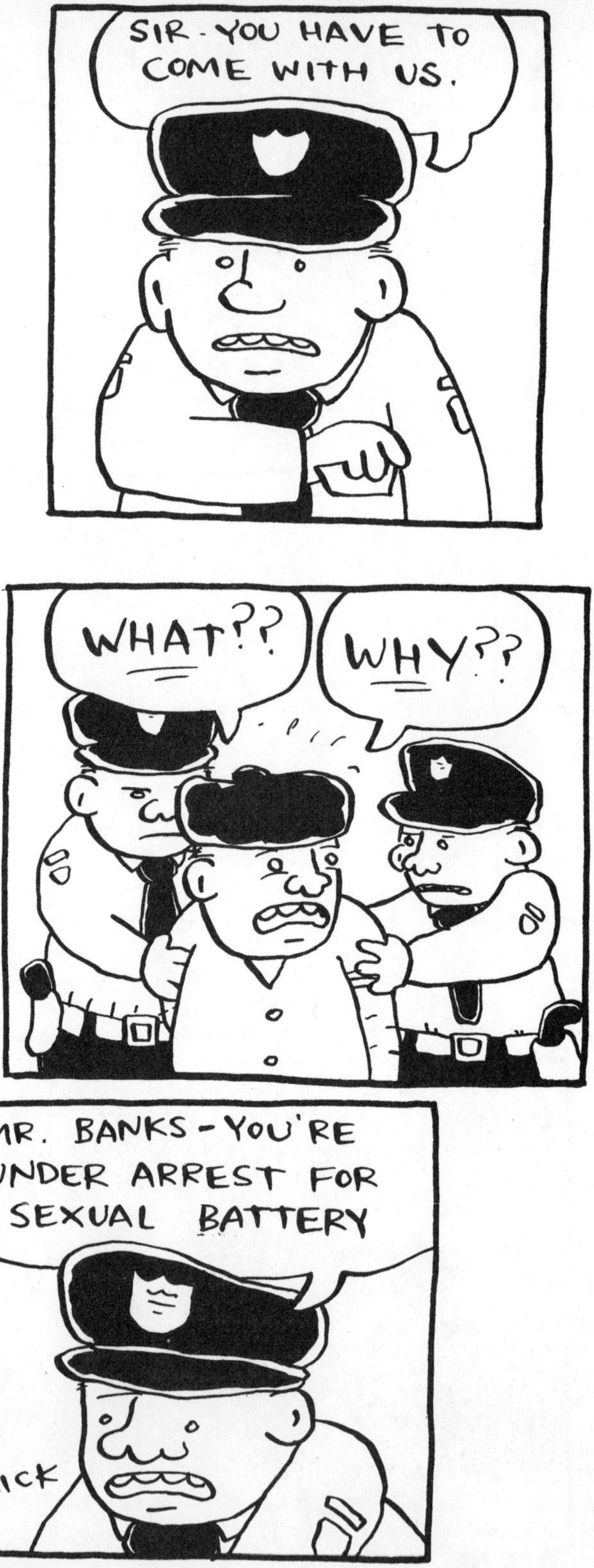
SIR - YOU HAVE TO COME WITH US.
WHAT??
WHY??
MR. BANKS - YOU'RE UNDER ARREST FOR SEXUAL BATTERY
CLICK

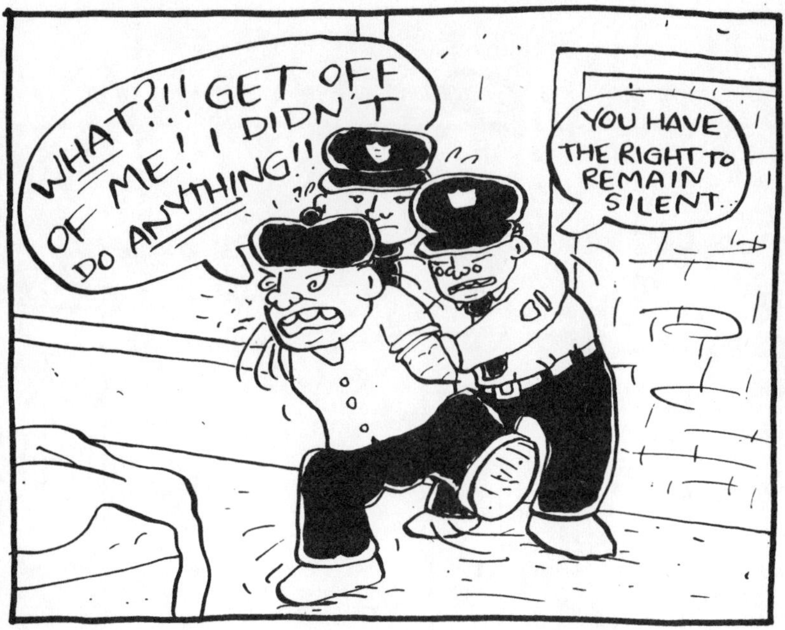
WHAT?!! GET OFF OF ME! I DIDN'T DO ANYTHING!!
YOU HAVE THE RIGHT TO REMAIN SILENT...

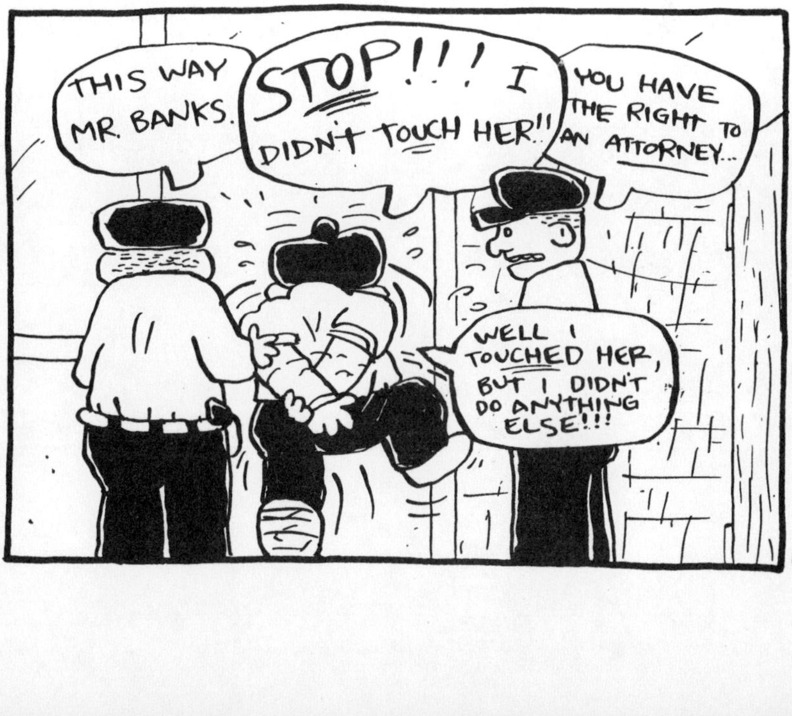
THIS WAY MR. BANKS.
STOP!!! I DIDN'T TOUCH HER!!
YOU HAVE THE RIGHT TO AN ATTORNEY...
WELL I TOUCHED HER, BUT I DIDN'T DO ANYTHING ELSE!!!

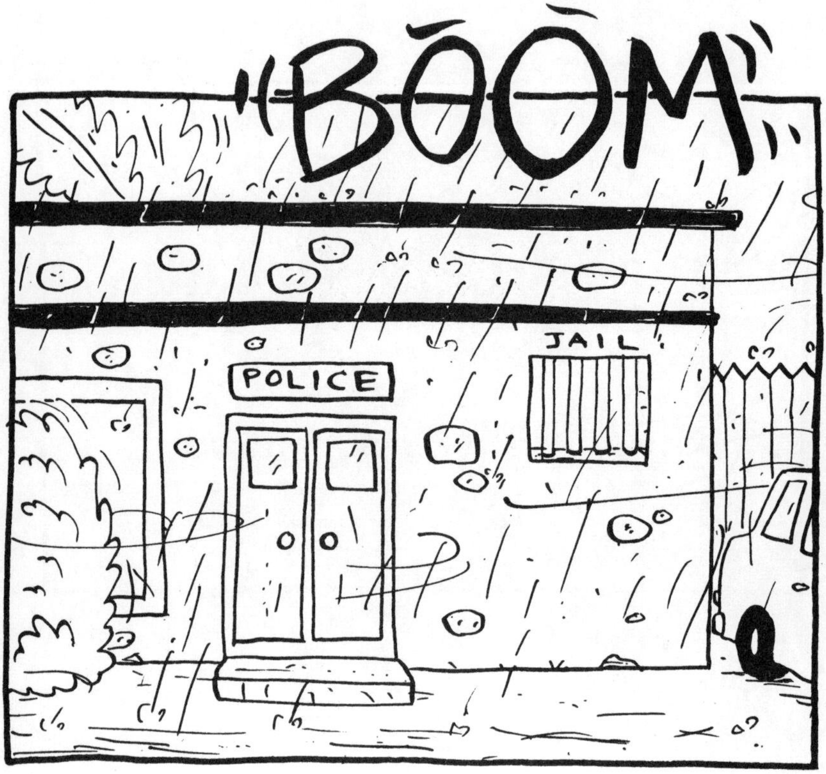
BOOM
POLICE
JAIL

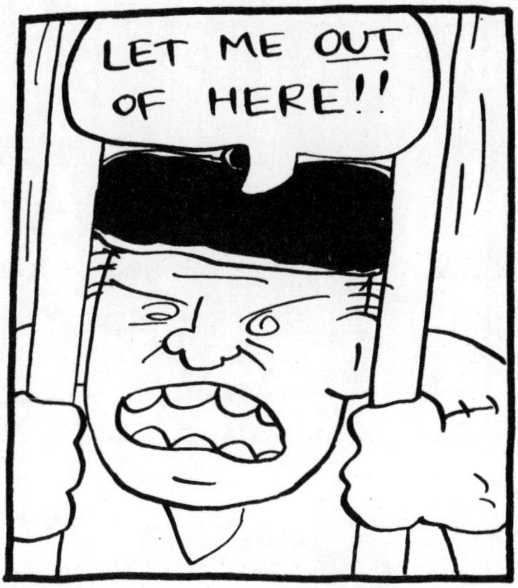
LET ME OUT OF HERE!!

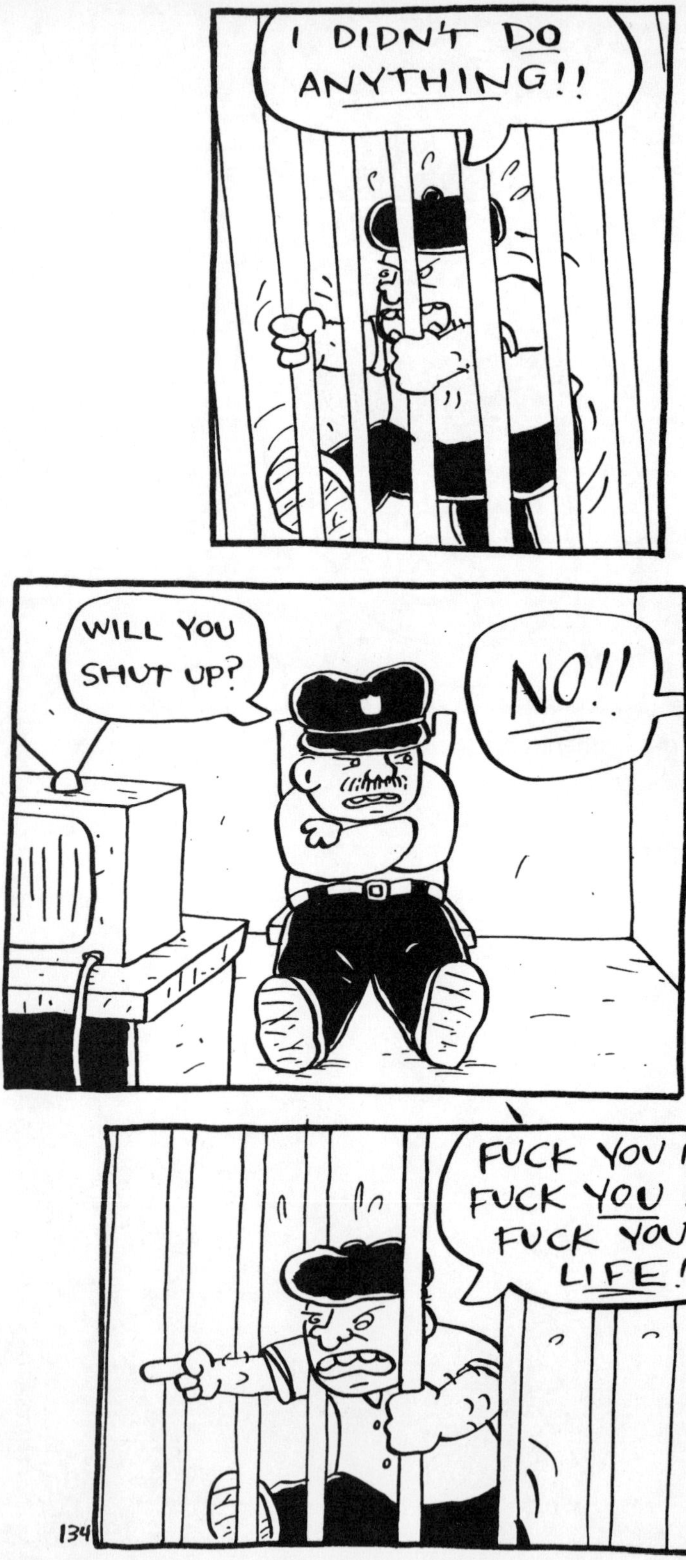
I DIDN'T DO ANYTHING!!
WILL YOU SHUT UP?
NO!!
FUCK YOU MAN!!
FUCK YOU AND FUCK YOUR LIFE!!

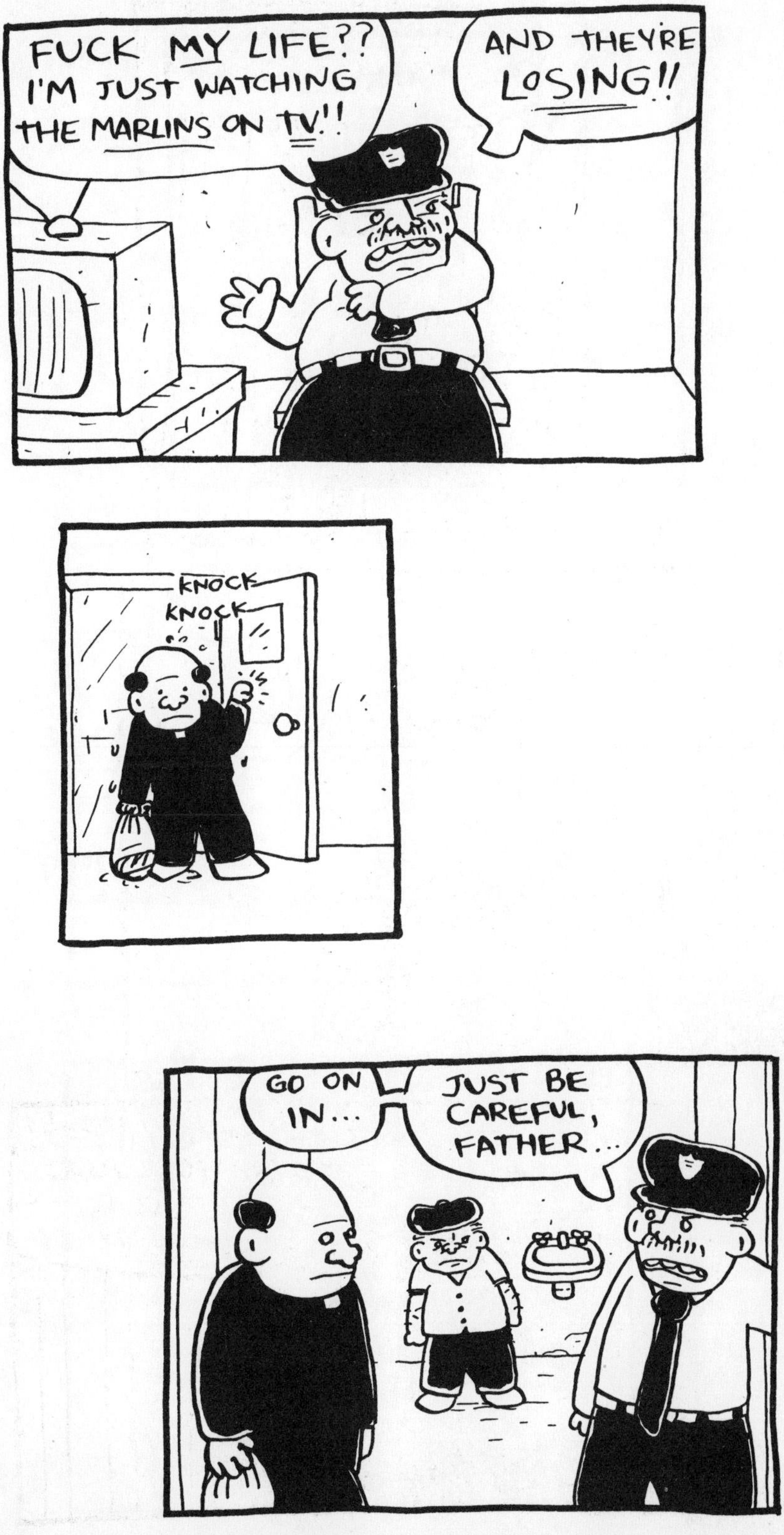
FUCK MY LIFE?? I'M JUST WATCHING THE MARLINS ON TV!!
AND THEYRE LOSING!!
KNOCK KNOCK
GO ON IN...
JUST BE CAREFUL, FATHER...

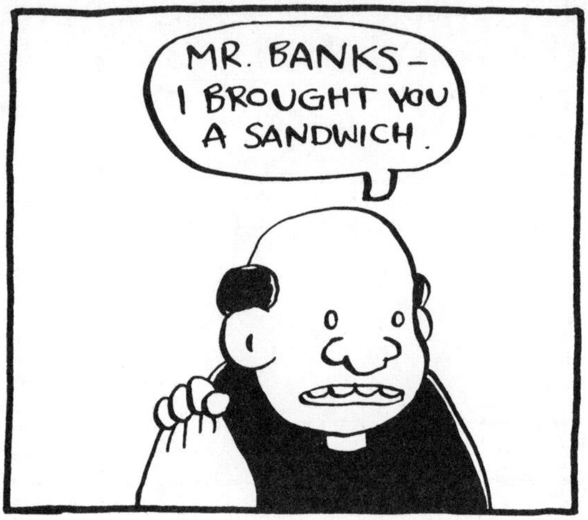
MR. BANKS- I BROUGHT YOU A SANDWICH.

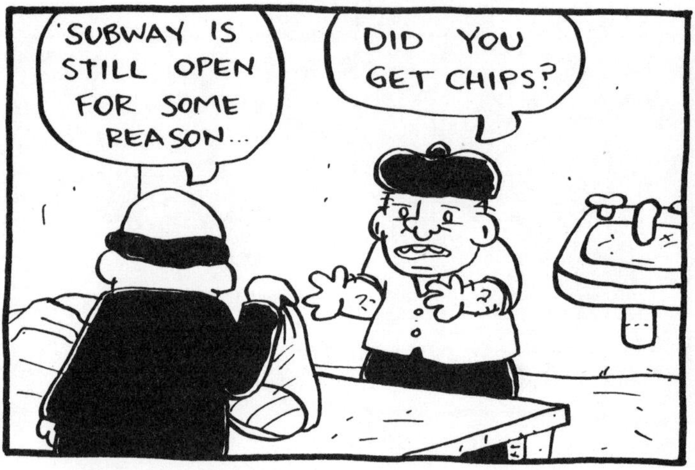
SUBWAY IS STILL OPEN FOR SOME REASON...
DID YOU GET CHIPS?

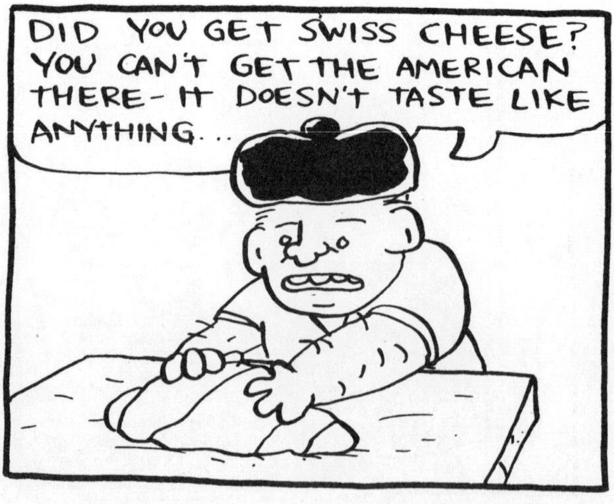
DID YOU GET SWISS CHEESE? YOU CAN'T GET THE AMERICAN THERE- IT DOESN'T TASTE LIKE ANYTHING...

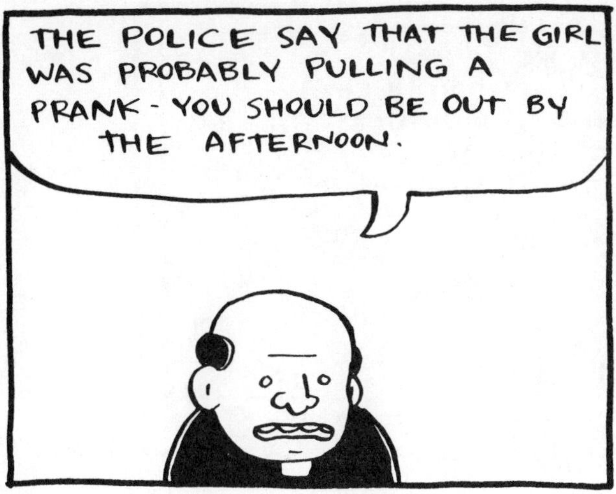
THE POLICE SAY THAT THE GIRL WAS PROBABLY PULLING A PRANK - YOU SHOULD BE OUT BY THE AFTERNOON.

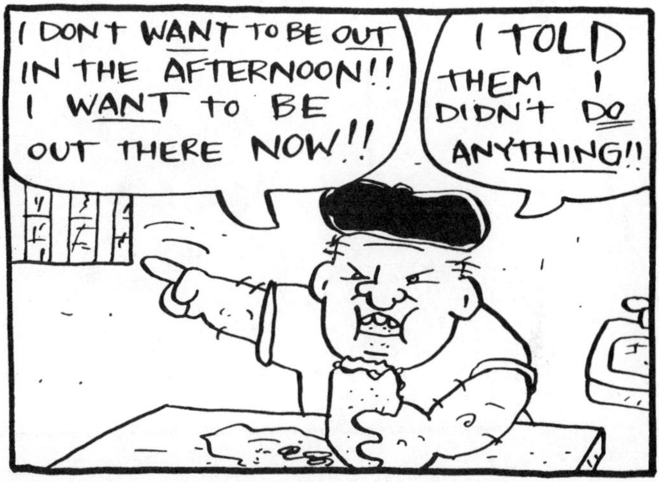
I DON'T WANT TO BE OUT IN THE AFTERNOON!! I WANT to BE OUT THERE NOW!!
I TOLD THEM I DIDN'T DO ANYTHING!!

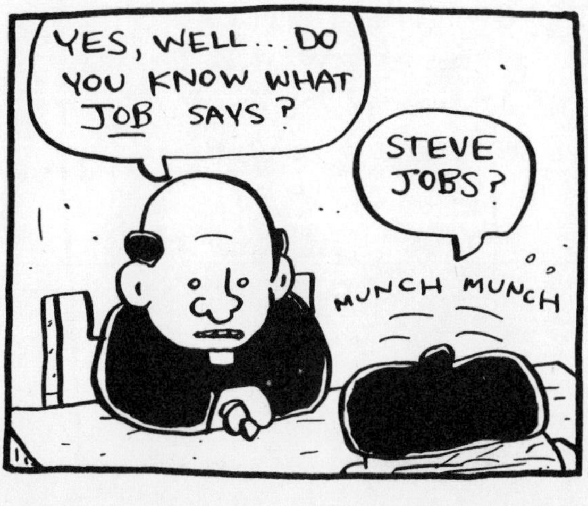
YES, WELL... DO YOU KNOW WHAT JOB SAYS?
STEVE JOBS?
MUNCH MUNCH

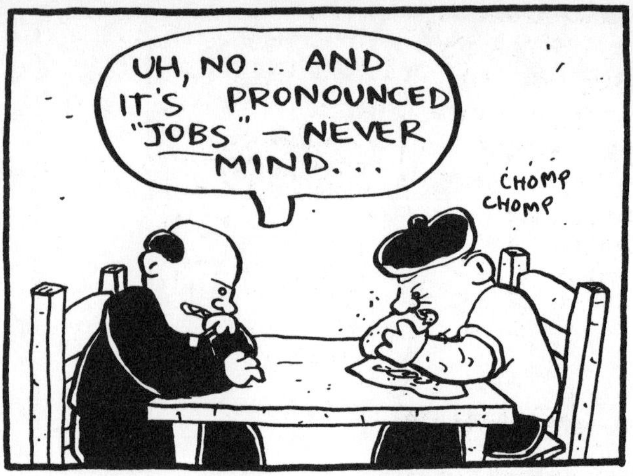
UH, NO... AND IT'S PRONOUNCED "JOBS" — NEVER MIND...
CHOMP CHOMP

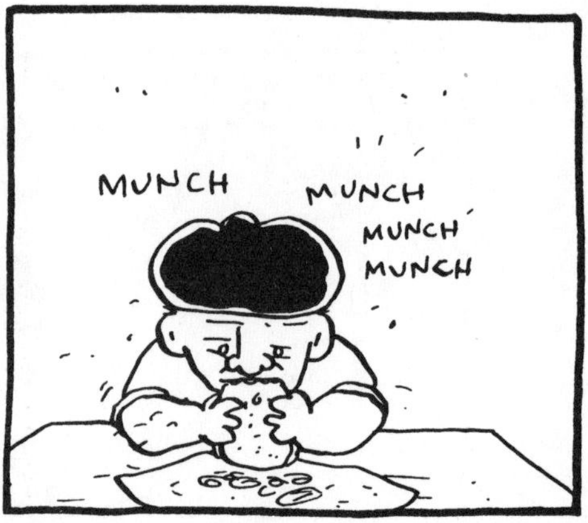
MUNCH
MUNCH
MUNCH
MUNCH

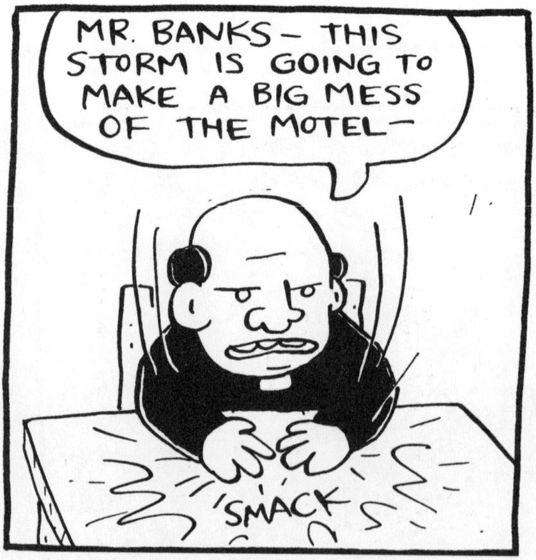
MR. BANKS — THIS STORM IS GOING TO MAKE A BIG MESS OF THE MOTEL—
SMACK

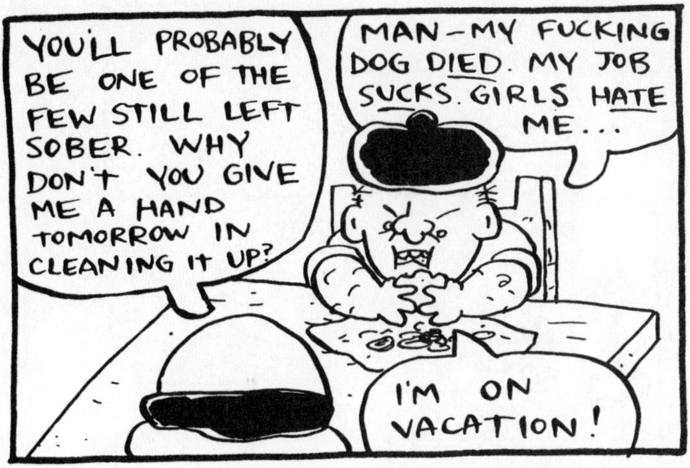
YOU'LL PROBABLY BE ONE OF THE FEW STILL LEFT SOBER. WHY DON'T YOU GIVE ME A HAND TOMORROW IN CLEANING IT UP?
MAN—MY FUCKING DOG DIED. MY JOB SUCKS. GIRLS HATE ME...
I'M ON VACATION!

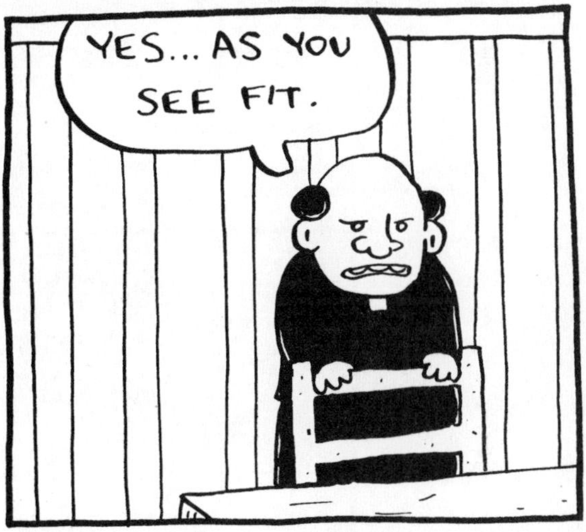
YES... AS YOU SEE FIT.

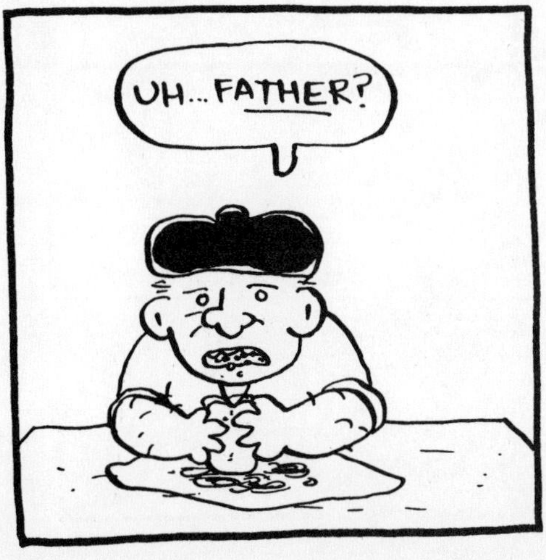
UH... FATHER?

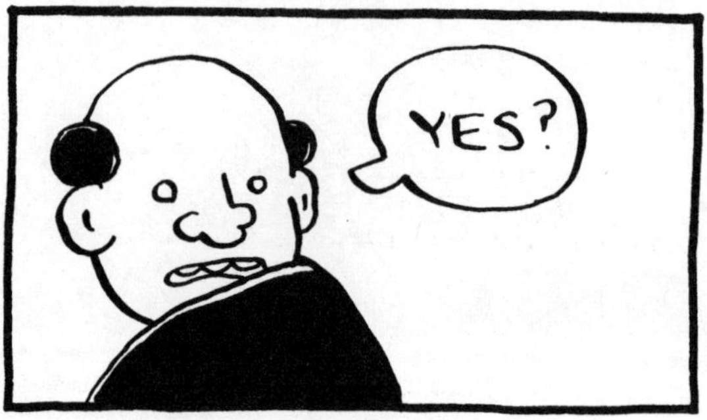
YES?

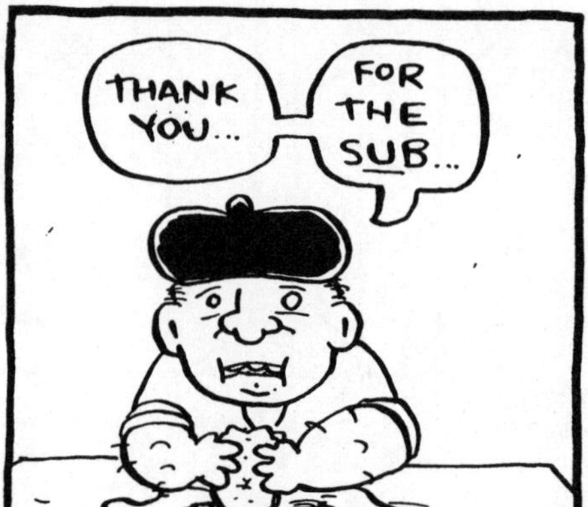
THANK YOU...
FOR THE SUB...

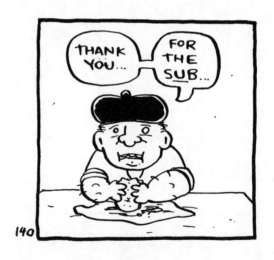

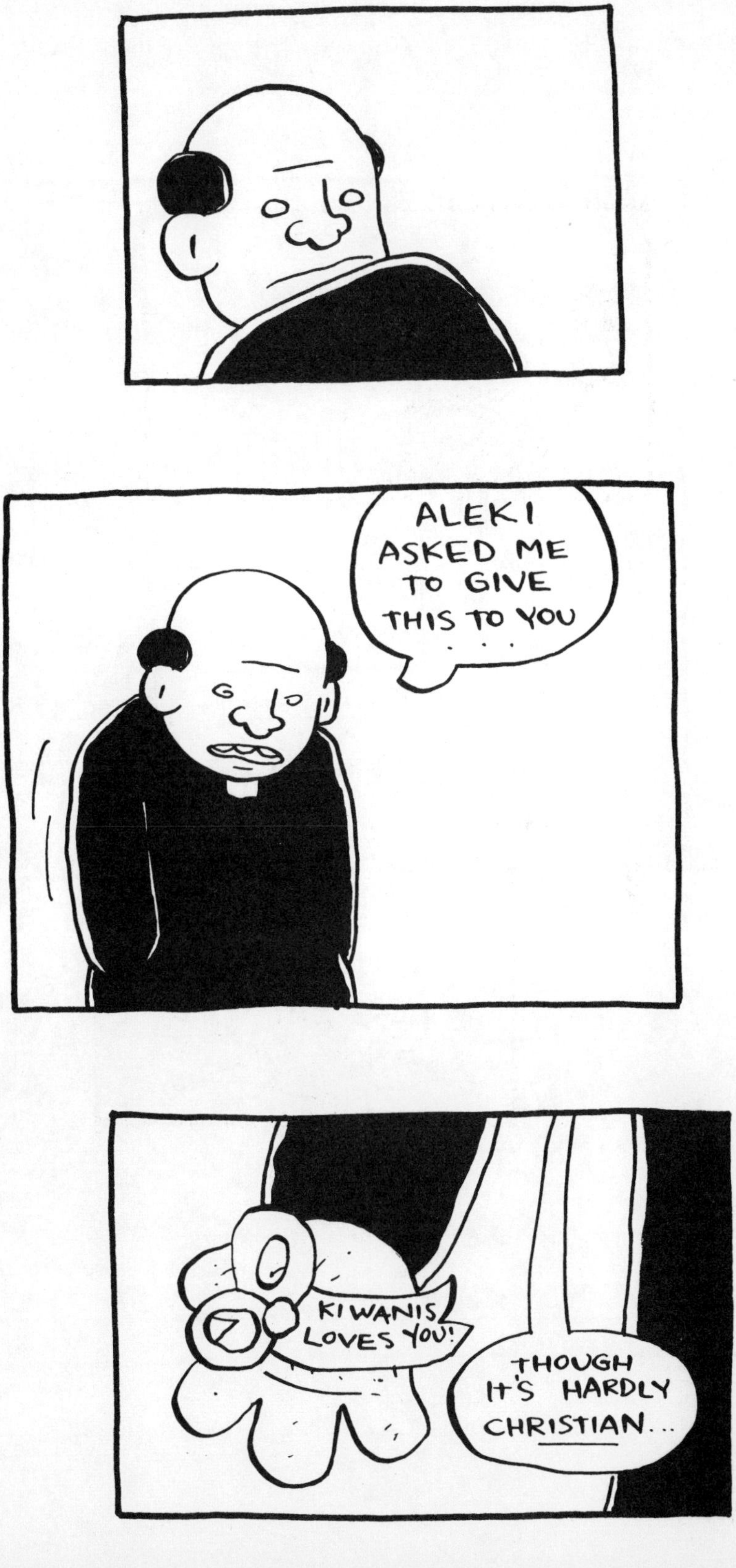
ALEKI ASKED ME TO GIVE THIS TO YOU . . .
KIWANIS LOVES YOU!
THOUGH IT'S HARDLY CHRISTIAN...

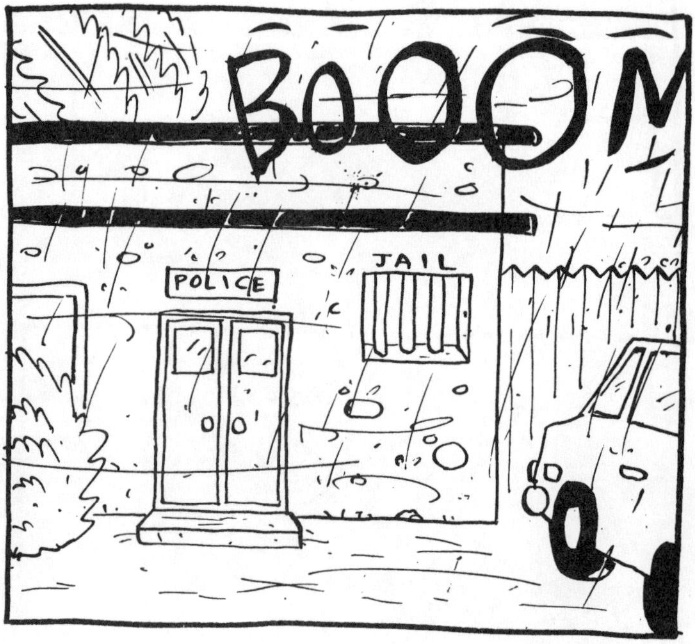
BOOOM
POLICE
JAIL

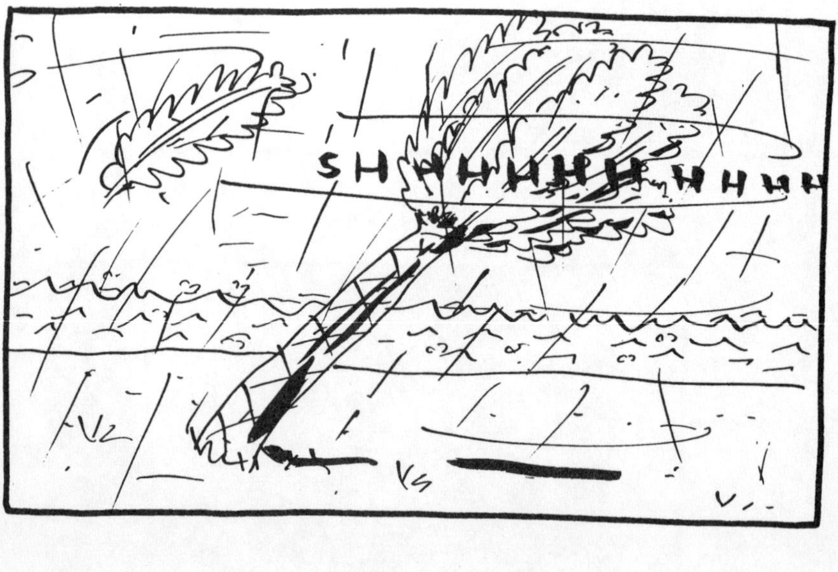
SHHHHHHHHHHH

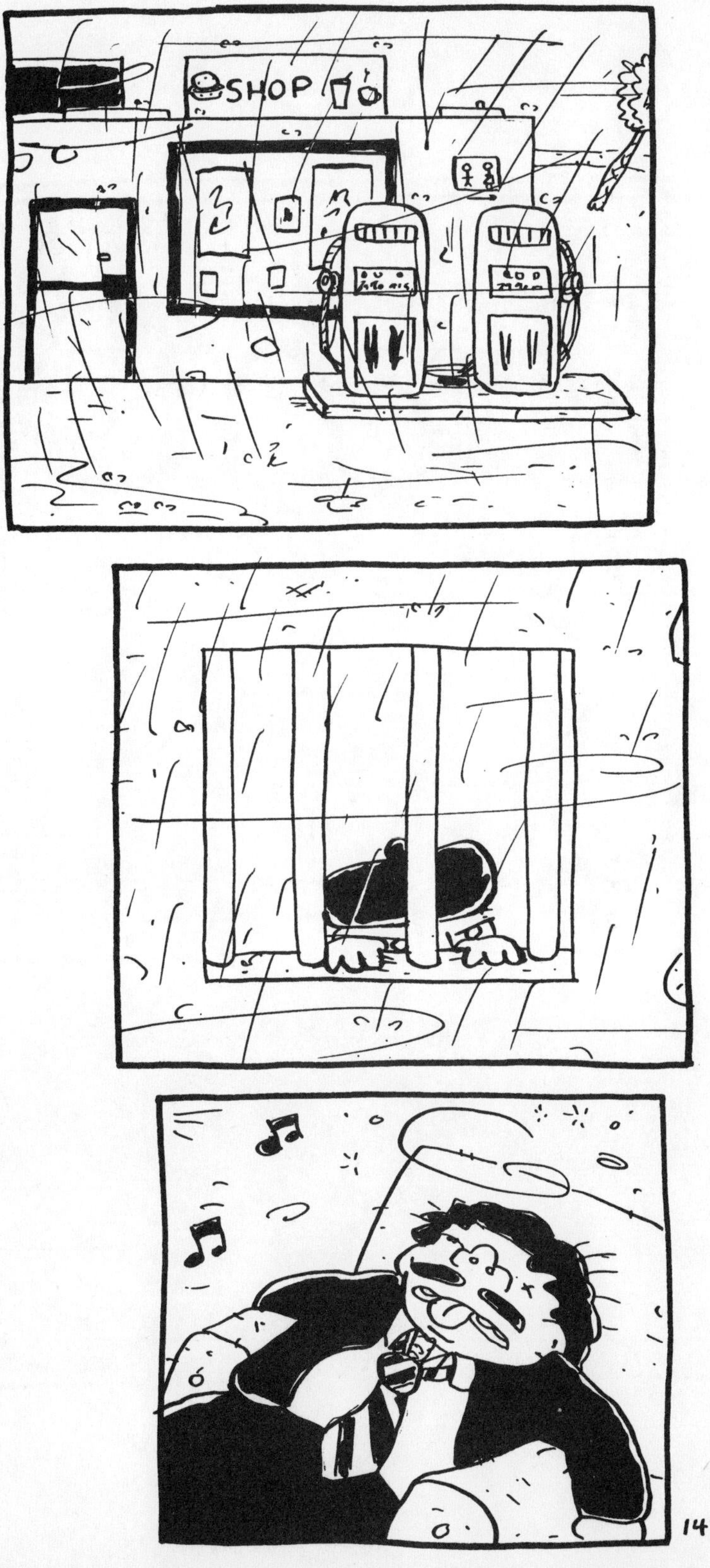
SHOP

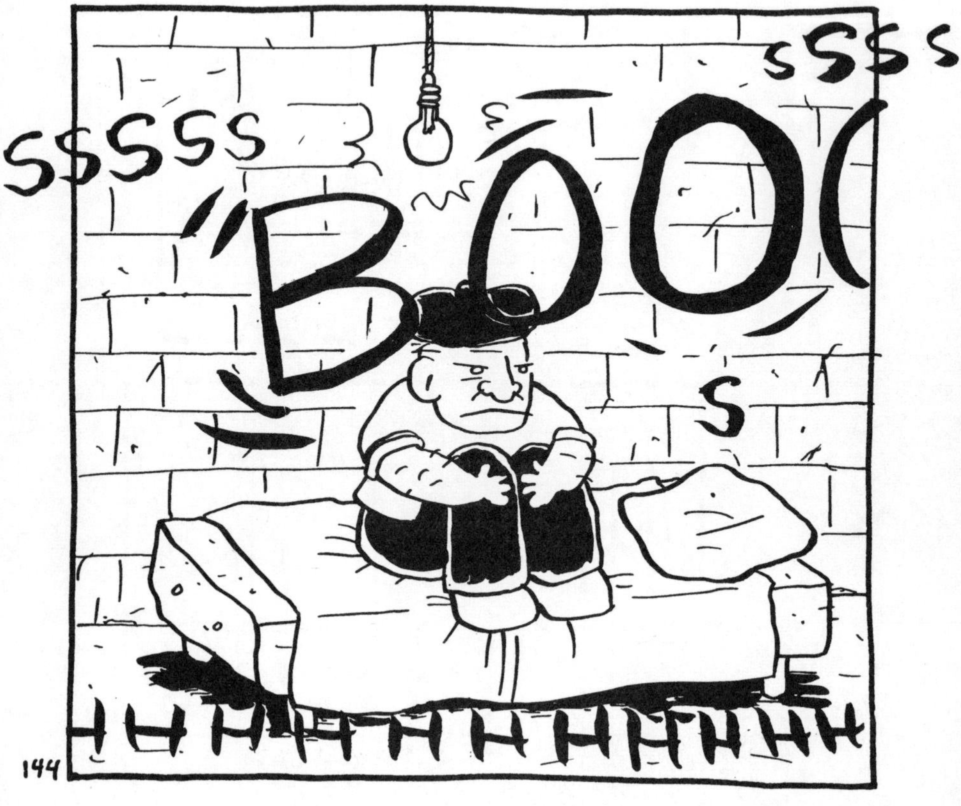
SSSSS
SSSS
"BOO
S
S
HHHHHHHHHHHHHHHH

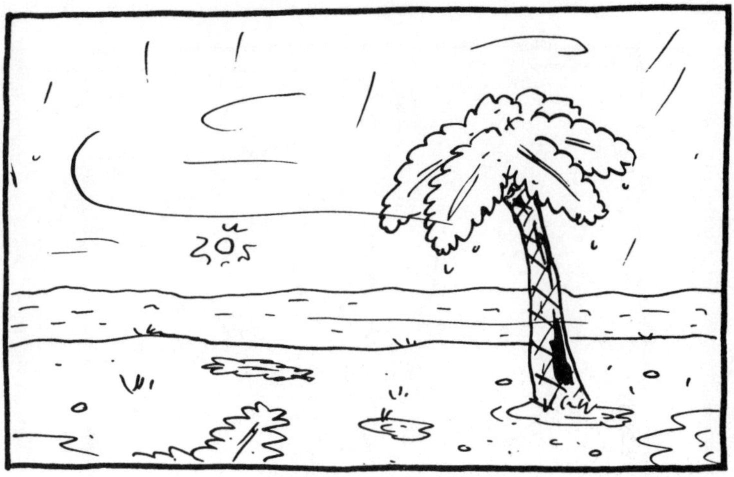

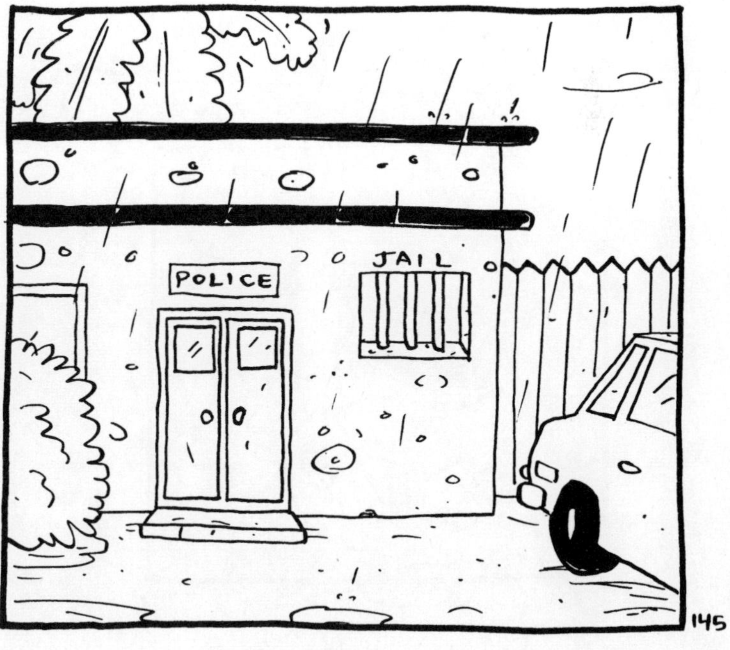
JAIL
POLICE

ALRIGHT, MR BANKS...

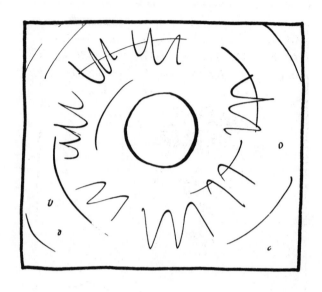

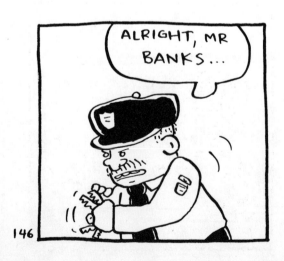

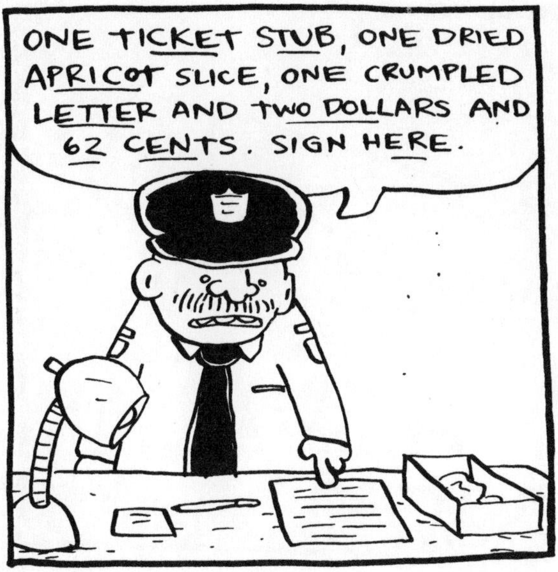
ONE TICKET STUB, ONE DRIED APRICOT SLICE, ONE CRUMPLED LETTER AND TWO DOLLARS AND 62 CENTS. SIGN HERE.

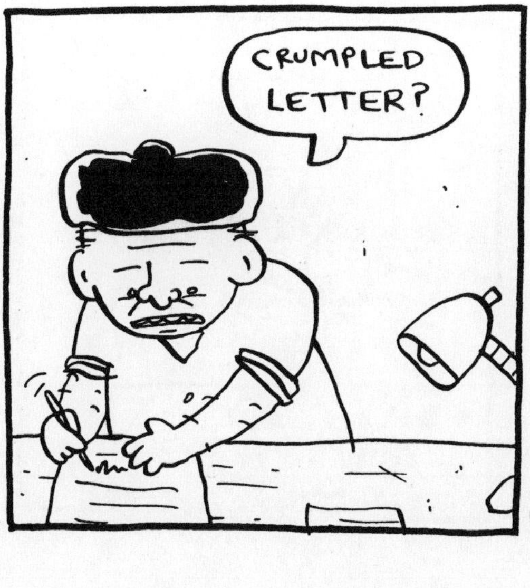
CRUMPLED LETTER?

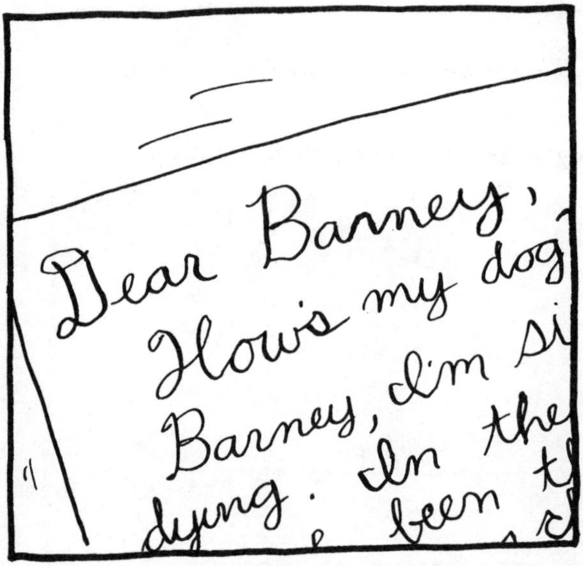
Dear Barney,
How's my dog
Barney, I'm
dying. In
been

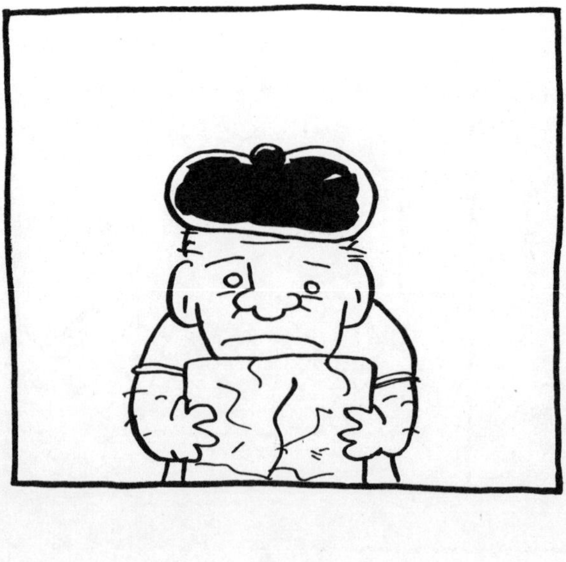

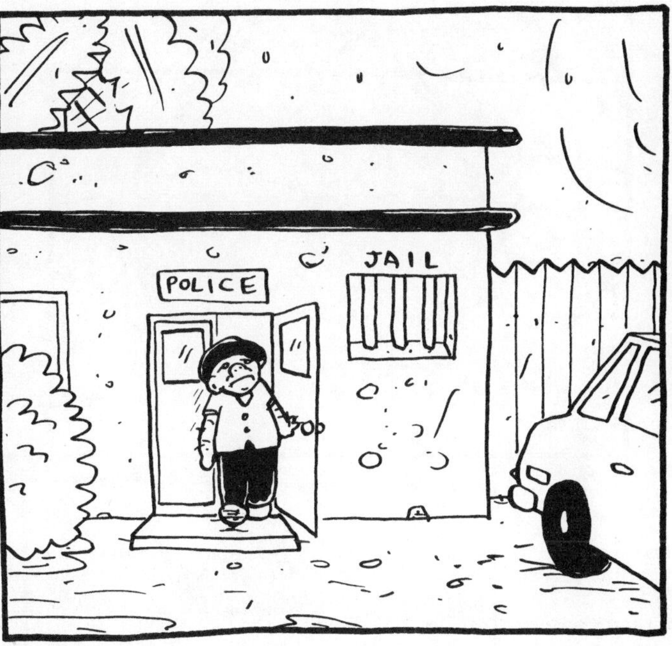
JAIL
POLICE

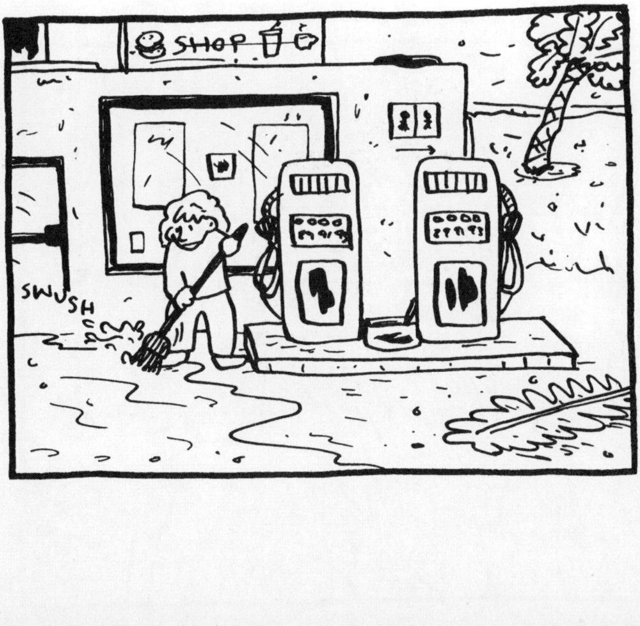
SHOP
SWUSH

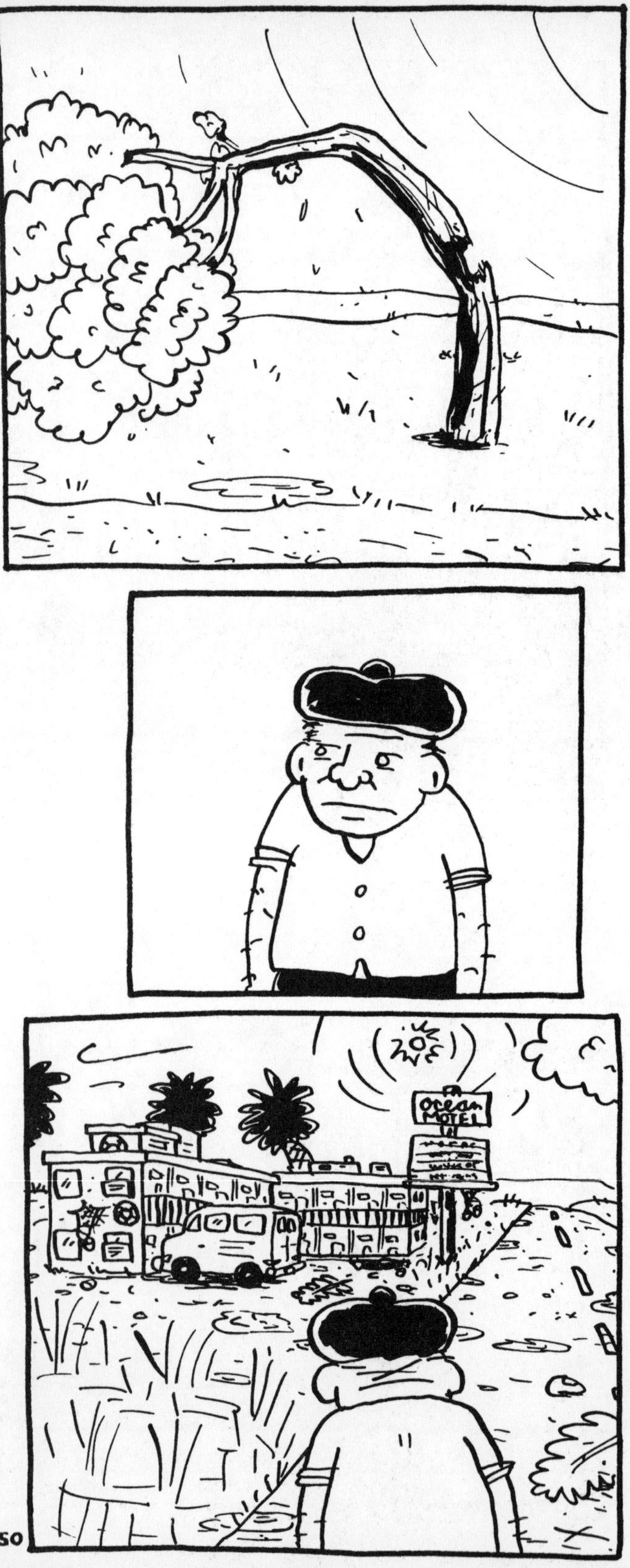
Ocean
MOTEL

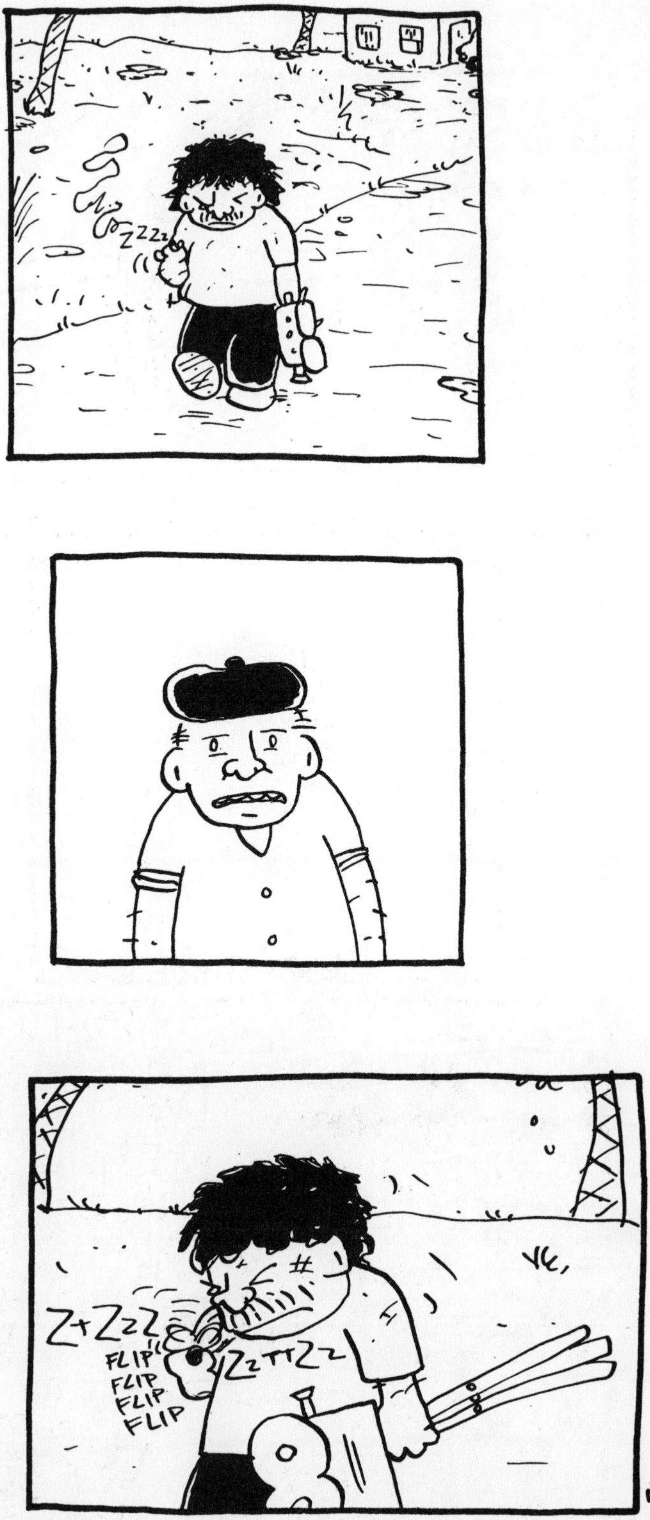
ZZZz
FLIP
FLIP
FLIP
FLIP

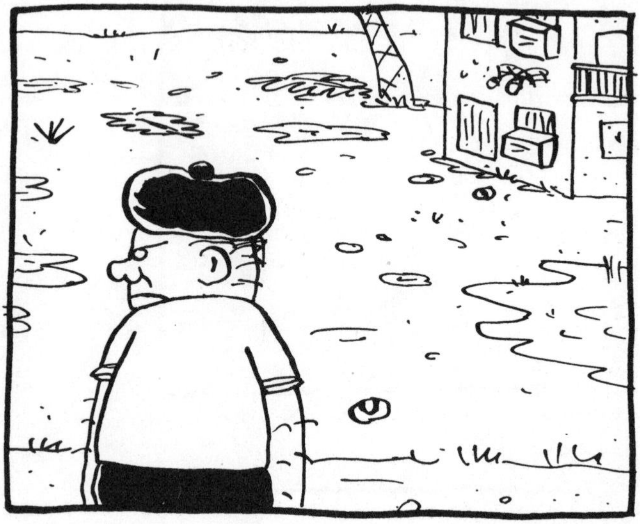

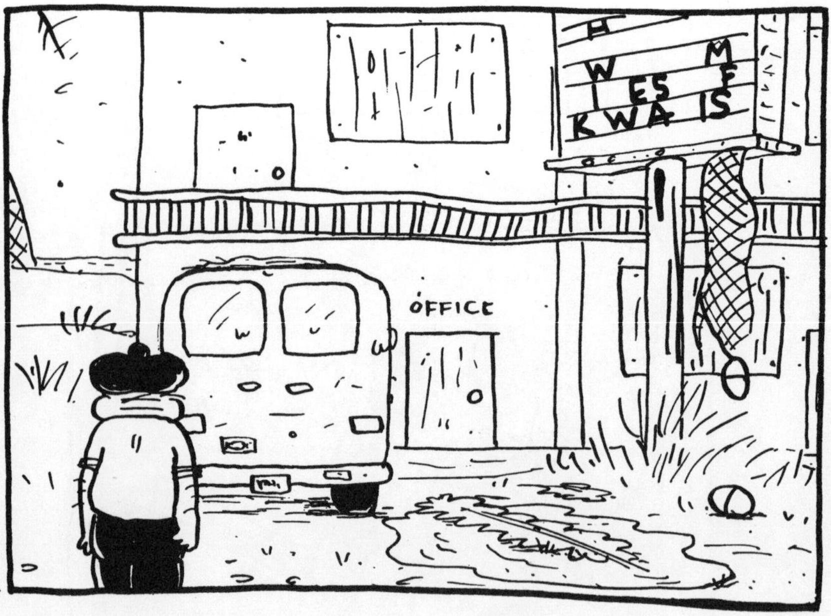
H
W M
ES F
KWA IS
OFFICE

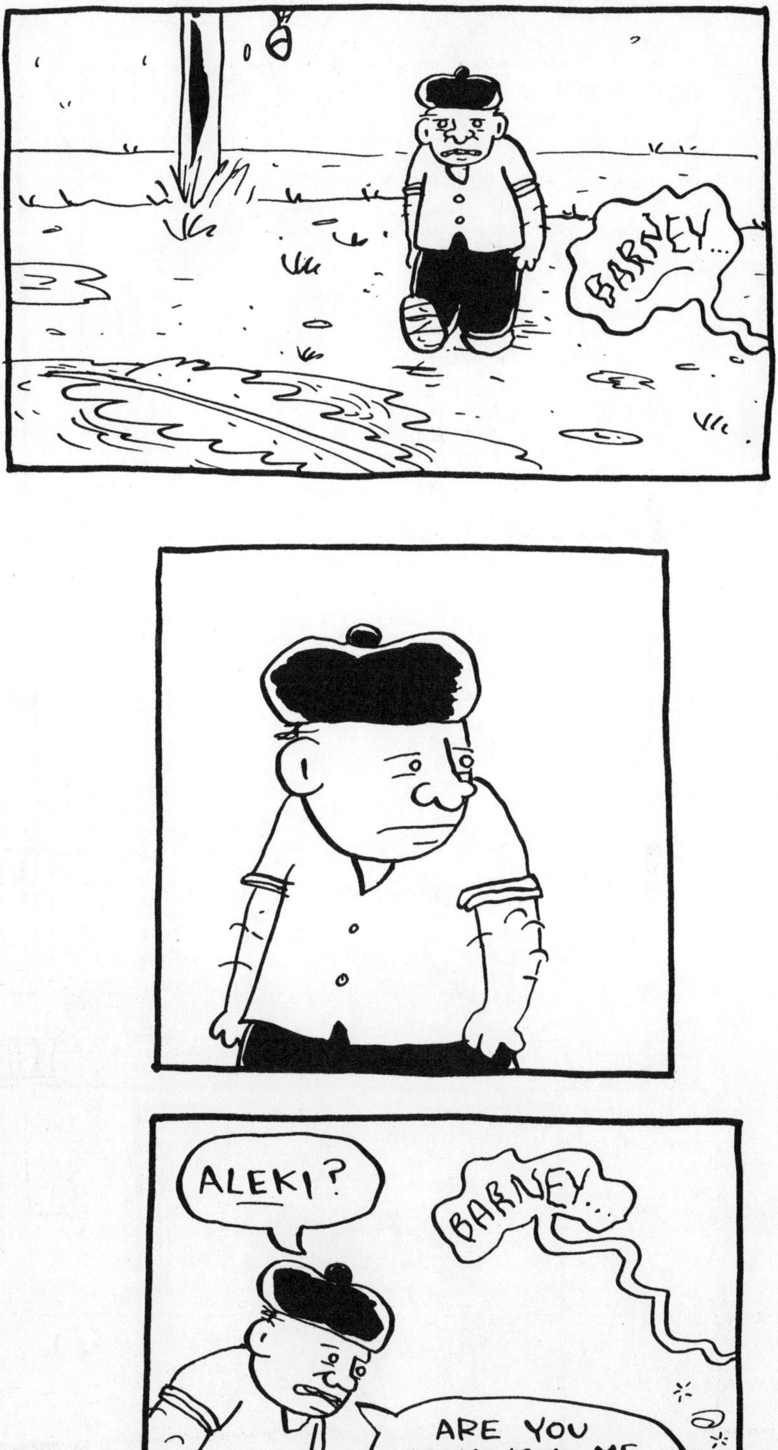
BARNEY...
ALEKI?
BARNEY...
ARE YOU TALKING TO ME OR THE STORM??

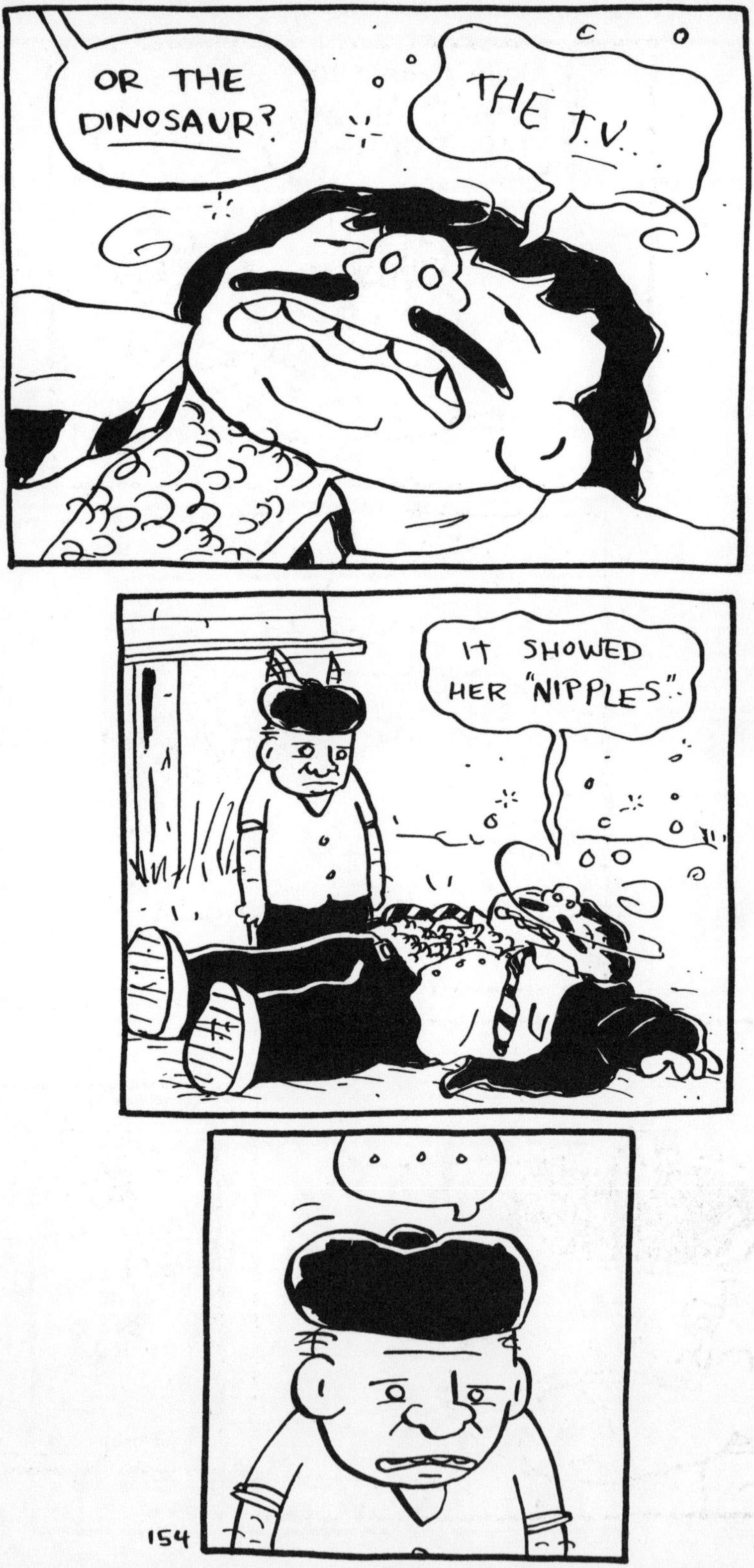
OR THE DINOSAUR?
THE T.V...
IT SHOWED HER "NIPPLES".
. . .

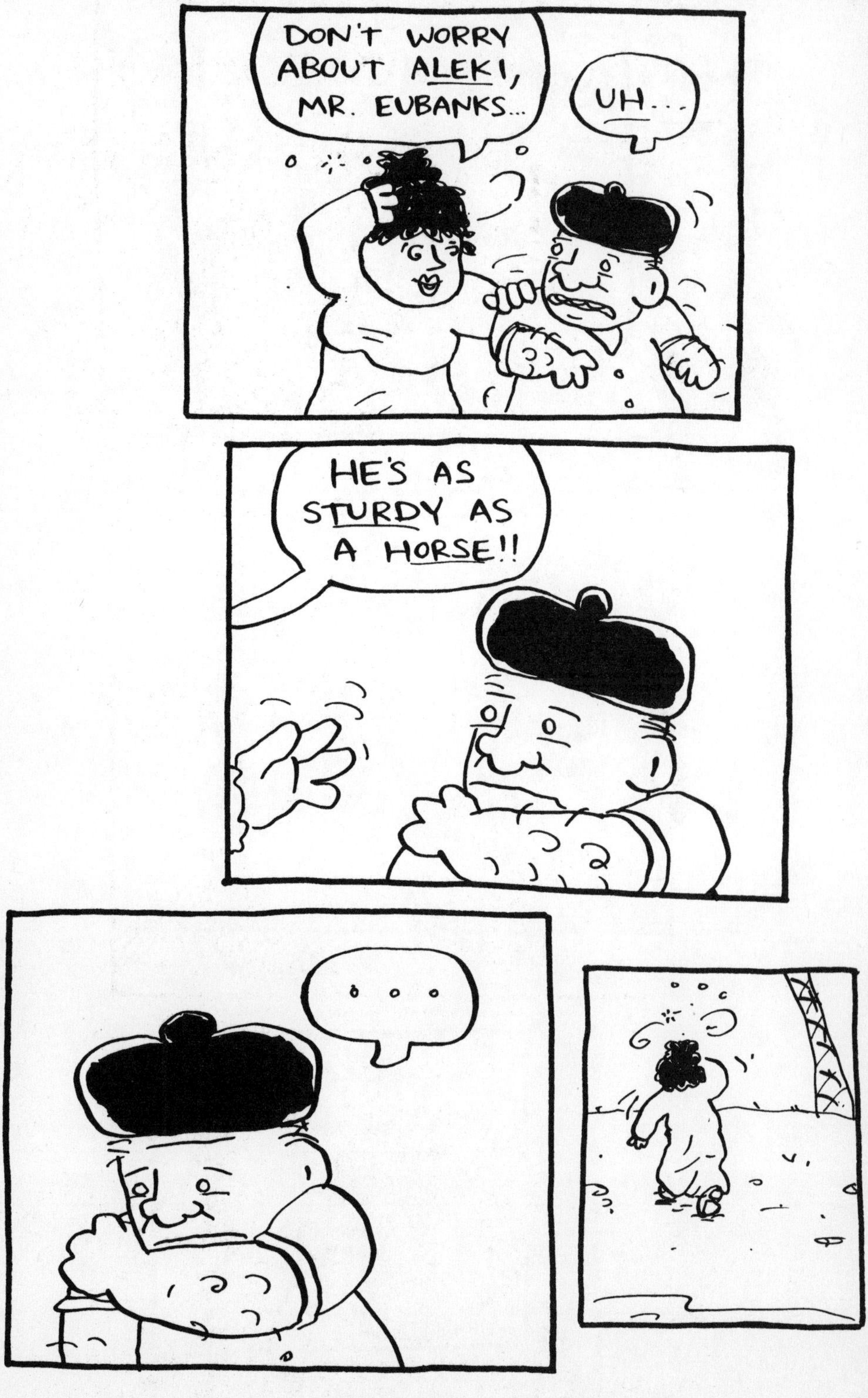
DON'T WORRY ABOUT ALEKI, MR. EUBANKS...
UH...
HE'S AS STURDY AS A HORSE!!
...

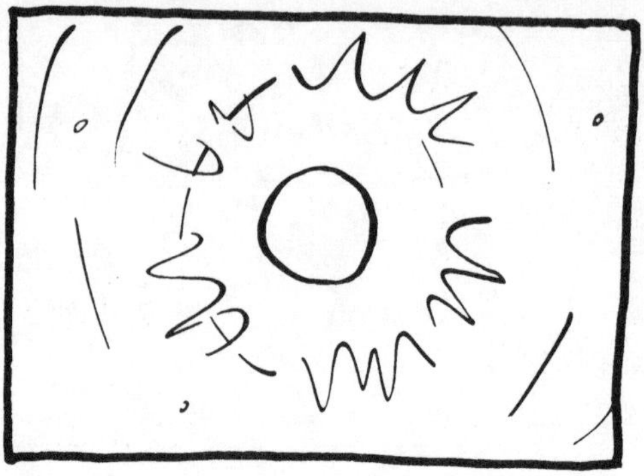

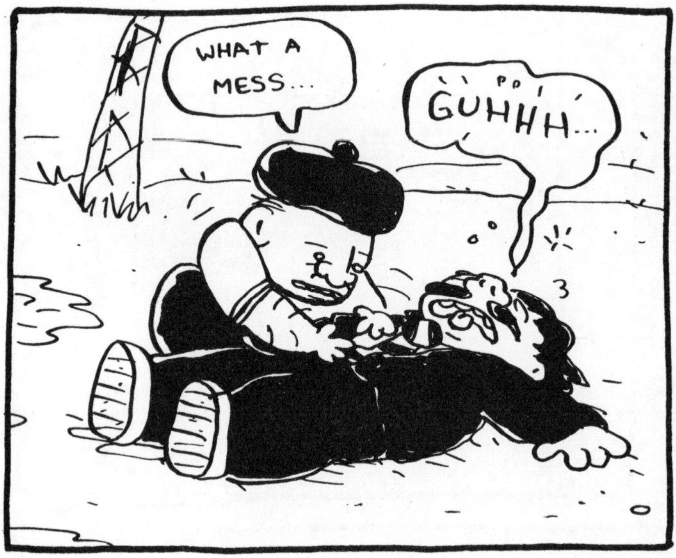
WHAT A MESS...
GUHHH...

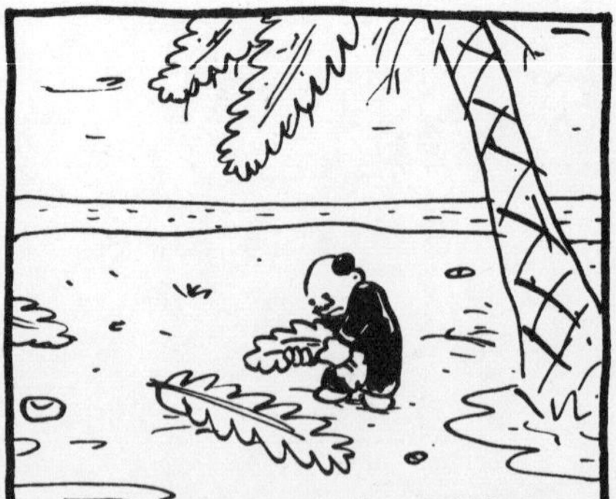

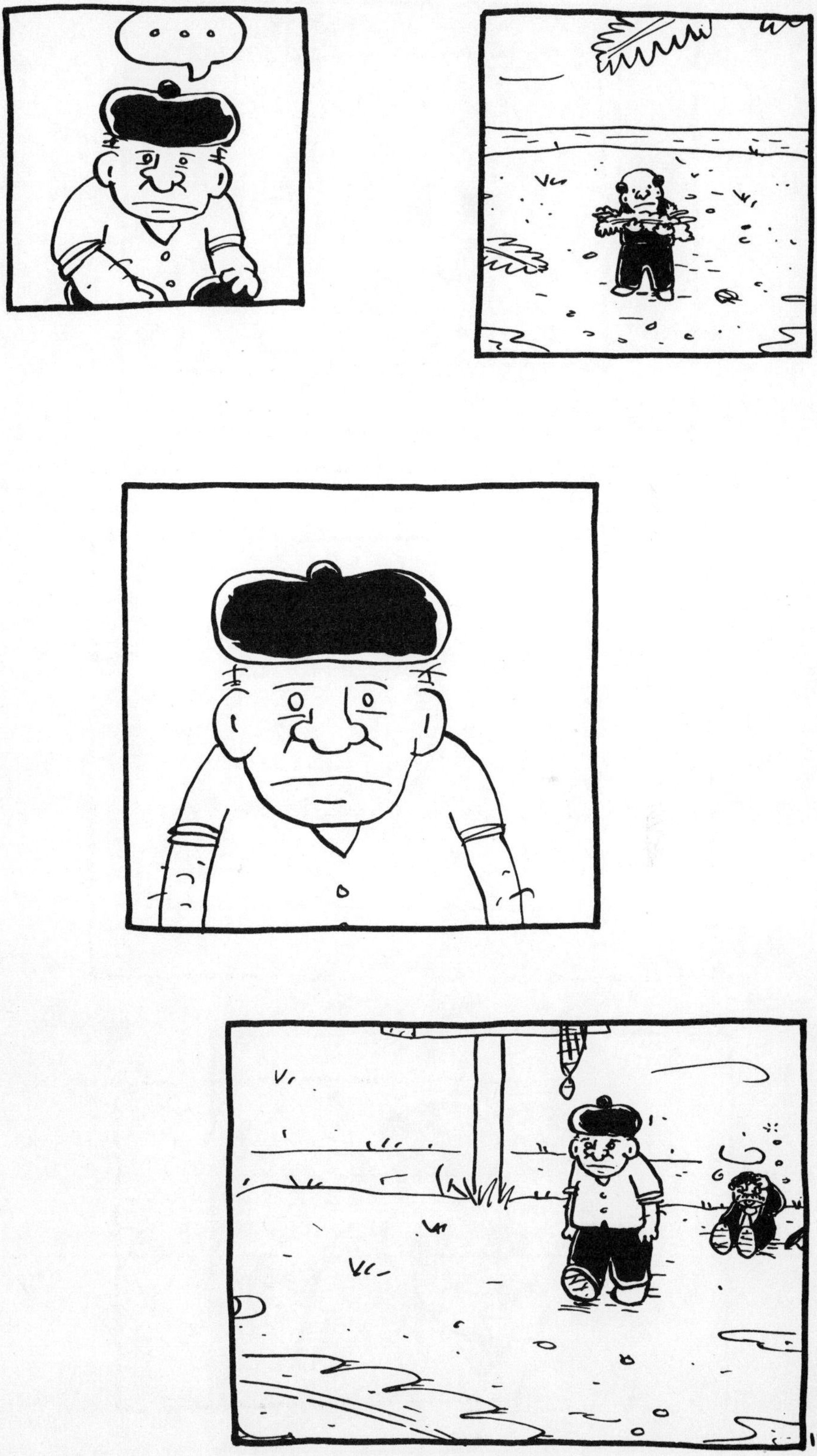
...

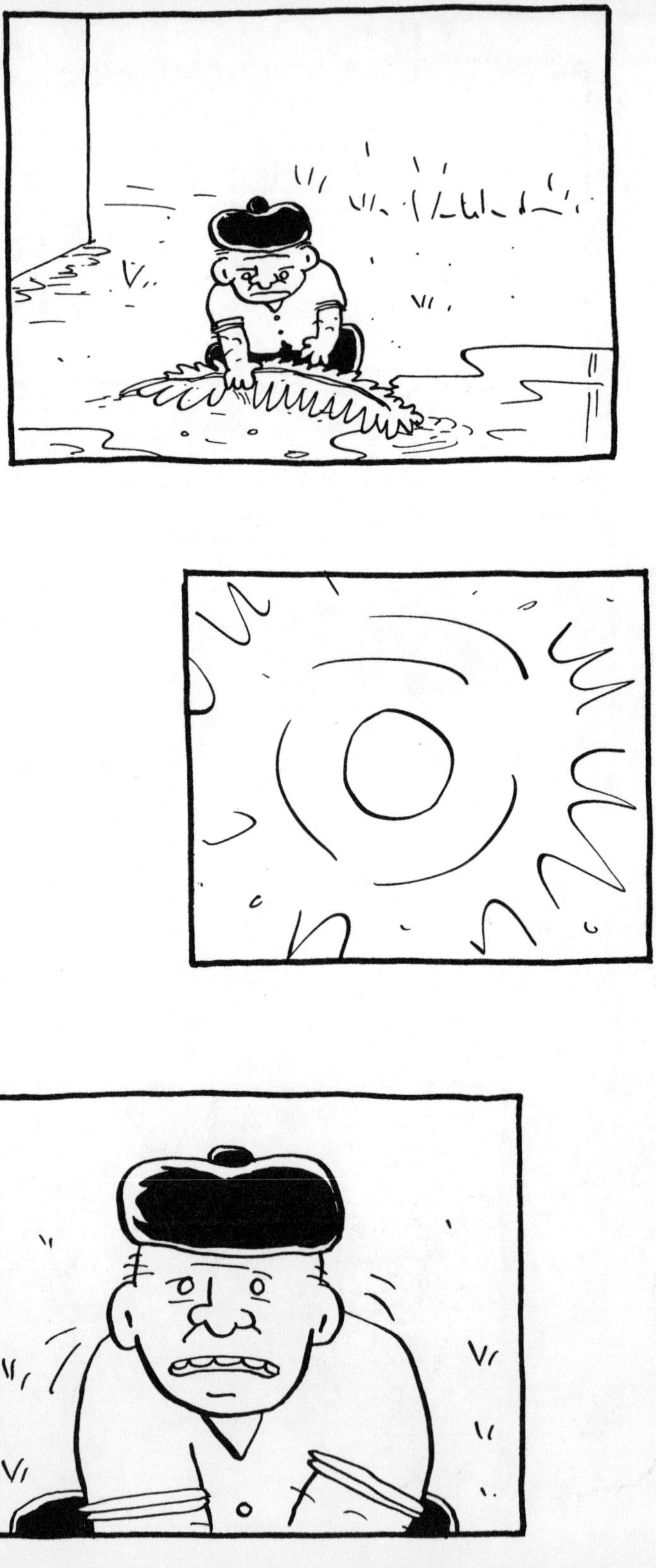

160